"It's not what you look at that matters, it's what you see."

— HENRY DAVID THOREAU

---

*D*emanding spirits barged their way into Aries's mind, each voice trying to outdo the other.

"Please stop," she said through clenched teeth.

For a moment they went away, allowing her to bask in the silence. But as soon as she took a step toward the school, their clamor started back up.

Aries ran behind a row of palm trees, shielding herself from streams of cars and pedestrians as the high-pitched aggravation attacked her senses.

"Not today...please not today," she begged no one in particular.

Out of sight, she dropped to her knees and picked at the grass as the noise escalated.

"Dammit. I said stop."

Giving in, she put her hands in her lap. With her index finger, she wrote the alphabet on her leg. She needed deep concentration to make the connection. She waited for a clear voice to come through, dreading - yet at the same time accepting - communication with the dead.

After tracing a Z on her leg, she started over with A as a faint whisper formed. Unable to make out any words, she slowed her pace and drew the letter B. She kept repeating this action, taking deeper breaths each time, trying to match the frequency of the spirit.

She'd almost given up when a clear voice said, "*You need to find out the truth, Aries.*"

"Shut up!" she screamed, covering her ears.

She wiped the sweat off her forehead, recovering from contact with that particular soul. He had unique ways of getting her attention, and he always had the same cryptic message.

Shaking out her hands, Aries stood up and stared at Newport Beach High.

Here's to new beginnings.

Nobody knew anything about her, or her past. And maybe her new school could help her forget about the last year-and-a-half.

She glanced past the running track, focusing on the field goal post. "Something isn't right about this school," she whispered. She glanced around to make sure nobody had witnessed her talking to herself before heading down the sidewalk toward the parking lot.

Slowing her stride, she tried to calm down as an intense wave of nausea hit. She could always walk back home. But that wouldn't solve anything. She might not be safe there either. The nauseating feeling left as quickly as it had come on.

She shook her head. "You're going to be okay," she mumbled to herself. "This is your chance to finally start over and have a friend." She smiled. "Or maybe even two."

In awe of the masses of students and expensive cars, she jumped when a luxury convertible flew past her with the horn honking and girls inside laughing and pointing at her. Her face flushed as she put her hand on her forehead.

Such an idiot. Why did she always make a complete fool of

herself? *Shut up and stop talking to dead people.* If only she could take her own advice.

As she made her way through the gate, the competing spirits came back, along with another noise like an emergency broadcast alert, the two of them drowning out the sound of the crowd around her.

A strong voice came through. "*Tell Ka— to keep playing piano.*" With the name muffled, all she could detect was a "Ka" sound.

Another voice said, "*I'm with J's dog.*"

Aries balled up her fists. *Stop.* She couldn't keep up with all their vibrations. The energy caused her head to ache.

A pleasant elderly woman materialized. "*Oh, sweetie, I don't mean to cause you any pain, but Cory's in trouble.*"

Cory?

She panicked, unable to control the throng on the other side, urgent to connect with the physical world. She hurried past a cluster of students, their loud voices melding with the ones inside her head. Picking up her pace with every step, she tried to run away from the madness.

The first bell rang, and masses of students scurried around her. Studying the numbers on the buildings, she found her first period class. Three girls, all with blonde hair, sauntered past her. Aries stumbled, running into the blondest of the three.

"Excuse you," the girl snorted.

Aries rolled her eyes. *Like she's never accidentally bumped into someone. Whatever, Miss Perfect.* She towered over the three girls with her contrasting height and dark hair. New school, fresh start? *Not so much.* Forcing a tight-lipped smile, she brushed off the bad feeling the girls gave her.

When the tardy bell rang, she froze in the doorway, unable to walk in as the loudest, most obnoxious soul penetrated her being. "*Tell B he drives too fast. SLOW DOWN. SLOW DOWN. SLOW DOWN.*"

"Leave me alone!" she screamed.

The whole class turned around, staring at her standing all by herself. The silence gripped her lungs, forcing out all the air.

Breathe. Take a breath.

"Um…um," she mumbled.

Ignoring the laughter and rude comments, Aries lowered her head to avoid eye contact. *Everyone, please face forward and stop staring. And could my cheeks please return to their original color?*

She took a wobbly step forward. *Great, Aries. New school, but same old freak.*

2

---

*O*f course, the only open chair happened to be next to Miss Perfect. Aries proceeded toward it with as much grace as she could muster, fighting every urge in her body to run home. She put her backpack on top of the table. Maybe it was a sign. Maybe they could start over and get to know one another.

"Hi," Aries said.

Her insecurity tripled when Miss Perfect put her foot on the chair.

"Sorry, this seat's taken, weirdo." Miss Perfect gave Aries a dirty look, while her two cohorts sitting at the table on the other side of her laughed.

So much for making new friends. *Guess it's just going to be me and the afterworld.*

The teacher stepped toward the girls. "Excuse me, go ahead and sit down for now. I'll be moving everybody into a seating chart in a few minutes."

Miss Perfect glared at Aries, causing her to remain standing.

"Well, aren't you striking. How tall are you?" the teacher asked Aries.

"Five-eleven, but my dad says I'm six feet of legs." *Why did I say that?* Her nerves got the best of her, causing her face to turn an even darker shade of red as she sat down.

The teacher laughed. "He's right. I wish you could spare some for me."

A light casting off the teacher displayed a unique aura about her. She looked to be in her mid-twenties. She had blue eyes, enhanced by her golden sun-kissed skin. She had a calmness to her, causing Aries to relax her shoulders.

The teacher's blonde hair swayed as she moved to the center of the room. "Welcome back, everybody. I'm Miss Townsend. I'm going to start with a seating chart. Each table sits two, and this will most likely be your partner for all of your wonderful projects." She scanned the room and smiled. "I can see the enthusiasm on all your faces."

Aries laughed.

"Teacher's pet," Miss Perfect hissed.

Under the table, Aries crossed her fingers. *Don't make me sit next to her.*

Miss Townsend began reading the chart. "Jamie Adler and Daniel Aguilar. Next table, Paige Bradley and Jordan Brown."

Paige, one of Miss Perfect's friends, moved to the next row and sat down. A foot shorter than Aries, and struggling to reach one hundred pounds, her skin revealed many days spent bathing under the summer sun. She ran her fingers through her thin blonde hair, causing her rose gold bracelets to clank together. Aries touched her cheap hoop earring and blushed. Every other girl in the class wore expensive jewelry.

As Aries waited for her name to be called, she glanced around the room, which looked more like a day spa than a class-room. Fake plants and trees landscaped the room. An oil diffuser let out a lavender aroma as relaxation music played at just above an inaudible decibel.

Miss Townsend glanced toward the door as a figure appeared

from the hallway. "Welcome, late comer. Just stand until I call your name."

Miss Perfect smiled and waved at the boy who'd walked in late. Aries tried not to stare at him, but his height and strong build had her spellbound. She liked how his wild brown hair escaped his NBHS baseball cap, and the way his smile displayed confidence, cockiness, and a warm soul all in one.

"Aries Dade," Miss Townsend said. "That's an intriguing name." She peeked up from the seating chart.

When Aries stood, Miss Perfect coughed out, "Stupid name."

Aries slouched as she walked over to her new table.

Miss Townsend smiled when she sat down. "I take it your birthday is either the end of March or somewhere in April?"

Wow, does she really understand astrology? "April third," Aries said in a low voice.

Miss Townsend raised her hand. "Fellow Aries; mine's the eighth. So, where's your famous Aries scar, face or head?"

Wide-eyed, Aries pointed to her temple. "When I was two, I fell, hitting the edge of a nightstand. Seven stitches."

Miss Townsend pointed to a small mark on her chin. "I came down on the safety bar of a roller coaster." Aries smiled as Miss Townsend asked, "Do we have any other Aries in the class?"

Miss Perfect rolled her eyes, while other students were either texting, staring out the window, or asleep.

"Alright, moving right along," Miss Townsend said. "Let's see who your lucky partner is."

"More like unlucky," Miss Perfect whispered.

Aries had experience when it came to the popular girls making fun of her; she'd learned just to ignore them.

"Cory Douglas."

"Cory," she mouthed. *Could he be the one who's in some sort of trouble?*

Miss Perfect directed her attention to the boy standing by the door, saying, "No way."

Aries attempted to acknowledge him, but she couldn't get past the disgust washed across Miss Perfect's face. She held her breath as Cory strolled over and flung his backpack around the chair next to her. Finally, good luck had come her way. The best looking boy in the class hadn't witnessed her make a complete ass out of herself.

"Hey," he said in a deep voice.

"Hi." She had trouble making eye contact with him.

He leaned back in the chair. Stretching out his legs, he winced when his knee whacked the under bar. "Ouch."

Aries smiled, relieved she wasn't the only uncomfortable, vertically enhanced student in the class. Cory had to be at least 6'3", maybe 6'4".

"Happens to me all the time," she said.

Curious to find out Miss Perfect's name, Aries listened as more students were seated. As she put names with faces, a light humming sound distracted her, but the noise didn't bother her like usual. In fact, she welcomed the warm energy. The sensation came from a pleasant soul, so she focused to make a connection.

Are you the woman from earlier?

Taking out a pencil and notebook, she scribbled an infinity sign. She repeated the motion, making the sign darker, until a pleasurable voice said, "*Yes.*"

A sudden pain jabbed at her chest. *Did you die of a heart attack? Or something related to your lungs?* She waited a moment as the pain subsided. *Are you still here?*

"*Yes.*"

Are you Cory's grandmother?

"*Yes. He needs you.*"

Aries jerked back, hitting her thigh on the under bar. *Why would he need me?*

Cory put his hand on her leg. "You too, huh? They need to sit us at the big kids' table." He smiled.

Aries put the back of her hand on her forehead, willing her cheeks to remain their natural color. A boy had never touched her like that before, and she enjoyed his a little too much. His hand remained on her leg, and for a split second she envisioned him kissing her.

Cory withdrew his hand. "Sorry. I didn't mean to touch you. Just, um, are you okay?"

"Yes, I'm fine." Her words came out strained. *Stop acting like a nerd.*

Miss Townsend distracted them by calling out, "Peyton Price and Michael Richardson."

Miss Perfect got up and sat down next to Michael, twisting around her sparkly tennis bracelet. Aries unlatched her cheap stopwatch and chucked it in her backpack.

Peyton Price…how fitting. True to her nickname, she looked as though she might have had plastic surgery. *Could anyone have a nose that perfect?*

Cory's grandma interrupted her. "*He could use your help.*"

Aries squeezed her feet together, concentrating. Forcing herself to stay in the present and not speak out loud, she asked, *How can I help?*

"*He's in a predicament.*"

I have no clue what I could do. I don't even know him.

"*He takes after his Grandpa Joe. He's named after him. Cory Joseph. I was the only one to call him CJ. Thought it was a cute nickname, but it didn't stick. They're both naïve and generous to a fault. That got CJ into a real mess this summer. And that womanizing, think-he-knows-everything lawyer father of his did a number on the family. My daughter finally left him after his third affair. CJ's still not over it.*"

Aries drew a dragonfly, making sure the connection stayed strong. *How long ago was that?*

"*About five years now. You'd be real good for CJ.*"

Aries continued to draw different pictures of insects. *What makes you so sure?*

"*Because he—*"

Cory bumped her arm. "That's pretty cool." He pointed to the butterfly she sketched. "I suck at drawing."

She couldn't believe Cory would even speak to her, let alone compliment her. "Thank you."

"What was that whole scar-Aries thing all about?"

Biting her bottom lip, Aries hesitated. *Don't sound like an astrological nerd.* He leaned closer, waiting for an answer.

"According to astrology, an Aries, the ram, leads head first, and at some point in their life they'll have a scar on their face or head."

"I have a scar on my head, but I'm not an Aries."

"It's not foolproof. Anyone can have a scar." She smiled. "It's probably all silly, really."

"Yeah, still kind of interesting, though. I'm a Leo. What are they known for?"

She smiled. "Ahh, you're a lion. Explains your hair, the lion's mane. Leos usually have great hair."

He laughed. "Never thought about that before, but okay. Thanks."

"Leos also like a lot of compliments."

He smiled. "Can't argue with that."

She nodded, quieting down when Miss Townsend said, "And finally, Brandon Young and Piper Zacora."

Piper, Peyton's other friend, sat down. Pretty and perfect as well, Piper had an aura about her, almost mystical, and Aries caught sight of a small Z tattooed on the inside of her wrist.

Aries dubbed the three pretty blondes the "P-pack." Apparently, to get in that club you had to be tiny, blonde, rich, and your name had to start with a P.

Miss Townsend made her way to the front of the class. "This

class is part of the Elite Scholars program designed for college credit. This is the only health class mixed with juniors and sophomores." She studied her clipboard. "Looks like we only have five juniors, Jamie, Daniel, Cory, Peyton, and Brandon." She wrote down something on the paper. "Sorry, that was more for me than you. Okay, your first assignment is going to be…" She wrote on the whiteboard "One Wish" and underlined it, then continued. "Write one or more paragraphs describing your wish, and why you chose it. This will help me learn a lot about you. Not to mention it's great for your mental and emotional health. Toward the end of the period, I'm going to have a few students read their wishes out loud."

Aries tried to blow a strand of hair out of her eye, while Cory wrote his paragraph. She did have a wish, but it was too private to share with anyone. She tapped her feet for a few more minutes, while Cory pulled out his cell. Keeping it hidden under his folder, he texted someone. Peyton giggled. Were they making fun of her?

Screw it.

Aries blocked them out and wrote a paragraph. She'd completed her last sentence when Miss Townsend said, "Alright, everyone should be finished by now. Do I have any volunteers?"

Paige Bradley's hand shot up. Miss Townsend looked at her seating chart. "Great, Paige, stand up and tell us about your wish."

Paige stood, holding out her paper. "I wish we could end world hunger," she said in a high-pitched voice, reminding Aries of a mouse. "Nobody should ever have to go without food, and—"

"What is she practicing for, Miss America?" Cory whispered.

Aries got lost in his brown eyes for a moment and smiled before focusing back on Paige.

After Paige finished, she gloated as she sat down.

"Thank you, Paige, that was very noble of you," Miss Townsend said.

Peyton rolled her eyes as she sat down.

"Any other volunteers?"

Peyton pushed her partner Michael's arm. He cleared his throat. "Yeah, I wish I didn't have to do this lame assignment. I chose this as my wish because it's a waste of time—"

The whole class burst out in laughter except Cory and Aries. Miss Townsend put out her hand. "Quiet down. I find it sad that out of all the possibilities Michael could have wished for, he chose not to do this assignment." She walked over to his table and took his paper, tearing it into tiny pieces. She threw the papers in the trash can and wiped her hands together. "There, your wish came true. I will not give you a grade, nor will I count it against you. It's like the assignment never existed. But I did learn something about you. Be careful what you wish for, class, it just might come true."

"Ooh, you got told," a boy sitting in the back shouted.

"Now, are we done with all the class clowns? I'd like to hear some real wishes." Miss Townsend checked her watch. "We have time for one more."

The class remained silent.

"Anyone?" Miss Townsend said, glancing in Aries's direction.

Aries kept her head down.

"Please don't make me have to pick someone." Miss Townsend held up her seating chart, her eyes shifting from the paper back to the class.

"Alright, Aries, will you please share your wish with us?"

"Loser," Peyton whispered.

Spoiled brat.

Aries liked everything about Miss Townsend so far and didn't want to get on her bad side by refusing to read her wish. She pressed her lips together as her cheeks flushed and a knot formed in her stomach. She didn't want the class to know anything about her, let alone her one intimate wish.

"Aries?"

Aries bumped the table as she stood. The P-pack laughed. Miss Townsend shushed them.

She gripped her paper. "I wish…" She swallowed and cleared her throat. "I wish my mother were alive." She paused, regaining her composure. "I'd fill her in on everything that's happened in my life the past year-and-a-half."

Flashing Miss Townsend a look, Aries hoped she'd have the decency to stop her. With no lifeline being thrown her way, she pressed on.

"She was smart, beautiful, and the life of the party everywhere she went. Everybody loved her. And I wanted to be like her. Beyond the obvious, I chose this wish because I haven't felt complete since she passed."

Aries stared out the window, unable to meet the eyes of anyone in the room. There wasn't a hole in the world deep enough for her to climb into.

Miss Townsend covered her mouth. "I'm so sorry, Aries. I-I'm at a loss for words."

The silence in the room caused beads of sweat to run down Aries's sides. She pressed her arms against her body.

Miss Townsend asked, "What happened? Was it sudden?"

Aries took a moment. Could she shout, "It's none of your f-ing business?" No, she had too much respect for Miss Townsend.

"I'd rather not say."

"Oh. of course not. How inappropriate of me. I was just curious if you had time to prepare, I mean not that you're ever prepared…" Frazzled, she shook her head. "If you need anything, anything at all, my door's always open."

The bell rang, and Aries slipped into her backpack.

Cory stood, adjusting his cap. "Sorry, man, that sucks."

Aries nodded and rushed out the door, colliding with Michael. Losing her balance, she fell flat on her butt.

"What the hell?" He stepped over her, shaking his head.

The P-pack laughed, whispering to each other as they walked past her. "Omigod, could anyone be more pathetic?" Peyton said.

Cory offered his hand, helping her up. "Are you okay?"

"Yes. Thanks."

"Rough morning."

Peyton circled back on Cory, wrapping her arm around his and pulling him away from Aries. "Where were you Saturday? The party was insane," she babbled on as they headed down the hallway.

Cory glanced back and waved.

Aries's eyes moistened. She blinked several times, forcing back the tears working hard to burst through.

Where are you, Mom? Why won't you contact me?

ARIES MADE it all the way to lunch without having another class with Peyton. Piper and Paige were in her history class, but they seemed to be the lesser of the three P evils. When the bell rang, Aries wandered around several buildings until she came across a group of trees in a courtyard. She walked past the lunch benches, overflowing with clusters of students. Avoiding the whole "You can't sit here" or "This seat's taken" ordeal, she slipped into the shade to eat her lunch unnoticed.

She rested against a tree trunk, stretching out her legs. Starving, she downed a ham and cheese sandwich, potato chips, and some juice. With 25 minutes to spare, she took out her notebook and drew. In-between pictures, she scanned the benches, spotting the P-pack. Unfortunately, Cory and a few other boys were with them.

She caught Cory looking over at her a few times. A moment later, she held his stare. He smiled, then continued talking to his friend.

As Aries went back to sketching, a fly landed on her leg. Instead of shooing it away, she studied it. The fly rubbed its front legs together, then hind legs.

Is somebody trying to communicate?

The appearance of flies, bees, dragonflies, or hummingbirds was usually an attempt to get her attention.

Turning the page in her notebook, she scribbled lines back and forth until she made the connection with Cory's grandmother. Her initial calling didn't bother Aries, as her voice wasn't as demanding as some of the others.

Hello, Cory's grandma.

"*Gladys. Call me Gladys.*"

Aries smiled. *Hello, Gladys.*

"*It's a pleasure, Aries.*"

Gladys, are you with others right now? Maybe Gladys could help her connect with her mother.

"*Did you tell Cory how special he is?*"

The fly tickled her leg as it moved toward her shoe. *How? It would be pretty awkward and weird to tell him that, don't you think?* She glanced in his direction. *Besides, he looks preoccupied with the perfect Peyton Price. What do I have to offer him? I'm a lanky, no-curves, flat-chested dork.*

"*You are beautiful, Aries, with a beautiful soul. That Peyton is fake, with a tormented soul. Things aren't always what they appear to be, Aries. Dig deeper, and you'll see. Cory needs your help. He's in trouble*"

The bell rang as the fly took off. *Trouble? What possible trouble could he be in?* she asked no one in particular.

With the connection with Gladys gone, Aries rose, grabbed her things, and headed toward her final class for the day.

Please don't let the P-pack be in there.

With the lunch benches empty, the only noise came from a horrendous buzzing sound overtaking her mind. She collapsed on a bench as the buildings and trees spun around her. Rubbing her temples, she regained focus as the buzz transformed into the cryptic voice.

"You're running out of time, Aries. You need to find out the truth. Now."

3

*A*ries arrived late to Spanish class, still shaken from her last connection. A guy with black hair, impressive green eyes, and a handsome smile stood at the door, tardy as well. He had a five o'clock shadow and looked too old to be a student. He gestured for her to walk in first, so she moved past him. He sat next to her in the back of the room.

The teacher walked over to them. "Bievenido. Me alegra que nos acompanes. Yo soy el Sr. Gutierrez. Cual es tu nombre?" Mr. Gutierrez asked.

"Mi nombre es Aries Dade."

"Buena. Senor?"

"Damon LeMoore."

Mr. Gutierrez jotted down something and directed everyone's attention to the front of the room. As Aries took notes, Damon asked her for a piece of paper. She hurried and handed him one, then got back to work. Cory sat next to Peyton a couple rows ahead of her. Setting down her pencil, she curled her lip. She hardly knew Cory, yet she hated the way he flirted with Peyton.

Damon turned to her. "Are you an Aries?"

"Yes," she whispered. It was bad enough to walk in late; she didn't want to get in trouble for talking.

"I guess that takes out the whole cheesy line, 'Hey, what's your sign?'"

She shrugged.

"Your parents smoke a lot of weed?"

"It's none of your business. Please stop talking. I'm trying to pay attention."

"Freshman, right?"

She sighed. "Sophomore. You must be a senior, or did you flunk a couple grades?"

He smiled. "Spunky...I like that. Yes, I'm a senior, and no, I didn't flunk. I had to take an elective class to graduate, so I picked this one. I haven't seen you before. New?"

"Yes." She continued to take notes.

"Where'd you move from?"

"Riverside."

He laughed. "Inland empire. This must be culture shock for you."

She ignored him.

Cory peeked over his shoulder, smiling at her. She smiled back, forgiving him for his association with Peyton.

Her smile faded when Cory shot Damon a dirty look and Damon glared back. The alpha dog communication between the two boys lasted a few moments.

Peyton glared back as well, then linked her arm through Cory's, pulling him to face forward, then whispering something in his ear.

She's acting like a freaking animal; definitely threatened and pissing all over her territory.

"That guy's a douche."

"Seems like you're the douche," Aries said.

Damon laughed. "You like him?"

"I don't even know him."

"But you have a psychic ability to know he's not a douche?"

"Something like that."

Mr. Gutierrez glanced in their direction, and Damon fell silent for a few moments.

"Since you're new, I'll help you out," he said.

"Now why would you want to do that?"

"I like you, Sophomore."

"You don't know me."

"True. But you're smart, sassy, and kind of hot."

A senior thought she was kind of hot? Aries tried to fight back a smile, unable to believe it.

"See, I knew I could get you to lighten up. You have a pretty smile, by the way. But in all seriousness, stay away from Cory Douglas. He's bad news."

Aries smirked, logging in to her computer. She answered the required questions, ignoring Damon for the rest of the period.

When the bell rang, Damon scooted back his chair and said, "See ya 'round, Sophomore."

Entranced for a moment by his piercing green eyes, she grabbed her belongings and headed out the door.

Aries strolled through the parking lot, stopping when she reached the curb as the P-pack piled into Peyton's champagne-colored convertible Mercedes. Closing her eyes, she tried to be grateful for the good things in her life. But she struggled, unable to come up with anything besides her father. He worked hard, trying to make up for the loss of her mother. But there was absolutely nothing he could do to take that pain away. And now the P-pack made the wound a little deeper by having the means to anything their hearts desired. Were they really happy, or was it all a facade?

A motorcycle roared up to the curb, causing her to jump back. The rider balanced the Harley and took off his helmet.

"Hey, Sophomore."

"Damon. You back to torment me?"

"No. Thought you might need a ride. You look a little lost."

"I'm good, thanks."

He held out a spare helmet. "C'mon. Hop on."

She shook her head.

"You know you want to."

She put her hands in her pocket and bit her lip. She'd never been on a motorcycle before. It could be fun. Dangerous, but fun.

"Beats walking in one hundred degrees," he said.

"Live a little and have some fun," a spirit said. *"You could use the distraction."*

I don't know.

She pulled out her cell. "Hold on." She called her dad. "Hi, Dad."

"Hey, Kiddo, I was just going to call you. How was your first day?"

"Alright."

"Listen, I can't get away right now. Can you wait in the library for an hour or so, until it cools off? I'd hate for you to have to walk home in this heat."

She glanced at Damon. Turning away from him, she whispered, "It's okay, Dad. I called to let you know I have a ride."

"That's great. You made a friend?"

"We'll see."

"There's money in the jar on the kitchen sink. Order take-out. I don't think I'll be home in time for dinner."

"Okay. Thanks."

"Love you, Kiddo."

She put away her phone and faced Damon.

He laughed. "The discount store called; they want their phone back."

"Shut up. Thanks for the offer, but I'd rather battle the heat." She walked away.

"Good," a different spirit chimed in. *"Stay far away from him."*

Why?

"No, you need to go," the previous spirit said.

Who are you two? You're confusing me.

Damon waddled the bike forward, following her. "C'mon, Sophomore, get on. I overheard your conversation. Besides, what do you have to lose?"

"My life."

"Trust me."

She stopped. "And why would I do that?"

"Because you want to." He held out the helmet one more time.

The P-pack sped past them, collectively yelling, "Loser."

"I see you have some fans." Damon smiled.

"Maybe they're yours."

A luxury SUV trailed Peyton's car. The driver side window went down. Cory waved from behind the wheel and then hit the brakes.

"Is he bothering you?"

Aries grabbed the helmet. "No." She waved. "Bye, Cory."

Cory looked worried for a second, which made him that much more attractive. He glared at Damon once more before pulling away.

"Alright, LeMoore, I'd like to arrive in one piece."

"You're in good hands, Sophomore."

She put on the helmet and saddled onto the motorcycle, gripping the seat.

"There's still time. Don't go with him."

"Stop scaring the girl. Go. Enjoy. You're in good hands."

"No, you're not."

"Yes, you are."

Shut up, both of you.

"Ready?" he asked.

"I guess."

"You have anywhere to be?"

"Not really."

"Then hold on," he said. He revved the gas and headed toward the coast.

She closed her eyes, smiling as the wind hit her face. The speed of the bike thrilled her. She'd never done anything remotely dangerous, and riding on the back of a Harley Davidson was both wild and exhilarating. It brought out a sense of freedom in her. Free from voices, free from always doing the right thing, free from her family issues. As the sun beamed down on her, she realized in that moment she didn't have a care in the world.

Damon had an edge to him she both admired and feared, but somehow he seemed safe. She could sense he wouldn't let anything bad happen to her. When he said, "Hold on to me. I'm going to show you what this baby can do," she had no worries obeying him.

She wrapped her arms around his waist, leaning into him. The warmth of his body and musk scent of his cologne gave her a spike of adrenaline.

She rested the side of her head against his back as they flew down the highway, taking in the clear blue sky, cascading waves, and cliffs that formed the coastline.

After a wide-open run of curving road, they hit some traffic as they worked their way south through Laguna Beach, down into Dana Point.

Aries didn't care how far Damon was going to ride. She hadn't felt that good since before her mother had passed.

Ten minutes later, he pulled off the road, heading into the next beach town. He parked in the lot next to the San Clemente pier, letting her hop off the bike first. He then took off his helmet and ran his hand through his hair.

With a sexy smile, he asked, "What?"

She blushed. Her attraction to him had gained momentum after the ride.

She handed him her helmet. "Nothing. Just wondering what we're doing."

"You hungry?"

"Yes, I'm starving."

"Cool. Me, too." He motioned with his head. "This way, Sophomore."

She glanced at the ocean as they walked along a beach trail.

"What'd you think?" he asked.

"About what?"

He nudged her. "The ride."

"It was alright."

He laughed. "Sure. I can see it in your eyes, you loved it."

She smiled. "Then why'd you ask?"

"Just wanted to make sure you actually can smile."

Making their way up the road to a pizza joint, she said, "It's going to take a lot more than a ride on the back of a motorcycle."

He raised his brows. "Really? You don't strike me as that kind of girl."

Her face turned crimson as she pushed his shoulder. "I didn't mean that."

He put his arm around her. "Okay, what did you mean?"

She removed his arm. "I meant getting to know you. The real you. I don't really have any friends, and I don't know...I just..." She turned away.

"Whoa, lighten up. I was just teasing you. Boy, Sophomore, I thought you had thicker skin." He opened the door for her.

The cool breeze from the restaurant made her relax. "I don't want you to get the wrong idea."

"Trust me, I don't."

She looked over the menu as Damon ordered two sodas.

"What sounds good?" he asked.

"Everything."

"Cool."

After their server dropped off pizza, pasta, and breadsticks, he asked, "So what's your story, Sophomore?"

He stared at her as she twirled her fork around some noodles. "I don't have a story."

He laughed. "Everybody has one."

"Okay, let's start with you."

"Ladies first. Why'd you move here?" He reached for a napkin and handed it to her. "You might need extra."

"Thanks. My dad's job."

"You have any brothers or sisters?"

"Just me and my dad." She dabbed her napkin on a slice of pizza, attempting to remove some grease.

"Where's your mom?"

"She passed."

He looked into her eyes. "I'm sorry. What happened?"

Shifting in her seat, she twirled the straw around in her glass.

"It's okay if you don't want to talk about it."

She glanced out the window. "I don't."

"Was she the one into astrology? Can you talk about that?"

"Yes." She smirked at him. "She was a Leo, which is a fire sign, so she really wanted her daughter to be one as well. When she found out I was one, she named me after the sign. She said as an Aries I'd start the party, then as a Leo she'd be the center of attention during the party; we're a perfect match. Her part was true. Me, not so much."

"You're young. I can see you as a leader."

"What's your sign?"

"I don't know. What's October twenty-seventh?"

She chuckled. "Scorpio. Explains your eyes."

"You like my eyes?" He smiled.

"I didn't say that." She grabbed her drink. "Is it my turn yet?"

He motioned for her to have the last slice, and she accepted.

"Go for it," he said, leaning back in the booth. "What do you want to know?"

"What happened between you and Cory?"

"I thought you wanted to get to know me?"

"I do. We'll get to that. I'm curious."

"It's a long story. We're going to need another date for that."

"Is this a date?"

"Well, yeah. We're eating, getting to know each other, and there's definitely a physical attraction."

She let out a nervous laugh. She'd never been on a date before. And she never imagined her first date would be with someone like Damon LeMoore.

"I'm not allowed to date 'til I'm sixteen."

The server cleared their plates and dropped off the check.

He shook his head. "I hope you don't get in trouble, then, cause this is a date, and I'm going to take you on another one Friday night."

"You're just giving me a ride home, and we decided to get food along the way. As far as Friday night, keep dreaming."

"I still have a couple days to work on you. If you want to know more about me and your boyfriend, you'll go."

"I don't have a boyfriend, and maybe I'll just ask Cory about it."

"Good luck with that." He paid the bill and stood up. "Ready?"

Or maybe I'll ask his grandma. Gladys, are you hearing this?

"Sure. Thank you," she said and followed him out.

They were silent on the ride home, but she didn't mind. The force of the wind and ocean view soothed her as the dipping sun filled the azure sky with wisps of pink and lavender.

When they stopped at a street light in Newport Beach, he asked, "Where exactly do you live?"

Pointing at a shopping center, she said, "You can drop me off over there." He might judge her if he saw where she lived.

"I'm making sure you get home safe."

The light changed, but Damon didn't move. A few drivers honked their horns. "Either you tell me, or you're going to piss off a lot of people."

"Eleventh Street."

He hit the gas. Several twists and turns later, he pulled up in the alley behind her place.

Handing him the spare helmet, she said, "Thank you, Damon. I had a lot of fun."

"Do I detect a compliment?"

"Don't push me."

"Friday night, Sophomore." He cranked the handle and sped away.

She hopped up the steps, smiling as she walked through the doorway. *What's your story, Damon LeMoore?*

As she locked the door, a spirit responded, *"You might not want to know the answer."*

4

After Aries finished her homework, she headed straight for the kitchen. Scavenging through the cupboards, she searched for something to eat. She grabbed a bag of cream-filled cookies and poured a glass of milk. Pulling apart the top cookie, she licked the filling, bringing back memories of her mother.

I wish you were here. I have so much to tell you.

She stared out the window into the darkness beyond, a low fog having camped out for the night. The only sound came from the distant breakers pounding the sand.

Aries pretended her mother sat down across the table to have a late-night snack with her, just like they used to do. Maybe the visualization and a make-believe conversation would create some type of real connection.

Regulating her breathing, she stared at the empty chair until she could picture her mom's wavy blonde hair, caring brown eyes, and contagious smile.

Aries visualized Elizabeth dunking a whole cookie into a glass of milk, making it extra soggy. After she finished the cookie, the image of her mother said, "Spill it, I can see the look in your eyes."

"There's this boy. He's perfect. For one, he's taller than me."

Elizabeth chuckled. "I knew it would be different in high school. You just needed to let the boys catch up to you. Go on."

"He's cute, and nice. At least he was in class today. You know what I mean?"

"Sweetheart, it's not the boys who are going to be mean to you. That's part of the reason why the girls are. So far, he sounds great."

"I get butterflies just sitting next to him." Aries grabbed another cookie, again peeling off the top. "I don't know if he'd be interested in me, and I'm not sure if he has a girlfriend. But there's definitely a popular rich girl staking her claim."

"Of course he's interested in you. He'd be a fool not to be. Just take it one day at a time."

Aries put down the rest of her cookie.

"What else is bothering you, sweetie?"

"Well, there's this other boy."

The visage of Elizabeth's mouth dropped. "I didn't see that one coming."

"He's cute, too, but in that bad boy, edgy kind of way. He's a senior."

Elizabeth's eyebrow rose, but she remained silent.

"I don't know what to do. I need your advice. Not just about the boys, but everything. I'm so lost without you."

She waited for her mother to tell her what to do and that everything would be okay. But the image of her mom faded, and her make-believe conversation failed.

Aries sighed. "Oh, Mom, where are you? What can I do to reach you? I have to know what really happened to you."

A faint smell of tobacco drifted through the air. "I want to talk to you, Mom, but I guess your grandpa will do."

Never having seen a picture of her great-grandfather without a tobacco pipe in his hand, Aries couldn't detect if the smell was real or not. But it didn't matter, because he made a solid connection and wanted to speak to her.

"Hi, Grandpa."

"Well, hello, beautiful."

"Tobacco is bad news, Grandpa, that's why you're on the other side."

He chuckled. *"Good thing it can only get me once."*

"Are you with—" Aries choked up.

"I'm always with her. She loves you more than you could ever imagine."

"Then why won't she talk to me?"

"She does."

"What?"

"You aren't listening, Aries."

"I don't understand."

"I think you're the one who's blocking her out."

She clenched her fists. "Why would I do that? That's ridiculous."

"Think about it."

Aries stood and paced across the tile. He might as well have been speaking a foreign language. She leaned against the counter, calming her energy to match her grandfather's.

"Grandpa," she called out, the smell of tobacco completely gone. "Me? Sure. What the hell are you talking about, Grandpa?" A vibrating sound filled the room for a moment. "Grandpa, are you there?" All the energy drained from her body as her mind raced with questions no one would answer.

She cleaned up the crumbs and rinsed her cup. Scheming up a new idea to get in touch with her mother, she walked down the hall and opened her dad's bedroom door. Pulling down a box from his closet, she carried it into her room. Setting the box on her bed, she stared at the words in black marker scribbled on the top, *Elizabeth's Dresser.* She hadn't yet been able to look through her mother's belongings.

"Is this what you mean by blocking her out, Grandpa?"

Unable to open the box, she closed her eyes. *Contact me, Mom.* With her index finger, she traced over her mother's name. *Please, Mom, I need your advice…I need you.*

Her tracing accelerated. Maybe she needed more energy to keep up with her mom's frequency.

Mom, what I really need is…

With no connection, she closed her eyes, frustrated at the world. Shuffling into the bathroom, she washed her face. Changing into pajamas, she sat next to the box, once again unable to look inside.

What am I missing? I want to hear your voice. I miss you so much. I need to tell you how much I love you. Please, Mom. She squeezed her eyes shut.

Something shattered inside the box.

Aries screamed and ran into the kitchen. The clock read 11:11, and her dad still wasn't home.

Where is he?

The still of the darkness outside escalated her fear as a buzzing sound burst into her head.

"Shut up and leave me alone!" she screamed, turning on every light in the apartment. Grabbing the remote, she flipped on the TV and cranked the volume, trying to tune out the overzealous soul.

The buzzing formed into a voice. *"Aries?"*

She sat hunched on the couch, rocking back and forth. "No, no, no," she whispered. She couldn't stand the sound of his voice.

"I'm trying to help you."

The lights flickered, then the electricity went off.

Stuck in the dark with the foreign spirit, she jumped up and searched for her phone. It had no service.

"What do you want?" she asked.

The electricity came back on as the volume from the TV echoed throughout the room.

Her father's truck pulling up outside distracted her. She smiled when her dad walked in, until she noticed he wasn't alone.

"Hey, what are you doing up, kiddo?" Ryan asked, surprised. He let go of his girlfriend's hand.

Kimberly smiled. "Hi, Aries. How was your first day of school?"

She shrugged.

Ryan glared at her. "Kimberly asked you a question."

Aries rolled her eyes. *Really? Hadn't noticed.*

She despised the fact that her dad dated someone who wasn't her mother. But more than that, she despised Kimberly. The complete opposite of her mom, Kimberly wore revealing clothes that exposed her fake breasts and overly worked-out rear. She tried way too hard to look young, wearing clothes Aries would wear, and she yearned for her father's attention.

"It was fine," Aries said, displaying a fake smile.

Ryan gave her a stern look. "Are you okay? Why is the TV so loud?"

"No reason. I'm fine." She turned off the TV. "Goodnight."

"Goodnight, Aries," Kimberly said. She turned and smiled at Ryan, brushing his hair off his forehead.

Aries observed the couple from the hallway. Her dad opened a bottle of red wine and prepared a plate of cheese and crackers, like he used to do for her mom when he'd come home late after work.

Aries slammed her bedroom door. She studied the box on her bed for a while. Picking it up, she placed it in her closet.

She'd buried the pain of her mother's death deep inside, in places she didn't have to look if she didn't want to. If she opened the box and saw her mother's belongings, she'd relive it all over again.

She grabbed her guitar and sat on the edge of her bed. Strumming lightly, she played a few of her mother's favorite songs, a strategy she used to make herself feel better. It also helped her try to connect to Elizabeth. She finished the last song, then put her guitar back in the closet.

What a crappy day.

Broken down from her father, great-grandfather, and the spoiled students at Newport Beach High, she didn't have the energy to block out the most demanding soul she'd yet encountered. She named him Mr. Overzealous.

Oh, what do you want now?

"The truth."

Something shifted in the box.

———————

5

*A*ries woke up from a sleepless night with one question stuck in her mind. The truth about what? She looked in the mirror.

The truth is, I look like crap.

Squeezing in a few drops, she attempted to remove the crimson streaks from her eyes. With a little help from white eyeliner and a few strokes of mascara, her eyes looked less swollen.

She curled her hair, adding plenty of hairspray and mousse, attempting to take attention away from her face.

She was in no mood to worry about the lack of designer clothes and shoes in her closet. She had only one mission: to get through the day.

She headed for the kitchen, only to find a half-naked Kimberly buttering some toast. "Oh, hi, Aries, I didn't hear you." She made no attempt to cover herself up. "Would you like some toast?"

Aries grabbed her backpack.

"Aries?"

"No. Tell my dad I'm taking the bus."

"Okay. Are you sure—"

Aries slammed the door. "Am I sure you're a whore? Yes," she mumbled as she stormed down the alley.

She'd rather wait a half-hour for the bus than spend another second in the same room as Kimberly. She sat on the bench, letting the early-morning rays chase the chill from the onshore breeze away. Closing her eyes, she meditated, thankful to be alone.

Several minutes later, a loud engine revved in front of her, breaking her reverie. Annoyed, she opened her eyes.

Of course, Damon.

She stared at him for a moment. "You know stalking is considered a crime."

"Hop on."

"No, thanks."

He glanced at his watch. "You do realize this bus is going to Long Beach, right? On the route you're headed, you might make it to school by noon. You even know what you're doing?"

She crossed her arms, avoiding his eyes. "What are you doing here?"

"Last time I checked, this is the direction toward school." He held up his spare helmet. "Let's go, Sophomore." He nodded toward the back seat.

Sighing, she got up, accepted the helmet, and swung her leg over the seat, adjusting herself behind him.

He smiled. "You get all dolled up just for me?"

She rolled her eyes. "Glad you think this is dolled up."

"Your hair looks good like that." Without waiting for her to respond, he sped off.

They arrived at school within minutes. Damon parked, adjusting his stance so she could hop off. She attempted to fix her hair but lost the battle due to hairspray and the knots that formed at the bottom from the wind.

Walking across the parking lot, she continued to work out

the tangles in her hair. "So, are you going to be my chauffeur for the rest of the year?"

"If only I could be so lucky."

From across the courtyard, Paige shouted Aries's name. Bouncing toward them, she said, "Hi," out of breath. "Wow, you look different with your hair like that."

"Thanks…I think."

"Oh yes, definitely a compliment. You look like you're twenty-one."

"Paige, do you know Damon?"

"Duh, he's practically my brother."

Well, how the hell am I supposed to know that?

He nodded, then turned back toward Aries. "Well, I'll let you girls chat. My class is over there." He pointed in the opposite direction. "See you in fifth."

Why was Paige acting as if they were best friends? After Damon walked away, Paige grabbed her arm. "Ohmigod, are you guys dating?"

"No." Aries freed herself from Paige's grip and headed toward her classroom, but Paige caught up and tried to match her stride.

"Do you like him?"

"I just met him."

"So that's a no?"

Please go away. "I guess."

Paige stopped as they entered the hallway and put her hand on her hip. "Hmm."

Aries stopped as well. "What's that supposed to mean?"

"You can't hide that kind of chemistry," she said. "Be careful."

Aries shook her head. "Whatever."

"Whatever? I know things about him. He's been friends with my brother since kindergarten. I'd hate to see anything bad happen to you. There's been too much of that around here lately."

Aries gave her a strange look.

"What?" she asked. "It's a girl thing. We need to look out for each other."

"Okay. But he seems pretty harmless to me."

Paige laughed. "Oh, honey, you have so much to learn."

Aries squinted as Cory appeared, heading toward the classroom.

He waved. "Hey."

Aries blushed. "Hi."

Paige scrutinized her before whispering, "Ahh. So, I guess you're *not* into Damon." She giggled.

"After you." Cory held out his hand as they walked past him into the classroom.

Paige stood on her toes to whisper in Aries's ear. "Word of advice, watch out for Peyton Price if you're headed down the Cory Douglas path." She bounced back into the hallway.

Aries shook her head. First of all, she might be new to the school, but she wasn't blind. And second, it was none of Paige's business what path she was on.

As soon as Aries sat down, the P-pack made their entrance, laughing and gathering the eyes of all the boys in the class.

Peyton glared at Aries and laughed. "Now I know where the birds' nest under my balcony landed. Nice hair."

Paige giggled, but Piper turned away from the pack and took her seat.

Aries brushed her fingers through her hair until they got stuck in another knot.

Peyton turned to Paige. "What, did her finger get stuck in a light socket?"

Paige shook her head before sitting down.

Miss Townsend walked toward the front of the room. "Alright, today before we get into our main lesson, we are going to do a little exercise for our mental and emotional health. I want everyone to take three long breaths. Ready?" After counting the third breath, she said, "You're going to keep that same rhythm as you close your eyes, letting go of all your thoughts, concerns, worries, etcetera. Just total relaxation. We're learning ways to cope with stress, and today we'll focus on meditation. Has anyone ever tried to meditate before?"

Aries raised her hand.

"It figures. Loser," Peyton mumbled.

Cory tapped Aries's shoulder. "Really? Or are you just trying to make Miss T feel better by having at least one person pay attention to her?"

"No, really, I like to meditate."

He nodded.

Miss Townsend turned on a computer, playing relaxation music at a low volume. "Get comfortable. I know it's tough in a classroom, but try."

Aries closed her eyes, attempting to let go of all her troubles. Her peaceful state lasted a few seconds before a buzzing sound intruded in it. The sound in her head grew louder, causing her to swat around her head a couple of times, like trying to shoo an annoying fly.

I must look ridiculous.

She stopped her hand motion, squeezed her eyes shut, and clenched her fists.

"Are you okay?" Cory asked.

Aries nodded as a piece of the ceiling fell and landed on Paige's head.

Paige screamed before she recovered and dusted debris out of her hair.

Miss Townsend scrambled for napkins, handing one to Paige as she picked up the chunk of ceiling tile.

Aries's fists remained clenched.

Cory brushed her arm. "Did you see that?" he asked, his eyes wide with amusement.

"Sorry. I'm sorry," Aries said.

Miss Townsend looked up. "For what?"

Aries's temperature rose as the whole class stared at her. "Um…" She'd caused the incident. Things like that had happened before, but she couldn't explain that to the class. "I meant for Paige. Are you okay?"

Miss Townsend ignored her, continuing to sweep up the mess.

Paige continued to fix her hair. "Yes, I'm fine," she said, with flushed cheeks.

Miss Townsend put away the broom. "Well, I guess that was enough relaxation for today," she said.

As she lectured them about self-esteem, Gladys's voice popped in.

"Hello, dear."

Hello, Gladys.

A warm light from Gladys appeared in her mind, causing Aries to smile from the inside out, her body light as a feather as she concentrated on the connection.

"Why are you wasting so much time?" Gladys asked. *"You need to pay attention to the sign."*

What do you mean?

"Puh-"

"Peyton?" she accidentally questioned out loud.

Cory looked her way. "What did you say?"

"The sign…" Gladys's voice faded, and the warm light disappeared.

Aries cleared her throat. "Nothing."

Miss Townsend distributed worksheets. "Take turns filling out the worksheet with your partner. There's nothing better than a few compliments to help boost self-esteem."

Michael blurted out, "Are we actually getting graded for this nonsense?"

"Of course. Please take this assignment seriously. You'll be marked down for inappropriate remarks."

After reading the directions, Aries began biting her fingernail.

Luckily, Cory said, "I'll go first."

She met his eyes for a moment, then he wrote something on the paper, handing it to her. After reading it, she couldn't look at him. Her cheeks were burning from amazement as her mouth curved up. She bit her bottom lip, trying to hide any reaction. She re-read the paper.

1) Give your partner a compliment:
Beautiful

"Okay, your turn." Cory displayed a smile, sending chills down her spine.

She shifted in her chair. She didn't have enough space on the paper for all the things she liked about him.

Trying to redirect the awkward moment, she said, "You give great compliments."

He laughed. "Good one."

"No, really, I like your hair." She picked up her pencil and wrote down the compliment.

He combed his fingers through it. "Right on. Everyone keeps telling me to cut it."

She shook her head. "Don't do that."

He nodded. "You have such cool eyes. Are they green?"

Shaking her head, she said, "Hazel."

"I added a new compliment," he said. "You're different."

"That doesn't sound like much of a compliment."

He put his hand on her arm. "Trust me, it's refreshing. You're witty and sarcastic, in a good way."

Miss Townsend walked up to the table, collecting the worksheet. "Aries, I'd like to talk to you for a few minutes after class. Nothing to worry about." She smiled, then headed back to the front of the room.

"I wonder what that's all about?" Cory asked.

Aries shrugged. She checked the time. Five minutes

remained.

Cory put away his computer. "Hey, I know it's none of my business, but I saw you with Damon LeMoore. I have to tell you to be careful."

She narrowed her eyes. *What is going on with these two?* "Don't worry. I'm a big girl."

"I'm sure. But since you're new and all, I'd hate to see you get involved with someone like him."

"Thanks for your concern."

"I don't want anything bad to happen to you." He settled back in his seat, checking his phone.

Bad? Why does everyone keep saying that?

The bell rang, and Cory stood. "Hope it goes well with Miss T."

She smiled.

After the classroom emptied out, she approached Miss Townsend. "You wanted to speak with me?"

"Yes. Relax, I just wanted to make sure you're okay."

"Yes, I'm fine."

"I noticed how some of the girls treat you, and since I am teaching about mental and emotional health, I wanted to check in with you to make sure it doesn't become a problem."

"I appreciate that, but really, I'm fine."

Miss Townsend's tone became more serious. "There is one other thing, Aries."

"Yes?"

"It's about your reaction to the ceiling."

Aries took a step back.

Miss Townsend regarded her intently. "Why do you think you were responsible?"

"I didn't...I don't." She fidgeted with the strap on her backpack.

"You sounded guilty when you said you were sorry, and I'm wondering why."

"I don't want to be late." Aries turned away. "Thanks for your concern."

She dashed off to her next class.

❧

ARIES COULDN'T CONCENTRATE throughout Mr. McCready's lecture about the Roman Empire. His mouth moved, and words were coming out, but she kept picturing the way Miss Townsend questioned her. Did she figure out Aries had a psychic gift? The thought scared the crap out of her. This secret of hers was between her and the dead, not the living. She tapped her fingers on the desk.

Stop being paranoid and pull it together.

Aries sighed when Mr. McCready put her in a group with Paige, Michael, and Piper. Thank God Peyton wasn't in the class.

Paige led the discussion. "Okay, I'll give the speech. Michael, you're great with technology, so you can come up with some type of slide show."

He saluted her. "Yes, ma'am."

She rolled her eyes. "Fine, you do all the talking, and I'll work on the computer."

He leaned back. "Loosen up, spastic nerd, I was only kidding."

She glared at him.

Piper applied lipstick, looking bored. "You're such an ass, Michael." She pressed her lips together. "Paige's just trying to get us all a good grade."

"Can everyone meet after school to work on it?" Paige asked. "We can go to my place."

Michael scanned the room. "I don't think anyone else really gives a crap about this assignment. I guarantee they're not working on it after school."

"Well, we're not everybody else," Paige said, annoyed.

He cleared his throat. "The only way I'm giving up my precious time is if we go to Princess's house, since she has the killer back yard."

"Fine. Is that okay, Piper?" Paige asked.

"Sure." She checked her cell.

"What, do you have to clock in with The Queen first?" Michael laughed.

Piper gave him a dirty look. "Peyton and I aren't joined at the hip." She wrote down her address with a code to get through the security gate and handed it to Aries.

"She can go with me," Paige said.

"Whatever. Okay, see you guys at my place."

ARIES SAT under her tree at lunch again, eating her sandwich in peace. No disturbances from flies, the P-pack, or the other side. She found herself a little too excited for Spanish class, which had nothing to do with the subject. Picturing Damon brought a smile to her face.

He's not my type, she repeated to herself as she walked toward the building. Cory, on the other hand…

She shook her head. *Stop thinking about boys.* It worked for a few minutes until the bell rang, then she wound up near both of them, filing into the room.

"Hi." Cory waved.

She smiled. "Hi." *Speak of the devil.*

He walked to his seat.

Damon brought her back to reality. "Glad to see you made it to class on time, Sophomore."

"And you as well." They both sat down.

"Sorry, did I interrupt something?"

"What?"

"You were all googly-eyed over your boyfriend."

She hit him. "Shut up."

They opened their laptops and started on the assignment. "Do you need a ride after school?" he asked.

"No, thanks."

"Do we really have to play this game again?"

She sighed. "What game?"

"Where you say no a couple times, then make me beg. 'Cause there's a new trend where seniors beg sophomores, and I'd hate to miss out on that."

"Thank you, but I have a group project to work on, and we're meeting at Piper's house."

"Piper Zacora?"

"Is there more than one Piper at this school?"

He shrugged. "I don't know. I find it hard to believe you're hanging out with her."

"I guarantee I wasn't her first choice, but our teacher assigned the groups. Anyway, she seems the most normal out of the P-pack."

"Huh?"

"Peyton, Paige, Piper." Aries rolled her eyes.

He laughed. "I was picturing something completely different. But you're right about that."

"How well do you know her?"

A strange expression flashed across his face before he changed back into his usual confident self. "I know she's a sophomore, her parents are loaded, she parties a lot and got a DUI over the summer, and she's hot."

What is he hiding? "You think everyone's hot."

He stared into her eyes for a moment. "No, I'm actually very picky."

"You said I was hot."

He smiled. "Like I said, I'm picky."

Turning away from his gaze, she asked, "Well, what about Peyton?"

He glanced over at Peyton and shivered. "She's sexy as hell, there's no denying that, but something about her creeps me out."

While observing Peyton, a spirit flashed Aries an image of a young boy in a wheelchair, sending chills down her arms.

Go away, whoever you are. Peyton is bad enough; I don't want any extra info about her.

"Are you okay?" Damon asked.

She cleared her throat. "Yes, fine. I feel the same way about her." She smirked, while Peyton interacted with Cory. "Does the whole school know about Piper's DUI?"

He nodded. "Hell, the whole school knows I gave you a ride home yesterday, and to school this morning."

"Really?"

He smiled.

"That must suck for Piper. She's not even old enough to drink."

"Or drive," Damon said. "That's the thing."

"What?"

"I don't think she was."

"Driving?"

"Yep."

They worked for the remainder of the class in silence. As the bell rang, Damon turned off his computer. "Be careful today."

"Everyone keeps telling me that."

"Then it might be a sign."

A sign? She tried to put the pieces of Gladys's advice together: something about Cory being in trouble, things aren't as they appear, and be careful. But could she trust anyone? Including Gladys?

Waiting until everyone cleared out of the classroom, Aries grabbed her bag and entered the empty hallway. She took a few steps when all the lights shut off.

"Hello?" she called out, picking up her pace.

When she reached the door, the lights turned back on.

6

---

*A*ries and Paige walked through an elaborate iron gate and up the quarter-mile path to Piper's house. The multi-million-dollar estate sat high up on the cliffs of Newport Coast, overlooking the ocean.

Aries's mouth dropped. "I can't believe she lives here."

"Wait 'til you see the inside." Paige knocked on the door.

The housekeeper greeted the girls. "Good afternoon, ladies, please come in. The others are outside in the back yard," she said.

Aries's mouth remained open as she followed their guide through the house to the back yard, careful not to bump into anything.

Piper lay on an outdoor bed, wearing a black bikini, over-sized black sun hat, and designer sunglasses. She looked like a model at some fancy resort. Michael sat on a barstool, at a bar and grill area larger than Aries's entire apartment, holding a bottle.

With her hand on her hip, Paige asked, "Is that beer?"

"Yep. You want one?" Michael flicked the bottle cap toward the trash can, missing.

"Really, Piper?" Paige curled her lip.

Piper flipped through the pages of a magazine. Without looking up, she said, "We have margaritas, too."

"This is ridiculous. You two never take anything seriously. I can't buy my way into an Ivy League like you. I don't have a famous dad." Paige let out a long sigh.

Who could Piper's father be? *Better not to be an even bigger freak by asking.*

Piper put down her magazine and took a sip of a frozen drink. She held it toward Paige. "Have a sip and try to lighten up."

"No. I have to meet the fam for dinner after this."

Michael lit a joint. "Then here." He held it toward her. "Anything to make you chill out. God, you're a major buzzkill."

Piper sat up. "Well, then help yourself. The bar's fully stocked. And there are plenty of non-alcoholic drinks." She looked at Aries. "You want a marg? It's no trouble. Marisol makes the best."

"No, thanks, I'll just have some water."

"Alright, Miss Goodie-Two-Shoes, where do you want to start?" Michael asked Paige.

Piper grabbed a towel and walked over toward the bar. "Yeah, Paige, what do you need?"

Paige reached into her bag, pulling out a laptop. "I want to focus on the demise of the Roman Empire, like Mr. McCready told us to do, but I was thinking we could tie it into the present somehow. Since history repeats itself and all. What do you guys think?"

"I think we need music," Michael said.

"That's what's missing." Piper walked toward the sink area and activated the outdoor sound system.

Paige cursed under her breath and pulled up pictures of the colosseum. "Do you think you could draw that, Aries? If not, we could just print pictures and make a collage."

"No. I can draw it."

"Sweet, an authentic picture would be cool," Paige said. "Piper, do you still have all the paint and boards from our science project last year?"

Piper nodded, turning up the volume. One of Aries and her dad's favorite bands blared through the back yard. A spirit tried to break through regarding the band, but Aries couldn't make a direct connection. When the guitar solo started, Piper shook her hair forward and started to rock out. Aries smiled, playing air guitar.

Piper glanced up. "Right on. Do you play guitar?"

"I try."

"You should see Piper sometime," Michael said. "It's in her DNA."

"Let's get the supplies, and I'll show you," Piper said as she headed toward the house.

Aries followed her inside, ascending a circular staircase. The upstairs matched the bottom level, with windows instead of walls, showcasing the Pacific Ocean. They walked into a room with guitars and records everywhere. A custom shelf held a couple of Grammys and giant picture of the band IDK covered one wall, with a signed guitar from the lead guitarist on a stand in front of it. Aries solved the mystery.

"That's your dad's guitar?" *Is that what you were trying to tell me?* she asked the unknown spirit.

"*Yes,*" he said. "*I was their manager. Bunch of as—*"

"One of many," Piper said.

"Ohmigod - Robby Zacora is your dad," Aries whispered.

"*Don't get too excited,*" the manager said.

Piper plugged the guitar into an amplifier, tuning it. She played her dad's most famous solo from the song they were listening to at the pool, then handed the guitar to Aries.

"Your turn."

Aries blushed. "I'm really not that good."

She could barely wrap the strap around herself, knowing a famous artist had used that same guitar. Starstruck, even though the star wasn't there, she got adjusted and played a classic rock hit.

"Like I said, the man is a complete…"

Aries concentrated on the notes, drowning out the manager.

Piper smiled. "That was the first song my dad taught me."

Aries finished, then attempted an IDK song.

"Nice," Piper said. "You're better than you think." She started dancing. "Not as good as me, though," she joked.

"Of course not." Aries smiled, finishing the song. She handed back the guitar.

Piper set it down, putting her arm around Aries. "We should jam sometime."

Aries nodded. Piper definitely had rock star blood in her. She oozed cool. Why would she be friends with uppity snobs like Peyton and Paige?

Making their way to a spare bedroom toward the back of the house, the girls grabbed the art supplies. They then joined Paige and Michael, who were standing so close, it appeared as though they were kissing. But as they approached the couple, they saw they were actually arguing about the assignment.

Piper handed Michael another beer. "Here, now shut up and do whatever she says."

Marisol placed a tray of various appetizers on the table and set down a pitcher of strawberry margarita.

"She doesn't care that you're underage?" Aries asked.

Piper looked puzzled, like the thought had never occurred to her. "For what my dad pays her, she doesn't question anything."

How sad. Aries glanced past the infinity pool, out toward the ocean. *Piper has it all, why would she feel the need to drink?*

The deceased manager tried to cut in again, but Paige broke Aries's concentration by handing her the laptop with a picture of the colosseum. Aries placed a poster board on the table next to the bar and began to paint.

After a couple hours, Aries had made progress with her painting. She reached for a hot wing, but the plate was empty.

"Dude, you'd think she was the one who was high." Michael laughed. "You didn't save any for us."

Aries put down the brush. "Sorry, painting makes me hungry."

"Marisol can make us dinner," Piper said. "She makes a killer carne asada."

"I'm out of here in ten," Michael said. "Cory's picking me up."

Aries's stomach dropped. "Um…I'm with Paige."

"Sorry, I just ordered a car, and it'll be here any minute," Paige said.

Piper made a sad face. "You guys suck. The party's just getting started."

"I can ask my dad if he can pick me up later." Aries picked up the brush, dipping it in paint.

Piper smiled. "Yes."

"Alright, whatever," Paige said. "Let's wrap this up."

Aries glanced up. "Is everything okay?"

"Yes, fine. I just want to make sure we have everything ready to go for the presentation."

Paige went back to work on her laptop as Aries painted. Michael and Piper lay on a cabana bed, sipping their drinks.

Aries scooted closer to Paige. "Are they a thing?"

"No." She curled her lip.

"Sorry, it was only a question. I didn't realize it was such an offensive one."

"It's not. I know you're new and all, but everyone always

thinks they are, so it gets annoying." She stopped typing. "Speaking of annoying things, what's going on with you and Damon?"

"Nothing." Aries switched to a thinner brush.

"Sure."

"Seriously," Aries said.

"Good. *So,* are you excited Cory's coming over?"

Paige's voice became even more irritating when she asked stupid questions. "No. Why would you think that?"

"Oh, I don't know, the way your entire face lit up when Michael said his name."

A loud splash distracted the girls. Michael had thrown Piper in the pool. She laughed and splashed water in his face as they began play-fighting. Piper screamed, then swam toward the steps.

"Is she okay?"

"She's fine." Paige flashed Michael a dirty look.

Paige is acting so strange. Why would she care if the two are flirting?

A couple bees flew in-between the girls before darting away. Paige screamed and jumped off her chair as Aries closed her eyes, concentrating to hear the spirit's message.

"Tell Paige nobody cares. She doesn't have to hide anything."

Paige sat back down, glancing around to make sure the bees were gone.

"Are you and Piper good friends?" Aries asked.

"Tell her."

She seems agitated. I don't think it's a good idea. Aries counted to three, clearing the spirit from her mind.

"I've known her since kindergarten," Paige said. "We're not BFFs or anything."

"Is it because of Peyton?"

"No. I don't even know if Piper is that great of friends with her. She's nice to everyone but doesn't seem to be close to anyone. Especially now after…" Paige shook her head. "Never mind. And she's never had a boyfriend either."

"Well, neither have I."

"Yeah, but she's Piper Zacora."

Aries went back to work.

"I didn't mean anything by that." Paige's voice reached an even higher pitch.

Aries smiled. "Trust me, I get it." She waited a moment before asking, "Do you think it has to do with her dad?"

Paige shook her head. "More like her mom. She's a model and lives in Milan. She didn't even fight for custody. Piper was only four. It's so sad."

Aries nodded. *What's worse, having your mom living but not want you, or having her betray you before she died?*

7

---

*C*ory appeared in Piper's back yard a few minutes after Paige left. He did a special handshake with Michael, ending in a fist bump.

"Ready, bro?" Cory hugged Piper, then walked over to Aries. "Hi."

She glanced up. "Hi."

He checked out her painting. "Wow, that's awesome. Is that the colosseum?"

"Yes. I'm painting a before-and-after picture."

"Screw McCready, you should sell that."

"It's not *that* good."

"Guys, check out Aries's painting." He waved them over.

"Later," Michael called out, grasping on to Piper.

She smirked. "Let go, I wanna see."

Pushing Michael away, she sauntered over. "Ohmigod, Aries, it looks professional. McCready's going to shit himself." She took a closer look. "The sunset looks familiar. Have you ever sold a painting before?"

Aries let out a laugh. "No."

"I've seen this before."

Michael grabbed her from behind. "Yeah, it's called a history book."

"Not the colosseum, dumbass, the background. I mean every color, from the different shades of orange to where the sun is and how it looks. Where have I seen this before?" She shook her head. "Crazy."

Aries shrugged. "I don't know."

"Are you done? Come play with us." Piper smiled.

"Aren't you guys leaving?" Aries asked in a tone she didn't intend, letting her nerves take over.

"Why, you want to get rid of us?" Cory asked.

"No, no, I just figured you were, is all." She swallowed, trying to act nonchalant.

"They're staying for dinner, right?" Piper batted her eyelashes at the boys.

Michael mouthed something to Cory, and Cory nodded.

Piper clapped. "I'll let Marisol know."

Aries kept working, doing minor touch-ups. Even though she'd already finished, she didn't feel confident making small talk with the boys.

Piper returned, lighting the fire pit and tiki torches. "Let's go in the Jacuzzi."

Aries sucked in her stomach. "I don't have a bathing suit," she said. "I can just dip my feet."

"We could all skinny dip," Michael said, raising his brow.

"Pig." Piper hit him. Turning back to Aries, she said, "You can borrow one of mine."

"I don't think I'll fit," she said, hating everything about her body.

Piper shrugged. "Alright, let me know if you change your mind."

Piper turned on the jets as they gathered at the Jacuzzi, easing in slowly. Aries sat on the side, letting her feet dangle in the water. She swirled her legs in the bubbles, trying to stay in the moment, blocking the other side from barging into her mind.

"How was practice?" Michael asked Cory. "Anderson ease up in this heat?"

"Are you kidding? He went harder." Cory switched his voice, imitating Coach Anderson. "This is where we separate the boys from the men. You need to stop for a water break or slow down, go call your mama, and don't bother coming back to the field."

"Man, what a jerk."

"He did end up giving us extra water breaks though."

"What sport do you play?" Aries asked.

Michael laughed. "You are clueless, aren't you?"

"Football. You're going to the game tomorrow night, right?"

"First I'm hearing of it."

They all looked at her as if she were from a different planet.

"Cory's the quarterback." Piper pushed his arm. "Big man on campus this year."

"You should go," Cory said as he held her gaze for a moment.

Aries nodded.

"Yes, and then you can go to the afterparty," Piper said. "Everyone will be there."

"I don't know," Aries said. *That must be the party Damon mentioned.*

"I want you to go." Cory nudged her.

"She's going," Piper said.

"I'll have to check with my dad first." She could always use him as an excuse if she chickened out.

"Tell him you're spending the night here. Marisol will cover for us."

"Where's the party?"

"Paige's," Piper said. "It's tradition. Her parents go on vacation this time every year. It started five years ago with her older brother."

"I don't think Paige would want me there," Aries said. "And Peyton definitely wouldn't."

"The only person Peyton wants there is Douglas over here," Michael said, splashing him.

"What can I say? I'm the man," Cory teased, wiping the water off his face.

"Are you guys a couple?"

His face lost all expression, and everyone remained quiet as tension filled the air.

Aries tapped the water with her foot, then covered a jet for a moment. "Well, are you?"

No one spoke. The Jacuzzi jets were now the only sound as everyone looked in different directions.

Aries sensed Gladys trying to come through. Her voice seemed far away, as if she knew Aries didn't want to be bothered, yet at the same time she needed to be heard.

Working over by the grill, Marisol broke the silence, calling out, "Miss Piper, all ready, senorita."

"Oh, thank God," Piper mumbled. "You guys hungry?"

"Starving," Aries said.

Michael and Piper walked over to the table. Cory stood, reaching his hand out to help her up.

"Thank you." She admired his brown eyes and sexy smile for a moment too long.

Aries's heart fluttered as her head spun. Cory excited her, yet at the same time he confused her. Why all the secrecy?

"What do you like on your tacos?" he asked.

"Everything."

"How many?"

"I'll start with two."

"Nice. Go sit down, I got it."

"Thank you." She enjoyed having a guy take care of her.

Michael and Cory brought the girls their plates. Piper had only one taco, making Aries feel like a pig.

"What do you want to drink, Princess?" Michael asked.

"I'm sick of margs," Piper said. "I'll have whatever you're having."

Michael handed her a beer. Aries couldn't imagine drinking alcohol, but Piper made it look fun as she dropped the lime in the bottle and took a sip.

"Douglas?" He offered him a beer.

"No, man, I'm driving."

"Suit yourself." He clanked Piper's bottle. "Cheers." Turning toward Aries, he asked, "How do you like Newport?"

He actually spoke to her. All day, he'd acted like she didn't exist. "I like it so far. The beach is amazing. But it's hard to start over, especially when a guy knocks you down and acts like it's your fault."

"Ooh," Piper and Cory said in unison.

"Yeah, why are you such an ass?" Piper asked.

He shrugged. "I have a rep to hold up. Don't all you chicks love the bad boy?"

"The hot bad boy, but not the a-hole," Piper said.

"Oh, so I'm a jerk, huh?" He tickled her.

Piper squirmed. "Stop. Now apologize to Aries."

"I'm so sorry," he said in a sarcastic tone.

Aries nodded. "Uh huh."

"Really. It'll never happen again."

She smiled.

"Especially now that I know my boy's—"

Cory kicked him under the table.

"Dude, that hurt."

"That was the point," Cory said.

"Alright, alright."

That his boy is what? Confusing? Amazing? Could possibly like her? She shook her head. If only her life worked out that way.

"Can I get you anything else?" Cory asked.

"No, thanks, I'm full. Plus, I think my dad will be here soon."

"No, stay the night," Piper said. "I get lonely all by myself."

"My dad won't let me on a school night."

"I'll stay," Michael said as he swooped her up and carried her over to a lounge chair. They flopped down, looking up at the stars.

"What does she see in him? She seems so out of his league."

"A friend," Cory said. "He's looked out for her ever since I can remember. It always looks like they flirt with each other, but they're just friends."

"But they hook up?"

"People think they do because they get wasted together and he stays the night a lot. But to my knowledge, they haven't done anything. She thinks of him as a brother. And he's very protective of her."

"That's sweet. You guys seem like a close group."

"The three of us are." He analyzed her for a moment. "To answer your earlier question, no, Peyton isn't my girlfriend."

"Then why didn't you just say that?"

"It's complicated."

"Not really. Either she is or she isn't."

He looked into her eyes, putting his hand on her knee. "It is, and she isn't."

Aries smiled, taking in the moment of being touched by him. She glanced up at the stars, feeling as though Gladys was winking at her.

"Where did you learn how to draw?" Cory asked.

"My mom. She was an amazing artist."

"Is that what she did for a living?"

"No, but that was her dream. I guess I got in the way."

"I doubt that. You were probably her inspiration."

Aries focused on a bug crawling over a crack in the ground.

"I can't imagine losing my mom. It was hard enough losing my favorite grandparents."

"What were they like?" she asked, interested to learn more about Gladys through his eyes.

"When's your dad getting here? There's not enough time in the world to tell you all the amazing things about them."

"We have a few minutes, please tell me."

His eyes lit up. "My Grandpa Joe would take me out fishing on the weekends I had free from sports. We'd head out toward Catalina Island, and we'd have these man-to-man talks." He let out a soft laugh. "Well, that's what he'd call them. I was six when we had our first one, I'll never forget. I actually felt like a man. But then he died when I was twelve. What really sucked is, it was like a double whammy, it happened around the same time…" He shook his head. "Enough about me, I want to hear about you."

"No, go on, I'm curious."

"Well, my dad left us." He stared at the moon.

"Sorry." Aries regretted making him have to say it out loud.

For a moment, neither one spoke. The palm trees framing the yard swayed in the warm breeze, creating a soft rustling sound that filled the void of their silence.

He swept his fingers through his hair. "But then my grandma picked up right where he left off, God rest her soul. She couldn't stand the tiny fishing boat. Made her seasick, but she still took me out. She wasn't into fishing, but she told me she wouldn't change that time spent with me for the world."

"You really miss them, huh?"

He nodded.

"Oh, I miss CJ so much." Gladys's voice came through. *"Isn't he just a doll?"*

"They're looking out for you, and they miss you, too."

He gave her a skeptical look.

"Well, that's what everyone tells *me* anyway." *I wish I could tell you Gladys is here.*

"Tell me something about your mom."

"Wow, where do I begin? She was my world. I didn't want to be like her; I wanted to *be* her. She was my best friend. I told her everything." Aries paused, collecting herself. "She wanted me to be smart and independent so I could be anything I wanted. Education was super important to her. She grew up in Riverside, too, but she would dream about living by the beach. She'd take me there during the summer, hoping one day we'd live there." Her voice cracked. She drew a breath, unable to meet his eyes. "I miss her so much, it hurts." Her eyes welled up.

"I'm so sorry." He put his hand on her shoulder. "Please don't cry. Because then I'm going to cry, and you know Michael will never let me live it down. The whole school will think I'm a wuss."

She smiled. "Okay, I won't for the sake of your reputation."

"My deepest gratitude. How can I ever repay you?"

"It's just nice having someone to talk to like this."

He placed the loose hair covering her face behind her ear. "I agree."

She nodded.

"I haven't even told those knuckleheads over there about my grandparents."

"Well, thanks for sharing with me," she said.

"Ditto. It's refreshing to hear how much you loved and respected your mom. Everybody around here despises their parents."

"I did…I mean I do, love her so much." *That's why her death doesn't make any sense.*

But she wasn't going to volunteer that information to him. She didn't even talk about it with her father. So far, Cory seemed trustworthy, but anybody could appear that way after a couple days. Better to lean on the cautious side for now.

"Do you mind if I ask how she died?"

Aries shrugged. "That's the thing. I'm not really sure."

"What do you mean?"

"Let me rephrase that. I know what *they're* telling me. But I don't believe it."

"They?"

"Doctors, police, my dad." She took a sip of water. "How'd your grandparents die?"

Cory analyzed her for a moment, not pressing the issue. "My grandpa had a heart attack, and I think my grandma actually died of a broken heart. *They* said she died peacefully in her sleep, and my grandpa went quick. It's good neither one of them suffered, but still sucks the same."

"Yeah."

They sat in silence as Marisol cleaned the table. Piper and Michael moved back to the Jacuzzi. When Marisol went back inside, Aries asked, "Do you ever see your dad?"

"When my mom makes me. Can't stand the guy."

"But he's your dad. You may not like that he left you, but at least he's alive."

He appeared to be deep in thought.

Aries checked her phone. "Speaking of dads, mine's at the gate."

"I'll walk you out."

"I don't think that's a good idea. I don't know how he'd react to boys being here, especially with no adult supervision. Wouldn't be a fun conversation." She stood.

He got up as well. "You have a point." He leaned in and hugged her.

She turned away. "Um, okay, bye, Cory."

"See you later."

She walked over to Piper. "My dad's here. Do you mind bringing the project to school?"

"Not at all." She got out, wrapping a towel around her. She hugged Aries. "See ya."

As Marisol showed her out, she couldn't wait to tell her dad about playing Robby Zacora's guitar. She ran up to his truck, only to find Kimberly sitting in the middle.

Ryan hopped out, opening the passenger door for her. "Hi, Kiddo. Wow, it's good to know people in high places. Look at these houses."

"Yep." All her enthusiasm drained from her body, replaced by nausea.

"Hi, Aries, did you have fun?" Kimberly smiled. With her mini dress hiked up her legs, Aries didn't want to look in her direction for fear of seeing her underpants. If she even wore any.

"Hi. Uh huh."

"Are you hungry?" Kimberly asked. "Ryan, we should stop for take-out. What would you like?"

"I'm not hungry."

Ryan raised a brow. "Since when?"

"I ate a big dinner."

"I know you can't pass up ice cream. What do you say?"

"I'm really tired."

Ryan gave her a puzzled look and put the truck in gear. They drove home in silence.

When they arrived, Aries said goodnight and headed for her room. After she got ready for bed, she turned off the lights, attempting to get some sleep.

Ryan cracked the door open. "Hey, Kiddo, you awake?"

She rolled over. "Yes."

He turned on the light and sat on the edge of the bed. "I know this is hard on you, and I just want you to know I'm proud of you."

She smiled. "Thanks."

"Your new friend, is she nice?"

"She's not my friend. We just worked on a school project together."

"Well, is your new classmate nice?"

"Yes."

He looked relieved. She told him some details about her day as they talked for a while. Ryan glanced at the clock. "I better let you get some sleep. I love you."

"I love you, too."

As Ryan closed the door, Aries pulled the sheets up to her chin. Her life had some meaning again, and she couldn't wait to go to school the next day, a sensation that rarely happened. She melted into her pillow, shutting her eyes as the buzzing started.

---

8

*A*ries spent extra time on her hair, French braiding it to the side. She tried on a few different outfits, settling for a denim mini skirt and white sleeveless blouse. Slipping on flats, she headed for the kitchen.

Ryan had already set out a plate with scrambled eggs and toast for her. She took a bite and mumbled, "Where's Kimberly?"

"Slow down, Kiddo. She didn't stay the night."

She swallowed. "Oh."

He examined her while taking a sip of coffee. "You look pretty. I like your hair like that."

"Thanks."

He smiled. "You look happy, too."

She nodded.

"And you survived your first week of school."

"The day's not over yet. And it technically wasn't a full week. Thank God we started on Wednesday."

"Yeah, but Fridays are usually easy."

"Not this one. We have to give our presentation in history class."

"You worked hard last night, and knowing you, you'll nail it. You definitely didn't get your work ethic from me."

"You work long hours." She hated that he had to work overtime any chance he could, and he also did odd jobs here and there to support them.

"I meant in school."

"Speaking of school, is it okay if I go to the football game tonight?"

"Sure, as long as you're home by ten."

Having a curfew sucked. It would take all the fun out of the night to have to worry about time. "Piper asked if I could spend the night at her house. Is that okay?"

He set down his coffee cup and stared at her. "I don't know."

"Pleeeeeease," she sang the word.

He thought for a moment. "I thought she wasn't your friend, just a classmate?"

"I'd like for her to be my friend. Can I?"

"Alright."

"Thank you, thank you." She bounced up and hugged him. "You're the best."

After clearing their plates, Ryan washed his hands and grabbed his keys. "Ready?"

"Yep." She found her backpack on the couch.

While they waited for the truck to warm up, a motorcycle roared by. Aries smiled. Damon was checking up on her.

Ryan played an IDK song on the ride to school, his way of trying to bond with her.

They pulled up to the shopping center near the high school. "Dad, you can drop me off in front. I'm not embarrassed."

"Really? I would've been," he said, continuing to drive toward the school.

Posters, streamers, and balloons of green and yellow decorated the buildings and gates. "Wow, they take their football seriously here," Ryan said.

"I'm finding that out." She hugged him goodbye, hopped out, and headed toward the courtyard.

As the bell rang, she spilled into the classroom with the rest of the students, and Piper found her.

"I dropped your board off with McCready. I was right, he shit himself." She smiled. "Nice work."

"Thank you."

Peyton walked up, giving Aries a dirty look. She pulled Piper away. "I've been trying to get a hold of you forev. What's going on?" They walked toward the back, out of earshot.

The tardy bell rang, with no sign of Cory. Miss Townsend explained the assignment, handing out worksheets. When she reached Aries, a spirit slipped into her mind.

"She's not sleeping at night. She needs to get more sleep."

It would be incredibly awkward for me to tell her that.

As she ignored the spirit, Cory strolled in wearing his football jersey. Miss Townsend stopped passing out papers. "Nice of you to join us, Mr. Douglas. Would you show up late to the game tonight?"

"No, ma'am."

"Tell me, class, what would Coach Anderson do?"

"Bench his ass," Michael blurted out.

"Excuse me?"

"Sorry Miss T, he'd bench him."

"How about if he were late to practice?"

"One hundred push-ups," Michael said.

"Alright, give me, um, ten push-ups."

"Seriously?" Cory looked puzzled.

"Yes." She smiled.

Cory dropped his backpack on the table and pumped out ten push-ups as the class counted. His face turned red as he stood up. He adjusted his cap before taking a seat.

"Hi," he whispered.

"Hey."

"What are we doing?"

"Writing our short-term and long-term goals."

He searched through his backpack. "You have a pen or pencil?"

She dug through her bag, handing him a pencil.

"Thanks. You're going tonight, right?"

"Yes."

"Cool." He wrote his name and date on the paper. "Paige's party, too?"

Her face lit up. With the way Cory looked at her, she had no choice but to say, "Yes."

Miss Townsend cleared her throat. "Since you two are so chatty this morning, why don't you tell the class your short-term goals? Mr. Douglas, you first."

He stared at his blank paper, pretending to read. "My goal is to not only beat CDM, but to pass for over four hundred yards and set a school record for the most touchdowns on opening night."

"Sounds like a good plan to me. Miss Dade?"

"My goal is to get straight As on this quarter's report card."

She smiled. "Another great goal."

"Nerd," Peyton mumbled.

Alright Peyton, you asked for this.

Aries faced Cory, putting her hand on his forearm. "See, I told you she doesn't like me."

"Don't take it personally. Like Michael said, she doesn't like anybody."

Aries giggled, pretending Cory said something funny. "Well then, I'm offended. I thought I was different. I wanted the honor of being the only one hated by *the* Peyton Price."

He laughed. "Okay, well you may be in the running for *most* hated."

"Who's my competition?" She ran her fingers along his forearm, stopping at his hand. She glanced at a girl sitting in the front with a sour look on her face. *What's her name?* She tapped her fingers on his hand. *Jamie?*

"Wait, let me guess…Jamie?"

He shook his head. "Jamie annoys Peyton, but she doesn't hate her. This freshman chick, I forget her name. Oh, and your buddy."

"Piper?"

"No, she's like one of her only friends."

"That's what I thought." Still touching him, she did her best to keep flirting. "Who?"

"LeMoore."

She removed her hand. "Why?"

He had a blank look. "The guy's nothing but trouble."

Was he telling the truth or hiding something? "Did they ever date?" she asked.

"Ha. No. Peyton hates the guy."

"She must have a reason." She tried to avoid eye contact as Peyton glared at her.

When the class ended, Aries packed up. "Good luck tonight."

"I'll see you in Spanish."

"See me, yes, but I'm sure I won't get a word in with Peyton next to you."

He laughed. "Probably true. Talk to you tonight?"

"Of course."

She walked down the hall, smiling. Cory ran up to her. "Your pencil." He handed it back to her.

"You can keep it."

"Alright. If we win tonight, you're going to always have to give me a pencil on game day."

"Deal."

◁≈▷

AT THE BEGINNING of history class, Aries tried to make contact with Gladys. Scribbling signs in her notebook, she said, *Gladys, please tell me what's going on with Cory and Damon. Everyone around here seems to have some sort of secret.* She waited a moment. *I wish I was better at this. How can I make a connection with you? I guess I can't, so I'll have to wait for you to come to me.* Frustrated, she put away her notebook.

Aries's stomach churned when Mr. McCready called her group up to the front of the room. She hated presentations. Michael set up the link to the video on the computer as Paige introduced them. After a few minutes, Aries began to relax. Besides the tone of her voice, Paige sounded like a news broadcaster. The presentation went off better than she'd anticipated.

Mr. McCready seemed pleased. As they sat down, Paige gave Aries a high-five.

"We're totally getting an A."

AN HOUR LATER, lunchtime arrived. Aries's hunger gained momentum with every step out of the building. It would be nice to join Piper and Cory, but Peyton wouldn't stand for it. She took the long way around to her tree, ensuring she wouldn't be seen. She then pulled out her lunch bag and scarfed down her sandwich.

"Hello, dear."

Aries swallowed, slowing down a bit before reaching for a chip. *There you are. Hi, Gladys.*

"You are pure sunshine, absolutely glowing. You make my grandson happy."

Tha—

Gladys kept talking as Aries worked hard to keep up with her frequency.

"Joe, come say hi. Come on. Oh well, he says hi. He just adores CJ. He's looking forward to his game."

Aries smiled.

"Aries?" Gladys's tone became serious, causing Aries to speak out loud.

"Yes?"

"You need to pay close attention at the paaa…"

Aries couldn't detect the last word. "Can you repeat that?"

Again, Gladys said something, but it sounded like a foreign language. "Gladys?"

Some leaves crunched behind her.

"Am I interrupting something?"

Startled, she said, "What?"

Damon had an interesting look on his face. "Sounds like you're having a deep conversation with yourself."

She let out a nervous laugh. "What are you talking about?"

"Nothing. Mind if I join you?"

She gestured for him to sit down. "Did you go by my place this morning?"

"Maybe." He displayed a cocky grin.

"Thanks."

"For what?"

She smiled. "For seeing if I needed a ride."

The corner of his lips curved up. "Are you going to the party tonight?"

Looking down, she picked at the grass for a moment. "Yes."

"See, I told you I'd get you to go."

"You, huh?"

He tilted her chin up. "Yes, me. Can I pick you up?"

"If you want to give my dad a heart attack."

"You're right. Well, can I meet you somewhere?"

"The football game."

He let out a sarcastic laugh. "You're going?"

"Why do you sound so surprised?"

He shrugged. "You don't strike me as someone who likes football."

"I don't."

"Oh, I get it now," he said, with a skeptical smile.

"What?"

"Your boy's the QB. Okay, that's fine. You won't take my advice about him. Looks like you'll have to find out the hard way."

"Ooh, I'm scared."

He put his hand on her leg. "Just be careful."

She stared into his eyes, shaking off the warm sensation of his touch. "I don't know what's going on between you two, but he says the same thing about you."

"What?" He stood, furrowing his brow.

"I've been warned by both of you."

"He has some nerve. He knows exactly what he's doing."

She jumped to her feet. "And what would that be?"

"The best defense is a good offense. He's trying to turn you against me before I—"

"Before you what?" She put her hands on her hips.

"Nothing."

"I'm not against anyone. I'm getting to know both of you, and so far I think you're both great guys."

"You have half that equation right."

She picked up her bag. "I didn't mean to upset you."

The cocky grin came back. "You could never upset me, Sophomore."

"You don't know that."

"True, although I doubt it. Frustrate, yes. Disappoint, yes. Especially if you end up with Douglas. But upset?" He shook his head. "You don't have that kind of power."

"You've never seen my kind of power."

He held up his hands. "Hello? What do you think I'm doing here?"

She shoved him. "I have no idea."

"I think you do." He took her bag from her and flung it around his shoulder. "C'mon, let's be on time."

In class, Aries stared at her Spanish book as Damon worked on the assignment. How on Earth could Mr. Gutierrez expect her to conjugate verbs when she sat next to one boy she liked and looked straight ahead at another?

Damon nudged her. "Stop daydreaming about your boyfriend."

"I'm not."

"Don't tell me you don't get the assignment."

"No, I understand it. Stop being so nosy."

He laughed. "Stop being so bossy."

"*Me?*"

"Yes, *you.*"

Cory glanced back, witnessing the two of them smiling. She dropped her head and worked for the remainder of class.

LISTENING to Kimberly and her dad in the other room made Aries want to puke. As she tried to get ready for the evening, Kimberly's muffled laugh escalated through the thin apartment walls.

Aries rolled her eyes. *She's so disgusting.*

Throwing open her closet, she tried on different outfits, hating the way everything looked on her.

"Ahh!" she screamed.

A few seconds later, Kimberly knocked on the door, cracking it open. "Aries?"

"Yeah?"

"Are you okay?"

Aries sighed. "Yes."

"Oh, it sounds like you're having some trouble."

"I have nothing to wear."

"Maybe I can help you find something?"

"That's okay." *I don't want to look like a hooker.*

"You want to look cute but casual, right? Make it look like you're not trying too hard?"

"I guess."

"Is there a boy you want to impress?"

Actually, there're two.

Kimberly scrutinized her. "I'll just assume so. May I look in your closet?"

Aries threw up her hands. "Go ahead."

While Kimberly rummaged through her closet, pulling out black trouser shorts and a matching halter top, pain shot through Aries's head like an instant migraine, followed by a voice.

"Her mother needs to have her blood pressure checked, and something is going on with her knee."

She rubbed her temple, even though her head no longer hurt. *Great. How am I supposed to relay that message?*

"You don't like it?" Kimberly asked.

"No, it's great," Aries said as she forced a smile. After she dressed, she said, "Thank you."

"Any time. If you like, I could do your hair and make-up."

Aries shrugged.

"C'mon," Kimberly commanded as she pulled her into the bathroom.

Thirty minutes later, Kimberly had Aries transformed into someone she'd never seen before.

Kimberly stepped back and admired her work. "Wow, I almost feel sorry for all the boys."

"Thank you."

"One last thing." Kimberly took off her gold watch and bracelet, handing them to Aries.

"I can't."

"I want you to." She took off her earrings, too. "Every girl must accessorize."

Aries put on the jewelry.

"Voila," Kimberly said.

Aries turned her eyes back to the mirror. "I don't know what to say. I really appreciate it."

Kimberly smiled, giving her a big hug. Aries gave in to her embrace. A small part of the wall she'd built up around Kimberly cracked.

Ryan looked worried as he said, "I trust you, Kiddo, but just be careful okay?" He walked over and hugged her.

"I know." She tried to reassure him. "I'll be safe."

"It's not you I'm worried about. I was once a teenage boy."

She sighed. "Is that what you're worried about? Boys?"

"Hell yeah, look at you. You don't look like you're in high school."

"Stop worrying, old man," Kimberly teased. "Aries is a good girl."

"Yeah, but she's my baby."

Aries's mom always used to say that. Her stomach dropped as a faint voice invaded her mind.

"*Aries...Don't go...*"

9

---

*A*ries purposely arrived during halftime. With the bleachers packed, she managed to squeeze in next to a group of girls sitting in the bottom row, making it look as though she were a part of their group. Peyton would definitely think she was a loser for going to the game by herself.

The cheerleaders were extra flamboyant, doing round-off back handsprings down the sidelines, yelling and flailing their arms, trying to get the crowd excited. Ignoring them and scanning the stands, Aries found the P-pack and their entourage at the far end of the top row, making it difficult for them to spot her.

Satisfied with her position, she couldn't keep her eyes off Cory. Standing several inches above the rest of the boys, he looked like a man on the field.

She flinched when Cory got sacked, fumbling the ball. The defense then took the field. When Cory reached the sideline, he pulled off his helmet, glancing into the crowd. He met her eyes, and his frown curved into a smile. Turning back toward the field, he ran his fingers through his hair, put on a cap, and talked to the coach.

"*Oh my, CJ is playing his heart out,*" Gladys said. "*He could play professionally, as long as he doesn't get involved with puh.*"

Wait, Gladys, come back. Involved with Peyton? Ugh, why is communicating with you so difficult?

When Newport High regained possession, Cory ran back on the field.

Aries had no clue about football, but the scoreboard showed her school winning 24-6. The band began to play as the crowd stood. The music carried her away as she danced along with all the other people, shaking off the nervous energy Gladys gave her.

Somewhere during the fourth quarter, somebody tapped on her shoulder from behind. She glanced back and stared into green eyes.

"You realize this is the first time I've been to a football game?"

"Well, then we have something in common," she said.

Damon stepped into her row, wearing jeans and a white T-shirt, looking sexier than ever. He looked even older with his black hair spiked up and extra stubble around his chin.

"Let's get out of here."

She glanced back at the field. "Don't you want to see the end?"

The crowd roared, and he glanced at the scoreboard. "It's now thirty to six, I'm pretty sure I know how it ends. Besides, this gives us a chance to grab a bite to eat."

She didn't want to leave the field with Cory doing so well. And what if he noticed her leaving with Damon? That might ruin any chance of him ever asking her out.

"Are you hungry?" he asked.

With the game almost over, and their sidelines going crazy, Cory seemed distracted.

"Well, I'm never one to pass up a meal."

She couldn't have asked for better timing, with a rush of

people amassed by the fence, blocking her view of the field. They hurried past the crowd, making it to the parking lot without attracting attention. They rode to a local fast food joint and ordered burgers, fries, and shakes.

Damon drenched his fries in ketchup. "Looks like your boyfriend had a good game."

She sighed. "He's not my boyfriend."

"I like giving you a hard time, Sophomore."

"How'd I get so lucky?"

"Key word being 'lucky.' You know how many girls would love to be sitting where you are?" he said, with a cocky grin.

"Ha. You're funny." She reached for some fries. "Okay, I'll bite, name a few."

"It would be easier to name the girls who wouldn't."

Aries bit into her burger. "Peyton," she said, with a mouthful.

"Wow, Sophomore, nice table manners. Yeah, I could get Peyton to go out with me," he said, with mischief in his eyes. "But I got a thing for brunettes."

They ate without speaking for a while. Breaking the silence, she said, "So tell me what's so great about this party."

"DB, Derek Bradley, started it. It's an annual thing. He's a good friend of mine, but he recently moved down south. I tried to get him to come up. He said next time. This particular party usually goes off. Although, I don't know, with Paige running the show, it could be lame. But with you there now, somehow I doubt it."

She took a sip of her shake. "Are you trying to get on my good side?"

They finished their meals at the same time.

"Wasn't I always? Or are you in the habit of hopping on the back of anyone's motorcycle?"

"You're definitely the first." She grabbed a napkin and wiped her fingers.

"I'm hoping for that," he uttered.

She smirked. "What?"

"Nothing." He grabbed their trays and stood up. "Ready?"

She followed him out. Twenty minutes later, they pulled up to a beach house on the southern tip of the Balboa Peninsula.

"I can't imagine growing up here. I mean, to have the beach as your front yard. It must be incredible," she said in awe.

He grabbed a leather jacket from under the seat. "It's not that great. Look how close your neighbors are, and there's little privacy, especially in the summer. You have to lock up everything on your patio or say adios to it. At least her house is away from the bike trail, so there's a little less foot traffic."

Music echoed throughout the neighborhood as streams of kids arrived from all directions.

"Are her neighbors going to complain?" she asked.

"Most are renters and will probably join the party. But I'm sure the cops will be here at some point."

Aries's temples throbbed as the spirit from earlier said, "*Be...*" His voice faded, along with the connection. She should go home.

"Damon?"

He stopped. "Yes."

"I don't know if I should go inside. I mean, I wasn't exactly invited, and I really don't think Paige likes me."

"Relax, Sophomore, you're with me."

They took a few more steps before she touched his arm. "Okay, the truth is, I'm feeling uneasy about this. I can't explain...it's just a gut feeling."

He regarded her for a moment. "Okay. You up for a walk on the beach? Maybe the feeling in your gut is what we ate." He nudged her shoulder. "Man, I've never seen a girl put away that big a burger before. Better be careful, or it's going straight here." He put his hand on her hip and gently tapped her behind.

Her body stiffened. "Shut up."

"It's impressive though."

"The way I eat?"

"Not what I meant," he said.

They walked across the sand out onto the rocks of a huge breakwater, as a yacht made its way back from the sea to the channel.

"This is the Wedge, great skim-boarding here," he said.

"Seems dangerous so close to the rocks. Do you do it?"

"Sometimes."

They turned around and faced the houses set in the cliffs across the channel. A light turned on in the biggest house as Damon's expression changed to stone.

"The bastard's home."

"Who?"

"One of Orange County's most honorable judges. Yeah, right."

A frantic male voice barged his way into Aries's mind. A quick image flashed, showing he'd died suddenly and at a young age. Although ages and time in the afterworld could be difficult to interpret, he was definitely in his teens when he passed. He gave her a message.

She blurted it out, "The Judge is your dad."

"How'd you guess?"

The voice wouldn't stop. She focused before saying, "I didn't…I knew."

"What?" He glared at her.

She shivered, trying to recover and tune out the boy's voice. Even though the boy was desperate to give Damon another message, she didn't have the energy.

"Um, I meant I could tell by the look on your face."

He kept staring at her.

"So, you grew up there? I'd give anything to live in a house like that."

"I'd change places with you in a heartbeat." He said as he turned, facing the ocean.

As the waves pounded down on the sand and rocks, the wind swept through her hair, bringing out goose bumps on her arms. He wrapped his jacket around her, running his hands down her arms. "You must be freezing. Ready to check out the party?"

The warning not to go to the party grew stronger. "Damon, would it be okay if you took me home?"

He slouched, glancing down for a moment. "Sure."

They walked across the sand, heading back toward the chaos. Kids were on the rooftop patio, shouting and laughing. Crowds gathered on the sand surrounding the house, and a boy and girl were making out on the lifeguard station. As they approached, Gladys came through loud and clear.

"You need to go to the party."

Gladys, my gut is saying no.

"Please, you must. There's something you'll discover."

Aries stopped Damon. "Maybe we could check it out for a little bit."

He wrapped his arm around her and smiled. "That's the spirit, Sophomore. Don't worry, nothing bad will happen to you. I've got your back."

"Last chance, do not go inside that house," the boy who'd died young warned.

Against her better judgment, she followed Damon inside.

s soon as Aries crossed the threshold, the rest of the voices started. Trying as hard as possible, she couldn't control all the souls telling her to get out of the house. But she trusted Gladys, so despite their protests, she continued.

A double-fisting boy Aries didn't recognize bumped into Damon. "LeMoore, my man." He handed him one of his cups.

"Hey bro, this is Aries."

With bloodshot eyes, the boy laughed. "Whassup, beautiful? You want one?" He held up his other cup.

"No, thanks." She wiped her hand on her shorts. Even though the temperature had dropped into the fifties, she was sweating.

Piper ran up to her. "You made it." She clung on to her, rubbing her hands through Aries's hair. "You're so pretty. Your hair is so soft. I love it."

Aries stepped back, staring at Piper's dilated pupils. "Are you okay?"

"I love you. Love, love, love, what a beautiful word." She pet Aries's hair again.

Aries moved away, whispering into Damon's ear. "What's wrong with her?"

"Ecstasy."

Drugs? She couldn't be at a party with drugs. A lump formed in her throat.

"Ahh!" Piper screamed. "Come with me." She grabbed Aries's hand, dragging her through the hall.

Aries glanced back at Damon and mouthed, "Help." He followed.

"Look!" Piper shouted, pointing to a painting. "Is that yours? I told you I saw your sunset before." She touched the frame, gliding her fingers across the glass. "Beautiful sunset, I love it. The glass feels so good." She giggled. "I love you guys."

Aries gasped as she stared at the picture. "Oh, my God," she whispered.

The music changed to a techno beat, distracting Piper. She twirled into the next room, dancing and running her hands through her own hair.

Damon appeared beside Aries. "What is it, Sophomore?"

She fixated on the painting.

"You look like you've seen a ghost." Damon read the inscription above the frame. "*Neptune's Window*? It's a picture of a beach with a killer sunset. Big deal." He squinted. "And all the women are covered in diamonds. I don't get it. Doesn't look like this has anything to do with the planet Neptune."

Aries didn't move.

"Alright, Sophomore, you're starting to freak me out." He rubbed her arm. "Do you want to leave?"

She ran her finger over the artist's initials at the bottom, tracing the letter E, then D.

"Do you know the artist?"

She spoke in a soft monotone voice. "Elizabeth Dade. My mom."

"Oh. Wow, that's cool."

"I've never seen it before." She stood in disbelief.

"Do you understand the title?"

She nodded.

"You want to explain for the layperson?"

"In astrology, the planet Neptune can possibly represent what you're oblivious to. Like maybe a character trait you have that others can see, but you can't."

"Okay." He looked doubtful. "So, what does *Neptune's Window* mean?"

"It's a glimpse of what you don't understand or pay attention to. Like, you're only seeing or comprehending half of something. These women on the beach, wearing diamonds, they think that's what makes them successful. See how they're looking at the diamonds, and not the sunset?"

"Yes."

"Now, do you see the bigger diamond hidden in the sun?" She pointed to the picture.

He stepped closer. "Oh, yeah."

"Her message is that life isn't about possessions. These women are on a beach with a gorgeous sunset, but they're blinded by diamonds, except for the one lady looking at the sun. She's looking through a metaphoric window, realizing what the other women don't."

"That's a pretty good interpretation for someone who's never seen this painting before."

"That's how I'd paint something like *Neptune's Window*."

She kept her gaze forward as Damon wrapped his arms around her from behind. "You're a pretty cool chick," he whispered. He inhaled slowly. "Mmm…your hair smells like coconut."

Aries leaned against him, staring at the painting. *Is this what you meant, Gladys?* She squeezed her eyes shut, concentrating, eager to make contact with her.

Damon moved her so she faced him. "Seriously, are you okay?"

She nodded.

"Can I get you something to drink?"

"I don't drink alcohol."

"I didn't think you did. How 'bout a soda?"

"Sure. I'm going to use the restroom."

"I'll find you," he said, with a concerned expression.

While waiting in line to use the bathroom, she tried to contact Gladys. Instead a man named Chuck blasted through with, *"Get out of the house now. You still have time."*

"I'm trying," she accidentally said out loud.

A girl standing in front of her turned around. "What?"

"Oh, nothing. I can't believe there's a line."

"I know, right?" She banged on the door. "Other people really have to pee here." She knocked again. "They're probably passed out. C'mon, I know where there's another bathroom. My best friend lives here."

"Paige?"

"No, her sister, Kaylie. I'm just a *freshman*," she mocked. "Michelle." She stuck out her hand.

"Aries," she said, shaking her hand. "Nice to meet you."

They walked through the master bedroom, ignoring the sign on the door to keep out. Aries used the facilities after Michelle. When she walked back into the bedroom, she said, "Thank you. I don't think I want to leave this room. It's so peaceful."

Michelle nodded. "This guy Michael is wasted and won't leave me alone. You mind if I tag along with you?"

"Not at all."

"Have you been on the rooftop yet?"

Aries shook her head.

"Wanna check it out? I don't think Michael's up there."

"Sure." Aries followed her outside to the rooftop patio.

Peyton stopped them. "What are you doing here?"

Aries tried to come up with something clever to say, but Michelle interrupted her. "Screw you, Peyton. Kaylie's my best friend. What the hell are you doing here, is the question?"

Peyton made a face as she scrutinized them. "Watch yourself, freshman. Figures, a couple of losers. This isn't even worth my time." She stormed over to the fire pit.

Aries tapped Michelle. "Nice."

"I'm so sick of her. She thinks she's God's gift, and she's so stuck up. I don't even think Paige really likes her."

Cory stood in front of a ping pong table with his hat on backwards.

"What are they playing?" Aries asked.

"Beer pong. If you play, get on Cory's team. He wins every time."

"Does everybody drink?"

"Pretty much. I've tried it a few times, but I can't stand the taste of beer."

Cory glanced back and smiled. He gestured for her to come over. "Hey, Aries, sweet, you made it. C'mon, get in on this."

Aries walked over and held up her hand. "I don't know how to play, and I don't drink beer."

"It's easy." He handed her a ping pong ball. "Try to make it in one of the cups on the other side. And don't worry, if they make one in, I'll drink it." He rubbed her back.

She concentrated, lining the ball up to the nearest cup, but his touch distracted her. She threw the ball, amazed when it landed in the cup. A boy on the other side took the ball out and chugged the beer.

Cory hugged her, giving her a high-five. "Sweet. You're a natural."

"Beginner's luck."

They finished the game, winning, and Cory had to drink only two cups of beer.

Aries checked behind her. Damon leaned against the balcony rail, watching her.

She turned to Cory. "Thanks for the game. I'll be back."

He wrapped his arm around her. "Hurry, you're my good luck charm."

Aries liked everything about Cory; the way he looked, felt, smelled, and most importantly how well he treated her. She didn't want to leave him, but then there was something about Damon. She walked over and leaned against the rail next to him.

"Hi," she said.

"I didn't know there was a bathroom up here."

"Very funny."

He reached over his right shoulder. "I swear I put your drink here."

She grabbed a cup off the rail on his left side. "It's right here." She took a sip.

"Are you having fun?" he asked.

"Surprisingly, yes."

Someone put their hand on her arm. "Save me," Michelle pleaded, interrupting them.

"He's back?" Aries asked.

"Yes. I can't get rid of him."

Cory glanced over a few times as she talked to Michelle. *Awkward.* She gulped down her soda.

Damon hadn't said much since Michelle appeared, and he looked bored. "Are you okay?" she asked.

"Fine." He peered into her empty cup. "I'm going to get another beer. You want anything?"

She giggled. "Yes." She flung the cup toward him as she rocked from side to side.

He gave her a strange look. "Stay up here."

When he walked away, she danced over to Cory. He put his hand on her lower back. "Good, you're back. I need the beer pong champ on my team." Handing her the ball, he said, "Ladies first."

She threw the ball over the balcony. "Whoa, easy there, slugger," Cory said.

She laughed.

One of the boys on the other side of the table shouted, "She has to drink for that throw."

Cory took a cup off a side table, handing it to her. "Don't worry, this is just ginger ale."

"Drink! Drink! Drink!" the boys on the other team chanted.

"Whoo!" Paige cheered from the couch next to the fire pit. She hopped up and brought a tray full of small cups. "Who wants shots?" she sang the words as she swayed back and forth.

All the boys around the ping pong table took one.

"Hey, I know you," Paige said. "You're in my health class."

Aries glanced down, towering over her. *Is she serious?* "Yesssh, and your hishtory class." *Why can't I talk? Something's off.*

Paige waved her hand. "Here, do a shot with me."

Aries's vision blurred, and she couldn't stand up straight without leaning against the table. "Thank you, but that's okay."

"C'mon." She handed her the cup.

Since Paige tried to include her, she took the shot, and it tasted pretty good.

Paige cheered. She put her arm around Aries. "You're fun." She grabbed another tray and headed toward a different crowd.

The rooftop started to spin as Aries grabbed her head, needing to sit down. She took a step forward, falling over.

Cory caught her. "Are you okay?"

Her mind went blank, and as she lost control, the voices in her head took over. With her eyes closed, she blurted out, "CJ, it wasn't your fault. Sshtop blaming yourself. You don't owe anyone anything. You weren't involved."

His grip tightened as he set her down on a sofa. "What the hell?" He flung his hands on his head. "What did you just say?"

Her head fell back, and she tried to get everything to stop spinning as he shook her. "Aries, what's going on? What do you mean I wasn't involved? What the hell are you talking about? And *CJ*?"

She couldn't respond or see anything clearly for a moment, but she could hear Cory pacing.

"Honey, are you okay?" Paige asked. "You guys, let's carry her to my bed. She can sleep it off here."

Aries stood, stabilizing herself. "Mom?" She pushed past Paige and made her way through the crowd of people, bumping into some of them and knocking over a girl. "Mom, is that you?"

The background noise cut in and out as she clutched at a table, knocking it over. Damon cursed in the background, but his voice came out muffled. Masses of kids gathered as some chanted, "Fight! Fight! Fight." Two boys crashed into the ping pong table, throwing punches at each other.

Glass shattered amongst the yelling all around her as she searched for the doorway. She stumbled toward the rail, away from the crowd. Cory and Damon shouted and cursed louder as she tried to reach the stairs.

"Mom, I hear you. I'm coming. Let me find the stairs."

Paige said something to her. Aries couldn't see her, but only Paige's voice could set her on edge. She blurted out something back to Paige, then clung on to the handrail as she stumbled down the stairs, falling but landing upright when she reached the bottom. She flung open the door, stung by the cool night air.

"Wait," a girl called out, starting after her.

Aries bolted across the sand, ignoring the voice behind her, driven by the one she longed to hear. She made it to the Wedge, half-running, half-stumbling its entire length, slowing only when she reached the end. The waves thrashed against the rocks, pelting her with icy droplets.

"I'm here, Mom." She held her hands up to the sky. "I hear you."

A huge wave splashed over the rocks, causing her to fall. Then everything went dark.

11

SCORPIO MOON AND GEMINI RISING

Stacy paced her living room as the boy walked up to her front door.

What the hell is he doing?

It took longer than expected for him to ring the doorbell. No one should ever make her wait. She'd made him meet at her house to strategize their game plan, and she wanted to get to it.

"You're late." She smirked as she opened the door.

"Whatever," he said.

He annoyed her again by coming in, sitting on the couch, and turning on the television. She shut it off.

"Focus."

He sighed. "Right." He directed his attention to her.

Turning on a computer, she checked out a website. "Okay, we need fake names for our Newport Dish accounts." She flashed him a wicked smile. "This is going to be fun. She's not going to know what hit her. Oh, how I love new girls."

"You're evil."

"I like to call it 'bored.' Sounds a bit more humble, don't you think?"

"Sure," he said. "What's your name going to be?"

"Hmm…" She thought for a moment. "Oh, Aries Dade, did you ever come to the wrong school. Let's stick with the stupid astrology theme."

"What's your sign?" he asked.

"Might be too obvious." She quickly researched information about astrology as he tapped his fingers on the table. "Do you mind?" she hissed.

"This shouldn't be that difficult. Just pick a fake name. You're Jenny. There, done."

"I feel like being creative." She scrolled through an astrology blurb. "Listen to this, the moon represents your emotions. I like that." She researched the twelve astrological signs to see which would be the best fit to represent her emotions. "This is perfect."

"What?"

"According to this, Scorpios are passionate, yet if you betray them, they can turn spiteful. Sting you with the scorpion tail, so to speak. I love revenge."

"Sounds like you." He took a sip of soda.

She rolled her eyes. "I thought it sounded more like you."

"Okay, I'll be Scorpio one, and you can be Scorpio two."

"First of all, I'd be number one," she said. "Okay, I'll be Scorpio Moon." She pressed her lips together. "But I can't call myself that. 'SM' will be my user name, but I have to fill in a first and last name. I'll be Stacy Martin." She typed in the name. "Now for you."

"John Doe."

"No, moron." She browsed a few more webpages. "Look here, according to this site, the rising sign represents who you show to the world. I guess kind of like your representative, not the real you. Oh, Gemini, the twins. You act a certain way in public, but I know the *real* you. It's like you're two different people, twins. Perfect." She typed "GR" for his user name. "Let's see." She glanced at the ceiling, then back at him. "You'll be 'Greg Reed.'"

"Fine, whatever," he said. "Stacy and Greg. I don't see what was wrong with Jenny and John."

"Because this has meaning, and that's more fun. You're deceiving, and I'm malicious."

"I think you're both," he said. "But yeah, sure, whatever. Do you have anything to eat?"

"Not really. Let me go check."

While she rummaged through the kitchen cabinets, he looked uneasy, but she needed him to stay long enough to complete their mission.

She came back with pita chips and hummus. "Will this do?"

"Yeah, fine."

"Okay, let's get started," she said, rubbing her hands together. "Our latest conquest kept calling for her mom. This is almost too easy."

"I don't know," he said, with his mouth full. "She's new, and her mom recently died. Maybe we should give her a break."

She curled her lip. "Do you really like her? What is it about this girl? This is a game, remember? Your specialty. Now stop thinking about her legs and get your head back in the game."

"I do love me some long legs."

She hit his arm. "Stop being such a typical guy and help me paste her picture on this freak's body."

"I don't know," he said again, shaking his head.

"I do know some things about you, remember?" She glared at him. "I could destroy you if I wanted to."

"If you wanted to, you would've already."

She grinned. "Scorpio Moon, remember? Spiteful emotions could erupt at any moment. Never forget I'm a girl, and that time of the month might roll around and make me all *emotional*."

He pinched the bridge of his nose and closed his eyes. "Okay, just stop talking about girlie crap."

"Good. Now show me how to do this."

Caving, he helped her create a not-so-flattering video of Aries.

"I still think this is too harsh," he said. "Even for you."

She shrugged. Clicking the post button with satisfaction, she laughed. "Let the games begin, Aries Dade."

12

a loud motorcycle engine revved, causing Aries to open her eyes. Unable to see, she pushed a plastic tarp off her and squinted from the harsh light reflecting off the ocean. Shivering in the cool breeze, she lifted herself up from a lounge chair and touched a lump the size of a golf ball on the back of her head. She moaned in pain. Her head pounded in sync with the waves as the bile in her stomach tried to find its way to the light. Everything spun as she fell back into the chair.

What happened?

With her mouth watering, she forced herself to stand, then disposed of anything left in her stomach into some unfortunate bushes. She wiped her mouth and observed the scene a few houses down. Plastic cups and beer cans were strewn all about the familiar patio. Making her way back to the chair, she held her head in her hands, regaining clarity.

Mom?

Noises came from behind her as a man and woman talked and bumped around inside the house. Not wanting them to find her on their patio, she pushed herself upright again and ducked under a window, making her way between the houses to the street. Since every step hurt, she couldn't walk all the way home. With her dad at work, she needed to find someone who could give her a ride.

She paced by the curb, reluctant to make the call. Low on options, she dialed Damon's number and sighed as it went straight to voicemail. She sat on the curb. With only one other person left to call, she'd almost rather walk. But when her mouth watered again, forcing her to spit a couple times, she gave in and made the second call. While she waited for her ride, she rested against a stop sign and passed out.

Aries awoke when Kimberly shook her arm. "Aries? Aries, ohmigod, are you okay?"

"Huh?"

"What happened to you?"

"Oh. Thank you, Kimberly. I didn't know who else to call."

"Of course. You look horrible."

"I feel even worse." Aries rubbed her head.

"What happened?" Kimberly asked, helping her up.

During the quick ride home, Aries told her bits and pieces, leaving out the parts about her mom.

Kimberly found a parking spot close to the apartment. "You don't remember anything else?"

"No."

"I have a feeling someone roofied you or slipped something into your drink."

"Damon or Cory would never do that."

"I'm not saying it was one of them. I'm thinking *somebody* at the party did, though."

"She's right," a spirit whispered. *"And tell her about her mother."*

But who? And why?

Kimberly headed straight for the kitchen. "You need to eat and hydrate."

"I just want to sleep." Nothing made sense to her, and the

one person who could answer her questions refused to answer his phone.

"Trust me," Kimberly said as she pitched a bagel in the toaster and poured a glass of apple juice. Reaching into her purse, she popped open a bottle of pills and handed two to Aries. "My hangover remedy: toast, AJ, and painkillers."

"Thank you." Aries gulped down the pills, polishing off the entire glass of juice.

Kimberly sat at the table, talking as Aries ate. Sharing some of her high school memories, Kimberly said, "I was the insecure girl doing keg stands and chugging beer bongs."

Aries smiled.

Kimberly's cell vibrated on the table, and her face lit up as she responded to the text. Glancing at Aries, she asked, "Is there anything else I can get you before I leave?"

She shook her head. "Was that my dad?"

"Yes." Kimberly set down her phone. "Don't worry, I didn't say anything about your night. I'll leave that up to you."

Aries nodded again. "Can I ask you a question?"

"Sure."

"Does he ever talk about my mom?"

"He does." Kimberly cleared the dishes, rinsing them in the sink before sitting back down.

Aries's eyes dampened.

"I'm so sorry, Aries. I can't even begin to imagine what it must be like for you."

She stared at a crumb on the table. "Do you guys talk about how she died?"

"He's mentioned it."

Aries slouched back.

"Oh, sweetie, please don't worry," Kimberly said in a soothing voice.

"What did he tell you?" The pain in her head intensified.

Kimberly took a moment before responding. "I really think this is a conversation you should be having with him."

"I'm just curious."

"I know." Kimberly tapped her fingers along the table. "But I don't feel right talking about it without your dad here."

Aries glanced out the window. A hummingbird peered in as a spirit tried to say something, but she couldn't make out any words.

If this is in regard to her mother, I don't know how to tell her, and I really don't care.

"I can stay here with you until he gets home if you want," Kimberly said. "It's no trouble."

She shook her head. "No, I'm going to go lie down."

They stared at each other in awkward silence for a few moments. Aries broke the stare, fidgeting with the bracelet and watch on her wrist.

Handing Kimberly her belongings, she said, "I'm so glad I didn't lose anything. Thanks again, for everything."

Kimberly nodded as she slipped the jewelry into her purse. She stood, reached in the refrigerator, and handed Aries a bottle of water and sports drink. "Make sure you have plenty of fluids today."

"Okay."

"Call me if you need anything."

Kimberly hugged her goodbye and left the apartment.

ARIES SLEPT until the late afternoon. Her head didn't hurt as bad as earlier, so she turned on the radio and cleaned the house. Since they were now officially moved in, she threw the last few empty boxes in the dumpster. After putting away the vacuum, she left Damon a message to call her back.

Sitting on the couch, she pondered what her great-grandfather had told her about blocking out her mother.

Like Neptune's Window. Is that what I've become? She had a window into other deceased souls' lives, but she'd become oblivious to her own mother.

She went into her bedroom and brought the box labeled "Elizabeth's Dresser" out of her closet, placing it on the bed.

"You can do it, Aries, go on," a familiar male voice said.

Chuck?

"That's right."

You tried to warn me last night. I should've listened. Thanks a lot, Gladys.

The sweet sound of Gladys's voice came through as a faint whisper. *"You needed to experience what—"*

Go away, Gladys.

"It was for you." Gladys's voice cracked.

Great. Well done, then.

"You'll see."

Chuck, are you still there?

"Yes, Aries."

Tell Gladys to go away.

The pleasant aura drifted as Gladys faded away.

"Aries, I'm here to help you," Chuck said.

Thanks. Are you related to someone I know?

"Yes. Sarah. I'm her father."

Sarah? The only Sarah I know is from my elementary school. But I'm positive her father is still alive. There's a Sierra in my trigonometry class. Do you mean her? It frustrated her because names could get altered in the transition from the other side. *Say the name again.*

"Sarah."

She shook her head. *I don't know a Sarah.*

"Yes, you do. Now stop stalling and open the box."

Aries found scissors and cut through the tape. Setting the

scissors on her nightstand, she hesitated before peeking inside. Holding her breath, she peeled back the flaps, removing a couple of camisole tops. She held them to her face, inhaling the faint smell of her mother's perfume. Resting her head on a pillow, she enjoyed the lingering fragrance.

A smile washed across her face as she recalled the day her dad gave her mom the perfume for their anniversary. Elizabeth opened her gift and screamed with delight.

A tear of joy trickled down Aries's cheek. She sprang up, rummaging through the box for the bottle of perfume, relieved it was her mother's crystal ballerina figurine that had shattered. She fished out two picture frames, placing them face down, not ready to look at the images they held. Reaching back into the box, she found the item she was looking for and sprayed some on her wrist, embracing the sweet floral smell.

"I'm open, Mom," she said out loud. "I'm willing to let you in. Talk to me. Give me a sign, something, anything." Her cell phone rang. Grabbing it off the desk, she said, "Hello?"

"Aries."

"Damon, I'm dying to talk to you."

"I know. Me, too."

"How the hell could you just leave me?" she asked, growing angrier by the second. "Overnight! On some stranger's patio!" she screamed.

"Hold on there, Sophomore. First of all, I didn't leave you. I stayed up all night, watching you to make sure you were okay. The Honorable Judge wouldn't stop calling me this morning, so when it was light enough and I knew you'd be safe, I took off. And second, you left me. You were whacked out of your freakin' mind."

She rubbed the back of her head, pacing as she tried to calm down. "Well, what happened?"

"You tell me."

"I don't know, that's why I'm asking, jerk."

"Jerk? Really?" Now he sounded pissed. "You have any idea what I've been through? It's not easy taking on half the football team."

She sat on the bed. "Oh, the fight. I think I remember a lot of cursing and stuff breaking."

"Yeah, like my nose."

Putting her hand on her forehead, she said, "I'm so sorry, Damon. I really don't know what happened."

"Well, I think I might. Can we talk in person?"

"Yes. My dad's not home. But I don't know when he'll get here, so we can't stay."

"Okay, I'm on my way to pick you up."

She covered the box and her mother's belongings with the sheets, in case her dad came home before she returned.

While she waited in the alley, Ryan's work truck approached, followed by a Harley.

Oh, no.

Aries ran up to the truck. "Hi, Dad," she said, sounding a little too excited.

"Hey, Kiddo. Now that's an awesome greeting to come home to."

"I'm starving. Can we go out to dinner, please?"

"How can I resist those eyes?"

"Thank you." She smiled, opening the door.

Aries gestured for Damon to keep going. He nodded without stopping and turned at the next street.

"Can your stomach survive if I go in and change?"

His jeans and hands were filthy, so she said, "I guess we can just order pizza."

Once inside, she ordered two large pepperoni and sausage pizzas, while Ryan took a quick shower.

The pizza arrived, and Ryan cracked open a beer, looking exhausted. He plopped on the couch and turned on the TV.

They watched a college football game while they ate. Aries

almost finished an entire large pizza, then leaned back in her chair, feeling satisfied. About to admit to her dad what had happened to her, she turned off the TV and cleaned up, as he'd passed out.

Making her way to the bedroom, she peeled back the sheets and grabbed the frames, ready to look at the pictures.

The first one was a picture of her and Elizabeth at the beach. Aries was eight at the time. They looked happy. They'd played in the waves, Elizabeth wanting to swim out past them, Aries urging her to stay by the shore, where she felt safe.

She kept looking at the picture as she recalled one of the best days of her life. They brought a picnic basket and sat on the sand, talking for hours until the sun went down.

Elizabeth said, "That is probably one of the best sunsets I've ever seen. Where's the camera?"

Aries snapped back to reality, reaching for the second frame, already knowing what she'd see. She turned it over and smiled at the picture of the sunset. The exact sunset both she and Elizabeth had painted.

She pulled more knickknacks and clothes out of the box. A business card had become stuck to the bottom. Furrowing her brow, she peeled it off and read, "Camden Brentwood Price the Third, CEO."

Price? As in Peyton Price? What could her mother have been up to? And how did her painting wind up at Paige's house?

A sudden annoying sound, like that of a thousand bees, resonated in her head before Mr. Overzealous's voice broke through the din. *"It's taking longer than I thought, but now you're on the right track."*

She had so many questions to ask him, but he was already gone.

13

Over the weekend, Aries disclosed some information about the party to her father. He hadn't said much since she broke the ice on the subject, and they drove to school Monday morning in silence. He pulled over to the curb, looking into her eyes.

"I'm glad you told me. I'm just having a hard time dealing with you growing up."

Aries glanced out the window, sick to her stomach about letting her dad down, and for having to face everyone who'd been at the party. Especially Cory.

"Thanks, I needed to hear that. Can't handle it when I think you're mad at me."

He leaned over, kissing the top of her head. "You're my world, Kiddo."

She pressed her lips together before saying, "I love you."

She jumped out of the truck and strolled through the parking lot toward her class. Spotting Paige in the courtyard, she waved, expecting to be grilled again about Cory and Damon.

Paige turned away. Figuring Paige didn't see her, Aries caught up to her inside the building and tapped her on the shoulder.

"Hi."

Paige smirked and scurried up the stairs toward the classroom, gathering at the top with Peyton and Piper. Aries followed her up the stairs, almost running into the P-pack standing in the middle of the hallway. When she walked around them, Peyton laughed.

"You sure know how to put on a good show." Paige sighed in disgust, and Piper looked disengaged, as if she had problems of her own to worry about.

"What do you mean?" Aries asked.

"You're kidding, right?" Peyton put her hand on her hip.

The bell rang, and Aries headed into the classroom and took her seat. While Miss Townsend walked toward the front of the room, Cory slipped in late without her noticing.

"Hi," Aries said.

He looked straight ahead, without a response.

During Miss Townsend's lecture about nutrition, Aries spotted a slight gash on Cory's cheek, and he had a swollen lip. What should she say to him? She didn't have an answer, so she continued to take notes.

Miss Townsend surveyed her classroom. "Alright, using the nutrition guidelines we just went over, you're going to come up with a healthy five-day diet plan. You can work with your partner or on your own." She passed out laptops, stopping when she reached Cory. "What happened to you?"

He cleared his throat. "Just messing around."

"Did it happen in the game?"

He shook his head. "Guy stuff, no big deal."

She scrutinized him. "Okay, but I'm going to keep an eye on you. By the way, congratulations. What a game."

"Thank you."

When Miss Townsend moved on, Aries whispered, "Are you okay?"

Cory squeezed the bill of his cap together and looked at the assignment.

Aries sighed. "You, too, huh? Paige won't talk to me either. And according to Peyton, I put on a good show."

This time he looked at her, his face expressionless. "It was something."

"Sorry."

He went back to the assignment.

Aries might as well have been sucker punched in the gut, knocking all the wind out of her. She couldn't do anything except make sure she didn't break down in tears. Minutes somehow turned into hours. It took all her will to stay put in her seat. If she ran out of the classroom, she'd be giving everyone more to laugh and talk about. At last, the class ended.

Her respite lasted only a few seconds. As she walked down the hall, a few students she'd never seen before whispered and laughed as they passed her. Two girls stood by the lockers, staring and pointing at her.

What the hell is going on?

Picking up her pace, she made it to the bathroom and hid in a stall. She peeked through the door. A group of girls entered and gathered by the sink.

One girl applied lipstick, then said, "I don't know, some girl named Ariel, I think."

A different girl corrected her. "No, it's Aries."

"Whatever," the first girl said, blotting her lips on a paper towel. "Sucks to be her. Did you guys see her on all the socials?"

"Was it on Newport Dish?" a different girl chimed in.

"Yes. It's funny as hell."

"Poor girl."

"Stupid is more like it."

They continued gossiping as they walked out.

Aries held the bridge of her nose, taking deep breaths. When she was the only one left in the restroom, she stepped out of the stall, washed her hands, and stared in the mirror. Why would someone blast whatever she'd done all over the Internet?

Her legs started to shake. She put her back against the wall, next to the hand dryer, and slid down to the floor. As the bell rang, she grabbed her knees, hung her head, and let out a few curse words.

I need you more than ever, Mom. I'm begging for your help. Please talk to me, give me a sign, something.

Staying as still as possible, the only sound came from the air conditioner.

She hid out in the bathroom for another forty minutes, missing her trigonometry class. She could justify skipping one class to her dad, but he'd be upset if she ditched the rest of the day. And she'd been through this kind of thing at her previous school. Better to face the rumors sooner rather than later.

Summoning all her courage, and channeling her best acting skills, she stepped out of the bathroom and back into the throng of students switching classes. She walked to her history class, playing the role of a confident student. With her head held high, she ignored the laughter, gawking, and finger pointing.

The room had a funk in the air as she received dirty looks from Paige and Michael. Michael looked a little disheveled, like he'd gotten caught up in the fight as well. Again, during class, time felt like it had stopped until the bell rang, signaling the end to this particular chapter of her misery.

She mustered up the courage to stop Piper on the way out.

"Do you have a minute?" she said in a timid voice.

Piper took a step past her, then hesitated. "Yes."

"I don't know what happened to me at the party, and apparently there's a video or something. Do you know what it's all about?"

"I hate to tell you this, but there's more than one. Look, I don't think it's that big of a deal to be wasted out of your mind; happens to all of us. But it looks like someone really has it out for you."

"Peyton?"

Piper tilted her head. "You know, I don't even think she'd pull a stunt like this."

Aries closed her eyes. Who else would have a problem with her?

Paige barged in-between them, flashing Aries a dirty look.

Aries sighed, looking after her for a moment. "And I have no idea why she's so mad at me. She won't even talk to me so I can find out."

"You haven't seen anything from the videos, have you?" Piper asked.

She shook her head.

Piper glanced around. "Hurry, get out your phone, and I'll show you."

"Um…well, I don't…I don't have Internet on mine." She put her hand on her forehead.

"Girls, move along. You're going to be late to class," Mr. McCready interrupted them.

They moved a couple inches, appeasing him. Piper pulled out her phone, scrolled to an app, then handed her phone to Aries, who stood with her mouth open for a moment.

"Oh wait, there's more," Piper cautioned.

"Videos of me?" Aries cringed.

"Yes. But here, real quick, this one will explain Paige." Piper found what she was looking for, handing her phone back to Aries.

She pressed play. Aries and Paige stood at the top of the stairs at Paige's house. Aries had her hands covering her ears as she said, "Stop talking. Your voice drives me insane." Paige stood with her mouth agape, mortified.

"Oh, my God." Her stomach dropped, and her mouth watered. She handed the phone back to Piper.

"That's probably the least of your worries. I'm gonna go, but don't sweat it. This will all blow over."

"I don't know." Aries shrugged.

"Trust me. You just have to wait for the next scandal," Piper said as she turned and headed down the hall.

Aries made it to lunch without any more incidents. She rested her head against the tree trunk, unable to eat. What could possibly be on the other videos? Maybe the boy trying to send her a message to give to Damon could help her.

Running her finger along the grass, trying to concentrate, she said, *Hey, did you go to Newport High? I need your help.*

She snapped back to reality when a half-eaten apple hit her foot. Then an orange flew past her face, missing by inches. She stood, turning in the direction from which it came. A group of girls laughed as one of them held up an orange.

Aries grabbed her bag and retreated behind the tree, making her way to the other side of the courtyard. Maybe Mr. Gutierrez wouldn't mind if she hung out in his room a little early, so she could avoid getting hit by any more flying fruit.

When she passed by a group of students near the entrance of the foreign language building, a girl called out, "Mom…Mom, is that you?"

A few students laughed as a boy said, "Wait, Mom, I'm coming."

Aries spun in the opposite direction, but before she could run away, a girl from the group ran up and stopped her.

"Hey, wait. Sorry," Michelle said. She turned to her friends. "Shut up, you guys." She turned back toward Aries. "They're so immature."

"Michelle, I don't mean to be rude, but I have to get out of here."

"I totally get it. Just wanted to let you know I'm here if you need to talk."

The laughter and jeers from the group started up again. Aries bolted through the building all the way to the classroom. She couldn't wait to see Damon.

The class had started, but Damon hadn't shown up. Aries bit her bottom lip in frustration. She needed him more than ever as she sat by herself. Peyton sneered at her a couple times, but Cory didn't acknowledge her existence.

AFTER SCHOOL, Aries hid in the library, waiting for the parking lot to clear out. She borrowed a computer from the librarian. After she tried to pull up three different social media websites, she gave up. They were all blocked by the school's security system.

Someone from the other side, please help me. She tapped her foot while she waited for a response. *Fine, I get it, it's only when you guys want to be heard. Do me a favor and leave me alone for good.*

She gathered her stuff and shuffled through the hall, stopping while a custodian mopped the floor. He waved her along, then got back to work.

She found her dad's truck; he'd been waiting for her ever since school had let out. He didn't act too pleased when she opened the door.

"What took so long, Kiddo?"

"Sorry, I was doing some research in the library."

He analyzed her as she buckled her seatbelt. "Everything okay?"

"Uh huh." She leaned against the side window.

Ryan drove off, turning on the radio. She tuned out the noise the entire ride home, lost in the events of the day.

Ryan pulled up to the side of the apartment, turning down the volume. "Sorry I have to go back to work. There's money in the drawer if you want take-out. It's going to be a late night for me."

"Okay, thanks for picking me up."

She ran inside and couldn't turn on the computer fast enough. She found the website Piper had used earlier. After creating a new account, she hit enter. Three pictures of her popped up. One was her school photo ID, and the second one showed her passed out on an outdoor sofa next to the ping pong table. In the final picture, she looked like the devil. The flash had made her eyes look red, and whoever posted the picture had added horns on top of her head.

Aries scrolled down to the videos of her and clicked the most recent one, posted forty minutes ago. The caption read, "NBHS's newest slut." Pressing play, she watched herself start to dance. Taking a closer look, her face had been digitally mapped onto some girl performing a provocative dance, gyrating her butt. The song playing in the background was a popular hip-hop song with her voice dubbed over the hook, saying "Mom, ma, ma, ma, ma, Mom, is that you?" The lyrics repeated a few times, then the girl dancing started to strip. She seductively took off her top, then teased as if she were going to take off her bra, but she didn't.

This is sick.

Anyone with a brain had to know it wasn't her. But not a lot of people at the school knew her. Maybe they'd notice how short the girl in the video was.

She found the video link of her and Paige. The title read, "Finally someone says what we're all thinking."

Paige couldn't have posted this footage. She would never write that caption.

But what if it was her way of throwing Aries off track?

She shook her head. Not wanting to see the video again, she

clicked onto the next link. This one showed Cory helping her onto the sofa, leaning over her. It appeared as though they were kissing. She pressed rewind a few times. Their lips never touched. She let the video play in its entirety.

Halfway through, Damon came out of nowhere, shouting, "Get your hands off her!"

Cory stood, holding up his hands. "What's your problem?" he shouted.

Damon shoved Cory, shouting a few choice words. Cory pushed Damon back, cursing as well, causing Damon to throw the first punch.

Aries flinched as the two got tangled up, thrashing into the ping pong table, causing it to split in half. One of the boys who'd been playing beer pong jumped in, punching Damon, too. A crowd formed around the boys. Kids were chanting as the furniture got rearranged and plastic cups flew everywhere.

Aries couldn't watch any more videos. She'd caused the fight. Her stomach dropped as she turned off the computer and called Damon. She left him a message when he didn't answer.

She hadn't had anything to eat since breakfast, so she put a burrito into the microwave and made a salad. Not hungry, she forced herself to eat. She found a package of red licorice, brought it back to her bedroom, and spread her homework across the bed. With her social life ripped to shreds, it took her much longer than usual to complete the assignments.

She put away her books and flopped back on the bed. How could she make things better? If people could see it wasn't her fault, maybe they'd leave her alone - and even better, maybe they'd like her.

As she closed her eyes, a pleasant light cast around her, and the sound of Gladys's voice drifted into her mind.

"Hello, dear."

Haven't you done enough?

"No, and that's the problem."

Well, you can leave me alone. Cory hates me, so I'm not going to be able to help you get any messages to him.

"He doesn't hate you. He's confused right now, but don't worry, he'll learn soon enough."

I'm mad at myself for listening to you, and it won't happen again.

"Wait."

Aries covered her ears, singing, "La, la, la, la, la."

"Are you finished yet?" Gladys laughed.

You think that's funny?

"Quite frankly, yes. Now if you're through being childish, I have something to say."

Aries screamed into her pillow.

"Okay, are you ready now?" Gladys asked.

Oh, go ahead.

"Your mother's painting."

Go on. Aries could barely control her frustration.

"And what happened to you."

"What happened to me?" Aries questioned.

A buzzing sound rang through, and the light aura slipped away. She traced her finger faster and faster in zigzag motions on the comforter.

Gladys, talk to me, Aries pleaded over and over, with no response.

14

The next morning as Aries awoke, she recalled a message from Mr. O. It may have been real or through a dream.

"Your instincts are right regarding your mother's death. She didn't betray you."

Now wide awake, Aries jumped out of bed and smiled for the first time since the party. As she dressed for school, she did a dance in front of the mirror.

After completing her outfit, she sat on the bed, putting on her shoes. She scanned the room.

Hey, Mr. Overzealous. C'mon, talk to me. Bring on your most annoying signal. Where are you now, tough guy?

She squeezed her eyes shut and clenched her fists, desperate to get his attention. When she relaxed, the hand mirror on her vanity cracked.

I'll take that as a sign you can hear me. Thank you, by the way.

"I'm *going* to find out the truth."

She had to wake up her father, since he'd slept through his alarm clock. After she roused him, he dashed through the apartment, setting a record for getting them out the door in five minutes. He drove like a maniac and dropped her off in time. She waited in front of the science building with a new focus. She didn't give a crap about the childish antics posted all over the Internet. The only thing that mattered was getting to the truth about her mother's death.

As she made her way upstairs with the rest of the students, her shoulders lurched back from someone tugging on her backpack. When she reached the top level, half of her belongings fell down the stairs. Someone had unzipped her bag.

Dodging the waves of kids flowing up the stairs, she managed to collect her things. When she stood, she met Cory's eyes. She turned and hurried back up to class to avoid being tardy. On her way in the room, Michael stuck out his foot, launching her forward. She grabbed onto a table before falling to the ground.

"Appears she's a klutz too," Michael said.

Aries's good mood deteriorated at a rapid pace. How long was this harassment going to last?

Cory smacked Michael on the back of the head. "What the hell, man?"

When Aries sat down, he asked, "Are you okay?"

She nodded, and that was their only communication for the rest of the period.

After class, she waited until everyone cleared out before walking up to Miss Townsend.

"Can I come in at lunch to ask you a few questions about last night's homework?"

"Of course." Miss Townsend wrote her a lunch pass.

The hallways remained the same, students staring, laughing, and name-calling as she walked by. Being used to the drill, she did her best to ignore everyone.

After history class, Paige still wouldn't talk to her, and Piper gave her a weak attempt at a wave goodbye.

Walking into Miss Townsend's classroom at lunch, Aries found her sitting at her desk, eating a salad.

"Hi, Aries, go ahead and sit wherever you'd like."

She sat down and pulled out a sandwich.

Miss Townsend took a bite, then put down her fork. "I looked over your homework, and I can't imagine what you're having trouble with. In fact, I want to follow your diet plan."

"Um…" Not actually having a problem, Aries made something up. "I'm wondering what healthy proteins I could add."

Miss Townsend gave her a skeptical look. "You wrote great examples in the plan. You had fish, egg whites; most students just write eggs. Aries, you don't have to make up an excuse if you want to eat lunch in here. My door is always open."

Aries nodded.

They ate in silence for a few minutes before Miss Townsend said, "I know about the videos."

"You do?" Aries slouched in the chair. "Did you watch all of them?"

"Yes. I wish there was something I could do to help you. This sort of thing happens a few times every year. I had my suspicions, but I was hoping it wouldn't happen to you. Unfortunately, the school has no way of knowing who's responsible. And since it's not on any school-regulated websites, we can't shut them down. Our hands are basically tied. If we do find out who's behind it, we can have that student expelled and file cyberbullying charges." She shrugged. "But I have a feeling it's not always the same student, or students, doing the bullying."

"What do you mean you had your suspicions?" Aries asked.

"Well, you're new and attractive, which usually threatens people."

"Oh." Aries finished the rest of her lunch without saying much.

"You're more than welcome to eat in here for as long as you'd like," Miss Townsend said.

"Thank you."

"There is one more thing. I'm worried about you, and not just because someone's bullying you, but because you look like you were drunk in the pictures. And I'm wondering..." She paused. "Have you had any counseling since your mother passed away?"

"No. Thanks for your concern, but I don't need a therapist."

"I would hate to see you turn to drugs or alcohol to cope."

"Miss Townsend, I didn't drink alcohol at the party. Someone put drugs in my soda."

"Really? That's terrible. I knew you were as bright as your transcript scores, and I figured you wouldn't give in to peer pressure. But I had to check. Some of the other students wouldn't surprise me."

"Thanks for believing me."

"You haven't given me a reason not to. Which makes me have to admit something to you. I looked up your mother online, and I found out her cause of death. That's when I became concerned for you."

"She didn't use drugs either." Aries could finally say that with confidence. "I know it says the cause of death was a drug overdose, but she wasn't a druggie."

Her face turned red, and her emotions ran hot. Not because she was upset with Miss Townsend, but because that was the first time she'd ever talked about how her mom died with anyone other than her dad.

"No, I didn't assume she was. It's really none of my business. I'm sorry. I never meant to upset you."

"It's not you."

Miss Townsend walked over and gave her a hug. "If you ever need to talk, I'm here for you."

The lunch period ended, and Aries threw away her trash. "Thank you."

She grabbed her bag and started to leave when Miss

Townsend said, "Don't worry about the dancing videos. Everyone knows that's not you. That's another thing that happens each year; same dancing girl, different face."

"Now that she's helped you, help her," a spirit said. *"She needs more sleep. Melatonin will do the trick."*

Fine. If she thinks I'm crazy, I'm never listening to any of you again.

"I don't mean to be out of line, but you look really tired," Aries said. "I hear melatonin helps if you're having trouble sleeping."

Miss Townsend put her hand on her cheek. "Wow, I must look fantastic. Thank you, I appreciate your honesty. I'll give it a try."

Aries smiled as she walked into the hallway. *Okay, I think that actually worked. By the way, who are you?*

"Indeed. An old neighbor."

Aries relaxed a bit on her walk to Spanish class. She sighed at the empty desk next to hers as Mr. Gutierrez explained the assignment. Damon had ditched another day of school. She searched in her bag for her phone to send him a text. She always kept her phone in the same pouch of her bag, but it wasn't there. Dumping everything onto the table, she still couldn't find her phone. She did a double take as the panic caused goose bumps to spread across her arms.

Mr. Gutierrez walked over to her. "Esta todo bien, senorita?"

"Yes, fine," Aries said.

"En espanol, por favor."

"Si, esta bien." Aries didn't have time to chat with Mr. Gutierrez. She had to find her phone.

"Muy bien." He smiled and walked away.

She spent the entire class going through her bag, with no trace of her phone. Her dad couldn't pick her up after school, and she'd originally planned on asking Damon for a ride, but now she'd have to take the bus. She again hid in the library, waiting for all the students to go home. She had the librarian print out a bus schedule for her.

Walking toward the bus stop on the opposite side of the campus, Aries passed the gymnasium. A boy popped out of a side door to the weight room and shouted, "Hey there, beautiful, I'll help you find your mama."

Two more boys walked out, whistling. Aries peeked through the window, hoping their coach would stop them. Cory put a bar of weights back on the bench press rack and stood up. He came out and walked over to the boys.

"Shut the hell up, freshmen." He shoved one boy back inside.

Cory walked toward her. She pressed her lips together as she took in the sight of his shirtless body. His chest appeared bigger than the average teenage boy's, and his chiseled six-pack could pass for the cover of a men's fitness magazine.

"Sorry about that," he said.

"I'm getting used to it."

"You shouldn't have to."

"Does this mean you're not mad at me anymore?"

"I was never mad at you, Aries. You just don't get it." He glanced back at the weight room.

"Get what?"

"Look, I can't talk here. We don't have practice tomorrow; we're just looking over some game footage. It shouldn't take long. I'll talk to you then." He turned and started back to the gym.

"Okay." Aries walked away, happy they were communicating again.

She kept picturing Cory's body while she waited for the bus to arrive. During the ride, she pulled out her required reading material for English class to distract herself. Deeply engrossed in the story, she missed her stop. The bus headed south in the direction of the houses across from the Wedge. She took that as a sign to go visit Damon.

She exited the bus and walked along the street, surveying the custom homes. The house in which the *Honorable Judge* had turned on the light was one of the larger houses, but looking at them from the front, they all looked about the same size as she passed by. When she got closer to the end of the row, she heard shouting.

A man yelled, "You no-good, lousy excuse for a son. You're a loser. A nothing." He was so loud, he was causing a scene out on the driveway.

"The Judge," Aries whispered.

The Judge pushed Damon, whose hands remained at his sides, and he didn't retaliate as his dad kept pushing him and yelling at him. Finally, Damon turned, hopped on his motorcycle, and sped off.

Aries hid behind a bush as the bike flew by. *Poor Damon.* Why did she have to miss her stop? She shuffled back to the bus stop and read for the next thirty minutes, with a knot in her stomach.

After arriving home, she went to the computer and checked the website to see if there were more mean videos about her. The latest one had been posted fifteen minutes ago.

The picture on the screen tortured her. Staring at it with her teeth clenched, she squeezed her fists, with her nails digging into her skin. She couldn't press play; she could only gawk at the picture of her and Elizabeth. The caption read, "Like mother, like daughter."

"No, no, no!" Aries screamed.

Her hands were clammy as she wiped a bead of sweat from her forehead. She imagined beating the living daylights out of the person who'd stolen her phone to get the picture now tormenting her on the screen. She punched the table, shouting obscenities. Her anger intensified, causing a rash to spread across her chest.

With morbid curiosity getting the best of her, she pressed play. The picture remained the same as a song about drugs played in the background. Bright red letters popped up: "Elizabeth Jane Dade, beloved wife and mother dies of a drug overdose."

Now the whole school knew how her mother had died.

15

*A*fter a restless night's sleep, Aries tapped on her father's door.

"Come in," he said in a groggy voice.

"Can I stay home today?" she asked.

"What's wrong?"

"I don't feel so hot." She put her hand on her forehead.

"You look fine to me."

Kimberly stirred under the covers, next to him. Telling Kimberly to get the hell out of their house might help her feel a little better.

Aries's eyes dampened. "You don't understand."

She closed his door, fighting the urge to punch it. A moment later, Ryan came out of his room.

"Hey, don't walk away from me. Tell me what's going on."

"Forget it."

"Tell me." He sounded annoyed.

"Truth is, I'm having some problems at school again."

Ryan sighed. "Why does this keep happening to you? We can't just pick up and move every time you have a problem. There aren't enough schools."

"Great, Dad, thanks a lot."

"What?"

"It's all me, right? I'm such a loser." She threw up her hands. "I'm not saying we have to move. I just want to stay home today."

"Hey!" he said, yelling louder than her. "Don't raise your voice at me."

"Never mind." She went to her bedroom and changed.

"You can't run away from your problems," he shouted down the hall.

She barreled past him, grabbed a granola bar from the kitchen, and headed for the door.

"Wait up," Ryan called out. "I'll give you a ride."

"I'd rather take the bus."

Kimberly walked into the room. "Ryan, maybe you should let her stay home today."

Aries glared at her. "Butt out, Kimberly."

Ryan pointed at Aries. "Don't you talk to her that way."

"You just don't get it."

Aries turned and walked out the door, slamming it on her way out. Feeling hopeless, she went in the opposite direction of the bus stop, heading toward the beach. She took off her shoes, letting the cold sand squish between her toes with each step. As she approached the water and had time to calm down, she took a long breath, inhaling the salty air.

With the breakers rougher than usual, the waves pounced on the wet sand, and she related to it, feeling as one with the ground underneath the crushing walls of water. Her world seemed to mimic the surf. Every time a set of waves finished their beating, a new set would roll in.

What would it be like to dive under the powerful swells and never resurface, to end it all? She'd tried so hard to be strong, but the world had won the game of breaking her down.

Reaching toward the sky, she yelled, "I give up! You win!"

She had more in common with the afterworld anyway, and the thought of seeing her mom again made her spirit soar. Seeing her mother would make every miserable moment of the past year-and-a-half disappear.

She stared out toward Catalina Island, unable to see the familiar landscape due to the overcast conditions. But with her gone, her father would be alone.

"No, he'd have Kimberly," she said, curling her lip.

Hypnotized by the sound of the ocean, she went back to her imaginary life in the afterworld. She crept to the water's edge, letting the freezing foam stab at her feet. Turning her head back toward the houses, she felt at peace and ready to leave that life behind.

"What are you doing, dear? Don't you dare do anything rash. The world needs more people like you."

Aries sighed. "I'm not going to do anything, Gladys. It was just a fantasy, a thought of making everything easier."

"Easier? Are you kidding me? That would be the hardest thing in the world for everyone who loves you. Not to mention the most foolish and selfish thing I could ever think of. You have people who love and need you, and think about all the people you haven't met yet who are going to love you. You are so young; you haven't even brushed the surface of life yet. And you have such an amazing future ahead of you. Shame on you for not thinking every breath you take is a precious gift."

"I know, it was just a fleeting thought, a what if," Aries said. "I wasn't really going to kill myself."

"I don't want you to ever have that thought again. When you feel like life's got you down, I want you to be grateful."

Aries snorted. "For what?"

"There's only one place to go, and that's up. And not only will everything get better, you'll be stronger for it, too."

"Thank you, Gladys, but I really don't need the 'Go Get 'Em' speech."

A couple of dolphins undulating through the water distracted her, and she lost the connection with Gladys.

Grabbing her bag, she headed for the bus stop. She'd missed her regular bus; however, the day did seem to be improving. Not only would she miss her first class as well, she also now had thirty minutes to spare. Gladys was right, things were starting to look up.

Not having to see Peyton Price first thing in the morning is always a plus.

She walked over to the donut shop near the bus stop and ordered a glazed donut and chocolate milk.

Sitting on a bench, enjoying the sugar rush, she missed the days of getting rides from Damon. She hoped he'd be at school so she could have an ally for the day ahead. Everyone at school knowing about her mom's death made her entire body ache.

Aries arrived at school a few minutes after second period had begun. She savored the benefit of not having to deal with the hallway experience, everyone staring and gossiping about her. But she dreaded walking into the classroom with all eyes on her. Luckily, her trigonometry class counted for college credit, so most of the students were focused on grades, and not the latest school drama.

She entered the classroom without too many prying stares. Mrs. Gardner handed her an agenda, without skipping a beat, as she showed examples on the document camera. Aries took her seat, trying to catch up with the rest of the class on the lesson.

She didn't want the class to end. She had history next, and she could do without whatever Paige and Michael had in store for her. Thankfully, she still had a couple hours before she had to see Peyton.

When the bell rang, she rubbed her hands together and stood up, ready to brave the noisy hallway. Receiving stares from all directions, she blocked it out. But this time, the students weren't even trying to be discreet by whispering. The words "drug overdose" and "druggie" came out loud and clear from various mouths as she made her way to the next classroom.

During class, Piper glanced over and nodded. Aries relaxed for a moment. When the period ended and her classmates began rushing toward the door, Piper approached her.

"Where were you this morning?"

"I missed the bus."

"I'm glad you made it," Piper said. "Miss Townsend gave a pretty cool lecture about cyberbullying. She didn't mention your name or anything, but I can tell she has your back. You're lucky, because everyone respects her."

"I wouldn't say lucky. But thanks for telling me."

"No worries."

Piper strolled off in the opposite direction, leaving Aries standing next to Paige. Paige flashed a sympathetic smile and turned toward the door. As Aries opened her mouth to apologize, Paige walked away.

Well, at least that's a start. Paige didn't give her a dirty look.

FORTY-FIVE MINUTES LATER, English class let out, but now Aries didn't know where to go. Should she eat lunch with Miss Townsend? She took a couple steps down the hallway and stopped. Since she'd missed health class earlier, she turned and walked toward the library to hang out there instead. Borrowing a laptop from the librarian, she inhaled her sandwich and completed her homework. Two other students were using computers near her, but their heads never veered from their screens.

Attempting to make a connection with the boy spirit, she concentrated. *Please talk to me. Or help me make a connection with you. I feel like you know the students here. How can I get them to accept me? I'm so...* She glanced up. *I don't know, lost.*

She returned the computer and walked toward her Spanish classroom a few minutes early to avoid the hallway scene. Crossing her fingers, she said a prayer. *Please let Damon be there.* As she neared the room, Peyton stood alone by the entrance. Who'd have known she could function away from the pack?

Would it be weird if she ran in the opposite direction? She smirked. Totally weird.

Maintaining her course, Aries walked up to Peyton, who smiled at her as if they were best friends.

"Hi," she said.

Aries forced a smile.

"Do you need to ask Mr. Gutierrez a question, too?"

Aries shook her head, then peeked down the hall, hoping another student would appear.

"Sorry to hear about your mom," Peyton said. "I think it's awful what people are posting."

Aries scrutinized her. Was she really being sincere, or could this be some sort of game?

"What, you don't speak anymore?" Peyton let out a fake laugh.

Now that was more like the Peyton she knew and despised.

"I can speak," Aries said.

"Okay, great, congratulations. I was trying to be nice. I feel bad for you."

Aries took a moment before responding. "I guess I'm wondering why. You haven't exactly been nice to me so far. In fact, it's been quite the opposite. So why do you care now?"

The bell rang, and the hallway bustled. The two girls removed their gazes from each other and fixed their eyes on Cory in the distance, walking toward them. Peyton's pupils dilated as her smile widened.

"Because you're not new and interesting anymore," Peyton said, with a grin. "You're just like the rest of us. Scarred, Internet royalty, and trying to pretend like everything's perfect." She directed her attention toward Cory. Locking elbows with him, she said, "Hey, where were you at lunch?"

"Going over plays with Coach." He glanced at Aries. "Now I don't have to meet him after school. I have somewhere else to be." He gave Aries a discreet smile.

Mr. Gutierrez opened the door, and they filed in. Aries sat down at her desk, turning so she could watch the back entrance for Damon. The class began, and no such luck. He'd missed three days now.

What is going on with him?

Peyton stood up, walking over to ask Mr. Gutierrez a question. When she reached his desk, Cory leaned back and threw a crumpled piece of paper on Aries's desk. Aries waited until Peyton sat back down before smoothing out the paper.

A,

Meet me outside the boys locker room five minutes after class.

C

She covered her mouth with her hand to hide her smile.

AFTER CLASS, she slipped into the library. The librarian recognized her.

"Good afternoon, Aries, would you like to borrow a laptop?"

"No, thank you, Mrs. Chou."

Mrs. Chou smiled and went back to her desk. Aries didn't take her eyes off the clock until five minutes finally passed.

Most of the students had vacated the school by the time Aries reached the gymnasium. A couple of boys threw a football back and forth by the locker room, and a group of kids on skateboards were getting chased off by campus security.

Leaning back against the wall, she waited for Cory. A moment later, he appeared out of the locker room.

"Hi. Thanks for meeting me."

She smiled. "Sure. What did you want to talk to me about?"

He looked around. "Not here. Do you have time to go somewhere private? We could go to my house."

A mixture of curiosity and nerves stirred inside of her. "Yes, but I can't stay too long."

"You'll be home before dark."

She agreed.

The walk out to the parking lot took forever. When they reached Cory's SUV, he opened the door for her. Once inside, she reached for the seat belt. As the door closed, a flash in the side mirror caught her attention. In the reflection, a champagne-colored Mercedes appeared.

The car's window came down, and Peyton's face startled her. Peyton's eyes narrowed as her lips tightened, glaring with pure evil.

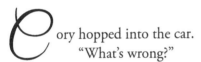ory hopped into the car.

"What's wrong?"

"Peyton's over there, watching us. She just gave me the most disturbing look I think I've ever seen."

"Impossible. There's nobody around. And besides, she takes off right after school on Wednesdays; she has horse riding lessons."

Aries turned back, pointing. "She's over…" Shocked, she said, "You're right. There're no cars around us. I swear she was there a minute ago."

"Must've been someone else." He started the engine, and a pop rock song came through the speakers.

"Is this IDK?" Aries asked.

"Yep. This is off their new album. It hasn't been released yet, but Piper got it for us."

"I like it," she said. "The beat's a little more techno than usual, but it's got a nice ring to it."

"It's one of the better songs. I'm not crazy about the album. I guess there're maybe two or three decent ones though."

"What kind of music do you normally listen to?"

Cory stopped at a light, flashing her a smile. The light changed, and he went back to driving.

"What? You're not going to tell me?"

"You'll laugh."

"No, I won't."

"I like all music. I'm not one of those types who doesn't like something just because all the cool kids say not to or it's not the latest hype."

"Wait a minute, aren't *you* one of the cool kids?" She poked his arm.

"Ha ha."

"C'mon, what do you like?"

He stared straight ahead.

"You know, sometimes getting you to answer a question is about as easy as checking out at one of those gigantic discount stores on Black Friday."

"Really?"

"Um, yes. Never mind, I can survive without knowing."

He laughed. "I like country music. When I'm by myself, that's what I like to listen to."

He turned south, heading toward Lido Island. She loved that part of Newport Beach. It had its own special charm. They passed by the movie theater, then a few shops and restaurants, and drove over the bridge toward the houses.

"I love country music," she said. "Why do you only listen to it when you're by yourself?"

"It's just easier than dealing with Michael bagging on it."

"Let's hear some," she said.

When he turned on a Blake Shelton song, she smiled. "Is Michael your best friend?"

"One of 'em. He's loyal."

"Seems like that should be a given quality in a friend."

He pulled into the driveway of a charming two-story house

with a white picket fence and neatly trimmed hedge. He turned off the engine and leaned back.

"You'd think. But pretty damn hard to find around here."

Before Aries had her seatbelt off, a little girl burst out of the front door and charged up to Cory's side of the car, hugging him as he got out. She wore her hair in two long braids and had on a surfer baseball cap.

"You're home," she said.

"Abby, this is my friend Aries."

"Hi." Abby smiled as Aries waved.

Abby grabbed Cory by the hand. "I have something to show you."

Aries followed them inside the house. Abby had a lot of energy. She held up a drawing of a cat and dog.

"I made it for you." She handed it to Cory.

"Wow, Abs, this is really good. Michelangelo who?"

Abby took a seat at the kitchen table, looking up at Aries with the same brown eyes as Cory's. "You want me to make you a picture?"

Aries smiled. "I'd love that."

Cory rubbed Abby's head. "Where's Mom?"

"Shopping."

"Aren't you a little young to be all by yourself?" Aries asked.

"I'm eight."

"Daisy's here," Cory said. "She watches Abs and cleans the house. We don't say the word 'babysitter' around here."

"Hey." Abby gave him a dirty look.

"I didn't say anything." He put his hand on the small of Aries's back, guiding her toward the table. "Can I get you something to drink? Lemonade, water, soda?"

"Lemonade would be great," she said, enjoying his touch.

"Me, too," Abby called out.

Aries sat next to Abby, while Cory poured the drinks. Abby drew a little, then put her work to the side and scribbled on a different piece of paper, similar to what Aries did when trying to connect with someone on the other side.

"What are you doing?" Aries asked.

Abby switched back to the original paper and drew again. "I was seeing what colors look good together."

"Oh, that's smart."

"Hi, Nana," Abby said, reaching for a crayon and continuing to color as Cory joined them.

With only the three of them in the kitchen, Aries asked, "What did you say?"

Can Abby hear you, Gladys?

"She calls Sunny 'Nana,'" Cory said. "Come here, good girl."

A golden retriever burst around the corner and brushed up against Cory before sitting obediently by his side. He reached down to pet her.

"Why do you call her 'Nana?'" Aries asked.

"She was Nana's dog. Sunny likes it when I call her that," Abby said, reaching for a different crayon.

Cory shrugged.

Sunny barked, then launched all 75 pounds of her frame into Aries's lap, licking her face.

"Whoa, good girl, what's going on?" Aries moved her head from side to side, trying to avoid the licks.

Cory pulled Sunny off her, but the dog jumped back onto her lap, whimpering and licking.

"Pet her chest and belly," Gladys said. *"Oh, my precious Sunny girl. I miss you so much."*

Aries followed Gladys's instructions. Sunny hopped off, rolled over twice, then stayed, exposing her stomach.

Gladys laughed with delight. *"My sweet girl. Keep rubbing her belly."*

"I've never seen her do that before," Cory said. "You must be the Dog Whisperer."

"Nana loves Aries," Abby said, hopping off the chair to pet Sunny as well.

"Thank you," Gladys said.

Sunny barked, wanting Aries to keep rubbing her.

No problem, Gladys. You owe me one.

Something broke in the other room, and Abby screamed. They all went over to investigate, Cory leading the way, and found a picture frame had fallen off the mantle. Cory picked it up, shaking his head.

"That's weird." He brought it to the kitchen and set it on the table.

Aries gazed down at a picture of Cory and a few other boys wearing baseball uniforms. She took a closer look at the boy standing next to him.

Damon.

"When was this picture taken?" she asked.

He glanced at it. "I'm guessing about three years ago."

Were Cory and Damon once friends?

Sunny barked, putting her paw on Aries's lap. She rubbed Sunny's head.

Is that a yes or a no, Gladys?

Sunny stood on her hind legs, licking Aries's cheek, causing her to laugh.

"C'mon, girl, give her a break." Cory grabbed Sunny by the collar and put her outside. He came back and asked, "Are you hungry?"

"Yes," Abby answered.

"Well, that's a given, but I was asking our guest."

Daisy walked into the room. "Oh, hi, Cory, I wasn't expecting you home so early. Sit down. I'll make you guys a snack." She smiled at Aries.

Cory waved her off. "That's okay. I'll take care of the ladies."

"I see, trying to impress your girlfriend. He's smooth, this one."

"Well, not anymore," Cory said.

Daisy laughed. Behind Abby's back, she mouthed, "Do you want me to take her to the park?"

Cory shook his head. "That's okay."

"I know you guys are talking about me," Abby said, without looking up.

"You're so conceited, little one. Why do you think everything is about you?" Daisy teased her. "I'll be in the laundry room if you need me."

"Here." Abby handed Aries a picture of a heart and rainbow.

"Thank you, what a great picture. I'm going to hang it on my refrigerator."

Abby gloated.

They let Abby do all the talking as they ate chips and salsa and finished with ice cream sandwiches.

"Have you ever gone paddle boarding before?" Cory asked.

"No."

"It's easy. You can borrow my mom's board. It's a great day to learn, so we can cruise around the channel."

"Okay." Aries stood, clearing some dishes and rinsing them in the sink.

Cory reached around her, taking a glass out of her hand. "Leave it." He finished for her, wiping his hands on a dish towel. "Alright, let's go."

She followed him out the kitchen door into the garage. He took down two boards from a rafter and grabbed the paddles. Opening the garage door, he put a board under each arm and said, "You mind getting the paddles?"

Aries gathered up the paddles and followed him out as Abby came running out the front door. "Can I come? Please, please?" She looked up at him with her most precious expression.

Cory glanced at Aries.

"Of course you can go," she said. "Who could resist that face?"

"Right?" Cory said, grinning at Abby.

She might not get the information from Cory she came for, but Aries admired the way he interacted with his sister.

It must be nice to have a sibling.

Cory managed all three boards, and they didn't have to walk far to get to the water. He put the boards on the sand, showing Aries how to stand. She stood, copying him.

"Perfect," he said.

Abby had already made her way into the water during Cory's instructions. "C'mon already," she called out.

"You can see who rules the roost around here," he said.

"As she should." Aries put the board in the water and pushed up with ease. They paddled past the houses, with relatively no wind and smooth water.

"Look," Abby said, pointing at a sea lion. She paddled after it.

"Be careful," Cory shouted.

He sat down on his board, motioning for Aries to do the same.

She balanced the paddle across the board and got comfortable, trying to adjust her eyes to the sheen off the water.

"It's messed up what's happening to you at school," he said. "I'm trying to put a stop to it."

"Thanks."

"Man, I don't know what I'd do if there was crap about my dad or something spread all over the Internet."

She ran her hand through the water, squinting from the sun's glare.

Gladys whispered, *"Be careful."*

"Of what?" Aries asked.

"Abby, get away from there," Cory yelled out.

Abby had paddled to within a couple strokes of a boat. "The sea lion is on it!" she shouted.

"I don't care!" he yelled back.

Abby did as Cory instructed and veered left, paddling away from the boat.

Cory grabbed Aries's hand. "I'm sorry, what did you say?"

"Nothing," Aries said, relieved he didn't hear her but disappointed she'd lost the connection with Gladys.

"I wanted to let you know Paige has more video of the party. They have a security system. You were definitely drugged."

She let go of his hand. "She has it recorded? Who did it?" Her pulse quickened.

"That's the thing, we don't know," Cory said.

"We? Who's seen it?"

"Let's see, Paige—"

"Obviously." Aries couldn't control her anxiety.

He gave her a moment, then continued. "Peyton, Piper, Michael, Danny, Brandon, and me."

"Who're Danny and Brandon? Did they drug me, or are they behind the stupid cyber videos?"

"Whoa, take it easy. They're both in our health class. Danny Aguilar and Brandon Young. They're on the football team, and there's no way in hell they're behind it, because they know I'd kick the crap out of them."

"How can you be so sure?"

"They were the guys we played beer pong against, and they were never out of my sight. Also, I've known them since kindergarten. We all go to the same church. They're not saints or anything, but they're decent guys who wouldn't think of doing something like that. Do you need me to go on?"

"Maybe." She broke away from his gaze, glancing back toward the houses.

"Hey, I'm on your side. I want to help you."

"Okay, then can I see the footage?"

"I want you to, and so does Paige, but when we suggested it, Peyton got really weird."

"Why? She did it, she's the one who drugged me. I know it. I need to get out of here."

He held on to her board. "Aries, listen to me. She might be a little abrasive, but she didn't do it."

"How do you know?"

"Because in the video there's a shot of someone putting a cup down next to you. All you can see is an arm. The person is wearing a black leather jacket, and Peyton was wearing some dress thing. She likes to show a lot of skin."

Aries sighed. "It was cold that night. She could've put on a jacket."

"I never saw her with one on," Cory said. "She may be a little jealous, but she's not a complete psycho."

His expression suggested otherwise, but he'd most likely keep defending Peyton, which infuriated Aries. Instead of saying something insulting, she said, "Okay, well, can you arrange for me to see the video without Peyton knowing?"

"I can try, but she and Paige are always together."

"Well, at least try."

He smiled. "For you, I can do that."

She calmed down and smiled back.

"There's something else."

"Yes."

He thought for a moment. "You called me CJ, then went on about how it wasn't my fault. What's that all about?"

Oh, no. Her mind spun. What could she say?

"You don't remember, do you?" he asked.

He gave her the perfect excuse. "Sorry, I don't."

"Well, at least tell me where CJ came from. How did you get that? I can't stop thinking about it."

She shrugged. "I don't know. I mean, the football roster has your full name. I guess I remembered from the game that night."

He shook his head. "But CJ?"

"I think the initials are cute. Sorry, I'll never call you that again."

"No, it's not that," he said. "I like the nickname. You can call me CJ."

"Are you sure?"

"Yeah. Reminds me of my grandma."

Abby started screaming. Cory shot up on his board, racing toward her. Reaching her, he flailed his paddle in the air as bees swarmed around them.

"Paddle, Abs, go, go!" Cory yelled.

Is this your doing, Gladys? Or are other spirits trying to get my attention?

The two made it back to Aries in record time, Abby paddling for her life, Cory flinging his paddle in the air for safety. But the bees had scattered away.

Out of breath, he said, "Man, I've never seen anything like that before. You okay, Abs? No stings?"

Catching her breath, she said, "No. I want to go home."

"We are." Cory reached for Aries's hand. "See, I promised I'd get you home before dark."

As they made their way back through the channel, Aries got lost in the serenity of the evening sky. Her mother would've loved it.

"Look at that sunset. It's awesome," he said.

"It is gorgeous," she whispered, falling for him even more.

She scanned the harbor, taking in the scene when the sun beamed off one of the glass façades, blinding her for a second. Averting her gaze to the next house, she did a double take. The window displayed a reflection of Peyton's face.

Her knees locked as prickles ran down her skin. When she remembered to breathe, she lost her balance, crashing into the water. With the water colder than she expected, she surfaced, gasping as she gulped in air.

Cory dashed to her, pulling her up onto her board. "What happened? Are you okay?"

She brushed her hair off her forehead, shivering. "Yes."

He rubbed her shoulder. "C'mon, let's get you out of here."

They didn't have much further to paddle. When they made it to land, Aries had already warmed up a little.

He grabbed the boards, trying to hurry.

She wrung out the bottom of her shirt. "It's okay. I'm not that cold anymore. It actually felt kind of good," she said, trying to reassure him.

"You sure?" He took inventory, making sure they had everything.

Abby pulled on Aries's hand. As she bent down, Abby whispered in her ear, "I saw her, too."

17

---

*A*ries threw off the covers, sitting up. The image of Peyton's face burned into her mind, keeping her awake. She waited for her eyes to adjust to the darkness as a fly crept up her window. The fly stopped and remained motionless as she heard a faint male voice try to make his presence clear. She couldn't understand him, so she slowed down her breathing, making an attempt to connect.

Hearing a certain inflection in his mumbling, she said, *Chuck, is that you?*

"Yes."

Leaning back into the pillows, she asked, *How can I help you?*

He laughed. *"I'm afraid it's the other way around."*

Right. I don't think anyone can help me. My life's a disaster. Unless you can help me contact my mom. Do you know who she is? Can you see her? What's the other side like?

"Slow down. It doesn't work that way. I'm here to guide you in this period of your life. But I want you to remember, you're always in charge of your destiny."

Great. My mom used to say that after she read me my horoscope.

Her digital clock blinked three times, then reset, flashing "12:00."

"I guess in a way, you could think of it like that," he said. *"Think of my guidance as an outline, and it's up to you to fill in the pages."*

Alright, so guide me. Let me hear some spiritual wisdom.

Something broke in the closet. Aries whipped her head in that direction, inhaling a whiff of Elizabeth's perfume.

No.

She sprang out of bed, turned on the light, and brought down her mom's box. Opening it, she found the perfume bottle intact. Part of the frame that held the picture of the sunset had cracked. She put her hand on her chest, relieved the perfume bottle didn't break.

Putting the box back and turning off the light, she asked, *Are you still there?*

"Yes. What did you notice inside the box?"

The frame broke. She sat on the edge of the bed. "My mom's painting," she said.

"That's right."

What was it doing in Paige's house? And who is this Camden Price?

"There's a start to your outline. I suggest you fill in the blanks."

Don't you think I would if I knew how? She covered her mouth with a pillow, letting out a muffled scream. *And what about Peyton? How do I prove she's the one tormenting me?*

"Are you sure she is?"

Yes.

"How?"

Let's see, she drugged me, she posted it all over the Internet, she stole my phone, and now she's stalking me.

"Has anyone else seen her do these things?"

I don't know, but I have. The stalking part, that is.

"Was that really her, or a figment of your imagination?"

Aries screamed into her pillow again. *Why are you messing with my head?*

"*Tell me then, why did you only see her face in the reflection on the window, and not her entire body?*"

Wait, Abby saw Peyton as well, so there, I'm not going crazy.

"*Abby said, 'I saw her.' She didn't say Peyton.*"

Aries covered her ears. *I can't handle this right now. Go away, go away, go away.*

"*Let's regroup,*" Chuck said. "*I'm suggesting you keep all options open for now. Don't assume anything. When it comes to finding your truth, make sure you have actual proof. But for now, lead with your instincts. When you get a feeling, follow it. You have natural intuition, and you need to tap into that ability of yours.*"

Aries picked at her comforter. *Okay, but my gut still thinks it's Peyton.*

"*But you'll keep an open mind, right?*"

I guess.

"*Good.*"

She sprawled out, pulling the sheets over herself. *Chuck, one more thing?*

"*Yes?*"

She turned on her side, facing the window. *Who's Sarah?*

The fly fell on the ground, and Chuck was gone.

Questions ricocheted throughout Aries's mind the rest of the night, causing her to toss and turn until her alarm went off. She snapped her head toward the clock, then checked her watch. The clock showed the correct time. She didn't have the energy to figure out how that was possible when it clearly had shut off during her conversation with Chuck.

Moving like a zombie, she went through the motions of getting ready for school, then headed for the kitchen. Her father was wearing a nicer pair of jeans than he usually wore to work, and a collared shirt. He didn't say anything as he fixed her a plate with bacon and eggs and poured her a glass of orange juice.

Sitting down at the table, she asked, "You don't have to work today?"

He analyzed her for a moment. "I'm going in late." He leaned against the counter, watching her.

She took a bite, unable to swallow as her father continued to stare at her. A moment later, she asked, "Aren't you going to eat?"

"I did." He juggled his keys in his hand. "Is there anything you want to tell me?"

"No. Why?" Avoiding his gaze, she took a couple more bites, then sipped some juice.

"Oh, I don't know."

She smirked. "Okay, you're acting strange. What's going on?"

"You tell me."

"Obviously I don't know, so you tell me." She finished her breakfast and carried her plate to the sink.

He analyzed her. "Is everything okay?"

No! she wanted to shout at the top of her lungs. "I guess."

He studied her for a moment, then nodded. "Alright, let's go."

"It's early, we still have time."

"I need to get you there early."

She panicked for a moment. More time for everyone to make fun of her. "Okay," she dragged out the word. *What's going on with him?*

They drove to the school in silence. Ryan pulled into the parking lot and turned off the engine.

"What are you doing?" she asked.

He stepped on the emergency brake and pulled out the keys. "I got an interesting phone call from one of your teachers last night, and I'm supposed to meet with her a half-hour before school starts." He got out of the truck.

She followed him. With her temperature rising, she managed to say, "Um..."

"You want to direct me toward your health class?"

Oh, God.

They headed toward the building. "I can explain. I-I missed class be—"

He held up his hand. "Save it, we're late."

They found Miss Townsend waiting by the door. "Hello, Mr. Dade. Thank you for taking time out of your busy day to meet with me. I really appreciate it." She held out her hand.

Shaking her hand, he said, "Of course, and call me Ryan."

She smiled. "Come in." Shifting to Aries, she said, "Do you mind waiting in the hall? I'd like to speak with your father in private." She didn't give Aries a chance to respond and shut the door behind her.

Aries sank to the floor, imagining the worst. She'd do anything not to have her dad upset with her. Why did she miss the stupid bus?

Twenty minutes later, Ryan opened the door. She stood, attempting to analyze his mood but was unable to read him.

He regarded her for a moment, moisture invading his eyes. Her eyes mirrored his.

"Sorry," she managed to say.

"Don't be. I'm the idiot. I had no idea." He hugged her like he hadn't seen her in years.

She sniffled, never wanting to let go of him, but she forced herself to pull back so she wouldn't lose it in front of him.

He held on to her. "It's going to be okay. We'll get through this. You and me, Kiddo, we're Dades, bulletproof."

She held it together, long enough to fake a smile and nod.

"I have to go, but we'll talk tonight." He gave her one last hug and walked away.

Aries cleared her throat and collected herself before Miss Townsend opened the door and greeted her.

"Come in, we have a few minutes."

Aries took her seat.

Miss Townsend sat on the table in front of her. "I told your dad what's going on with you, and I showed him the videos."

Aries's entire body went rigid as her hands balled into fists. Controlling herself so she wouldn't curse, she said, "Why would you do that to me?"

"Because I want to help you. And so does your dad. You should've seen how appreciative he was."

"Did you show him *all* the videos?"

"No, not all. I showed him the ones that involve your mom."

"Oh." Aries relaxed her shoulders.

The bell rang, but before any students poured in, Miss Townsend said, "Please have lunch in here today. I'd like to continue our conversation, if that's okay with you?"

Aries agreed as the room filled up.

Daniel Aguilar sat down in the front of the room, and Brandon Young took his spot in the back. Then the P-pack barged in, making their usual self-aggrandizing entrance.

Piper came up to her. "Looks like you're off the hook."

"What do you mean?"

"Jamie and Brandon broke up. He caught her making out with Troy. You probably don't know him, he's a senior. It's all over Newport Dish. Told you all you had to do was wait for the next scandal. Everyone's so ADD around here. This class is going to be interesting, though. She sits next to Danny."

"How's that interesting?"

"Danny's Brandon's best friend. He's gonna rip her a new one. Sucks to be her right now."

Cory sat down, giving Piper a special handshake and smiling at Aries.

"Talk later." Piper turned and walked toward her seat, which happened to be right next to Brandon.

Peyton whispered something into Cory's ear, then turned toward Aries. "Hi," she said and sauntered back to her table, gabbing away with Michael.

"See, I told you Peyton can be nice," Cory said.

"Sure."

He adjusted his cap. "And I found out she was at her riding lessons yesterday."

"According to her, right?" She had to point out the obvious.

"Peyton wouldn't lie to me."

She kept quiet, finding it useless to try and convince him otherwise.

"Abby sure liked you," he said. "She keeps asking me when we can all go paddle boarding again."

Aries smiled. "She's sweet. I had a lot of fun."

"Maybe this weekend?"

She couldn't resist the look in his eyes. "Maybe," she teased.

He leaned back. "I can accept that."

At the end of class, she said goodbye to Cory, and he held her gaze longer than usual.

Content with going back to being a nobody, she navigated through the masses in the hallways. All the rumors and gossip focused around Jamie Adler.

Since things were starting to go back to normal, she had the courage to approach Paige after history class. "Hi Paige, I want to apologize to you. I don't know why I made that horrible comment to you. I think everything about you is darling."

"Darling?" Paige smirked. "You sound like my mom. You really hit a nerve, though. It's one of my biggest insecurities. I hate my voice, too." She shrugged.

"Please don't. It's fine."

"C'mon, we all know how you really feel. But it's okay. At least you said it to my face. Everyone else just talks behind my back."

"Can we start over?"

Paige smiled. "We don't have to start over. I like knowing the truth. I'm not gonna lie, I was pissed. But I appreciate your honesty."

"Okay, good, I guess."

Aries turned and headed for her next class. She peered over her shoulder. Paige stood in the same spot, glaring at her.

When lunchtime arrived, Aries wanted to be alone and sit under her tree, but she'd made a promise to Miss Townsend. She entered the classroom and sat in her usual seat.

Miss Townsend looked up from her desk. "Hello, Aries. I'm glad you came. I wanted to check in with you and make sure you're okay."

"I'm fine."

"I noticed there haven't been any more videos posted. That's a good sign."

"Yes."

"Also, I hope you understand why I told your father."

She nodded, even though she didn't, and Miss Townsend should mind her own business.

"He mentioned the two of you don't really talk about your mom."

Aries should've talked to Ryan about her mother, but it never seemed to be the right time. She became saddened by the lack of communication between them.

"No, we don't." She lost her appetite and didn't feel like discussing her personal life any further. "Do you need any help? I can clean the tables for you or something."

"You know, that's a wonderful idea. I'd love for you to grade some papers. That gives me a chance to get the next test ready for tomorrow." She walked over and explained the grading process. "These aren't from your class. This period is a little behind, so I don't think you'll have trouble knowing the answers."

As Aries graded the papers, a spirit broke through. *"She's hurting."*

Miss Townsend?

"Yes. Broken heart."

Aries wanted to say something encouraging to Miss Townsend, but instead she handed her the graded papers.

"Wow, you're fast," Miss Townsend said. "Thank you."

She pressed her lips together, fighting the urge to say she was sorry.

"Everything okay?" Miss Townsend asked.

Aries nodded, regretting not speaking up as she walked out of the classroom and headed over to her final class for the day. When she rounded the corner, she came to an abrupt halt. Someone had grabbed her backpack from behind. Standing with her mouth agape, she narrowed her eyes as Damon flung her bag around his shoulder.

"Hey, Sophomore. I can tell by your expression you're happy to see me."

His eyes had a faint yellowish green tint under them, and his nose was still swollen. "Are you okay?" she asked.

"Good as gold."

"Your face. I'm sorry."

He wrapped his arm around her. "You should see the other guy."

"Unfortunately, I have," she said. "And he didn't look as bad."

"Way to kick a man when he's down."

She elbowed his arm. "No, I didn't mean it like that."

"It's okay, we'll see how Pretty Boy does when it's just me and him."

"No. Please let it go. Don't do anything."

"Sorry, Sophomore, I'm afraid you can't protect your boyfriend this time."

She rolled her eyes. "You know he's not my boyfriend."

He glanced down the hall. "Let's get out of here."

"I can't. I have to go to class."

"If you go with me, I'll consider dropping it with Douglas."

"But—"

"Hurry before we see him. There're things you need to know."

She paused for a moment. "Can't you tell me after class?"

Clusters of students entered the building.

"I can't look at the guy for an entire hour," he said. "I don't know what'll happen."

"You're going to have to face him sooner or later."

He directed her toward the back exit. "I choose later."

She stopped him. "I'll get in trouble."

"No, you won't. My buddy's an aide for the attendance office. He'll hook you up with a pass."

She hesitated as Chuck mumbled something.

"There's something I want to show you," Damon said.

"You might not like what you find out," Chuck said. *"But then again…"* His voice faded.

Damon held out his hand. "Let's go."

Clasping his hand, she said, "Okay." She took one final look back at the classroom entrance, unsure of her decision.

Cory stood in the doorway alone. His eyes locked on her and Damon.

18

Damon maneuvered down the coast at a speed that made Aries's stomach do somersaults. She liked the surge of adrenaline but worried for their safety. With her hair whipping her back and the wind buffeting her face, she focused on the ocean. They stopped at a traffic light, and she had enough time to catch her breath. With nobody else on the road, he accelerated to an alarming speed, causing her to gasp. Damon slowed down a bit after that.

As they traveled past Newport Coast, they passed the gated estates where Piper lived. A couple miles down, Damon veered off a side road toward the beach and parked. She removed the helmet, running her fingers through her hair.

"I'm glad we made it in one piece," she said.

He gave her a devilish smile. "I'm glad you liked it."

They walked toward a snack shack, and Damon ordered two cups of shaved ice, handing her one.

She took a bite. "Is this what you wanted to show me?"

"No. I just had a craving."

She followed him across the sand, sitting next to him on the edge by the water. They watched the surf for a few minutes. "I can't believe I'm missing class for this."

He gestured toward the ocean. "Why not? It's a great day, and you're with even better company." He nudged her. "You should be grateful."

"Why did you miss so many days of school?" she asked.

"Three's not that many."

"It felt like more."

With a serious expression, he said, "Honestly, I don't know what I would've done to Douglas. When I saw his hands on you, taking advantage of you…" He shook his head. "I lost it."

"He wasn't taking advantage of me. He was helping me."

"I know that now," he said. "That's why I came today."

"How do you know?"

"I don't live under a rock. I do own a computer."

"You know about the videos?" She flushed.

He faced the waves for a moment. "The stuff about your mom…that true?"

"Yes."

"Sorry."

"I don't think she did it on purpose," she said. "I think maybe someone might have killed her."

"What do the police think?"

"No foul play. That she used drugs and OD'd."

"Then why do you think she was murdered?"

Aries smoothed out the sand with her foot. "A hunch. And she didn't use drugs."

"You'd be surprised at what our parents hide from us," he said. "But you should look into it."

"How?"

"I can help you."

"Again, how?"

"I know people in high places." He smiled. "What?"

"You and that cocky grin."

"You love it."

She turned her head away. "Maybe."

"I like you, Sophomore." He kept his gaze straight ahead.

"Thanks, LeMoore. I guess I like you, too," she said.

He laughed. "Promise me you'll never get drunk again. Not a good look for you."

"Well, it wasn't on purpose."

"I know. That's why I'm going to take you somewhere in a minute."

"Promise me we'll get there at a normal speed."

"I can do that," he said.

"Can you tell me what happened that night?" she asked. "What happened after the fight? And how'd I end up on a different patio?"

"I remember being on the bottom of a dog pile, punches thrown here and there. A couple of linebackers broke up the fight. Paige was screaming like a lunatic." He squinted, concentrating. "Everyone pretty much evacuated when they heard sirens. It was like turning on a light in a room full of cockroaches. I asked the chick who was with you all night where you went—"

"What chick?" she interrupted.

He shrugged. "Freshman, maybe."

"Oh, Michelle."

"I guess," he said. "Anyway, she pointed outside. It was dark, so I ran up and down the shore, calling your name. I checked by the Wedge, because that was where we'd last been outside together. And I found you passed out on the rocks." He pushed her arm. "Don't ever do that again either. You have any idea how stressful that was? I checked your pulse, relieved you had one."

"Sorry," she said. "And then what?"

"And then I carried you. I couldn't take you back to Paige's, because there were guys still looking for me. I couldn't throw you on the back of my bike, because you were too groggy. So, I found the patio with the best lounge chairs. I stayed with you until I heard you moan in the morning. I would've stayed longer, but I had hell to pay when I got home. The honorable a-hole was on a mission to find me."

"Sorry."

"Stop saying you're sorry. It's not your fault."

"Well, thank you, then."

"Then you're welcome."

"I saw you with your dad," she said.

He whipped his head in her direction. "When?"

"A couple days ago. I wanted to see if you were okay. He was yelling at you."

"I wish you didn't see that."

"Me, too. I felt bad for you. Is he abusive?"

"No. Well, maybe in today's world, he's considered verbally abusive. But nothing I can't handle."

"You sure?" she asked.

"Let's just say he's not a nice guy. Which is a good segue into what I want to show you."

"Okay." She gave him a skeptical look.

"You ready?" He got up, took her cup from her, and threw away their trash, motioning for her to follow him back to the parking lot.

Damon drove at a respectable pace. A few miles later, he swerved off the main highway and revved the engine, continuing up a steep, winding street. After the second bend, Aries glanced over the edge and had a slight panic attack. They came to another curve in the road, and her head started throbbing, accompanied by the obnoxious buzzing sound.

Leave me alone, Mr. Overzealous. Not now.

Damon slowed through each switchback, but he was still going faster than she preferred. The buzzing intensified.

Shut up.

When they reached a lookout point, Damon cut the engine. She hopped off the bike, pacing.

He walked over. "Are you okay?" he asked, taking the helmet off her.

The noise ringing through her ears caused her to grab her head. She managed to say, "Talk to me, ask me a question." If she were in a conversation, maybe Mr. Overzealous would go away.

"Come look at the view," he said. "It's amazing."

The ocean was majestic from that height. To the left, she admired the open land masses of hills with dirt trails, a rarity in Southern California.

"That's pretty, too." She pointed toward the trails.

"You feel any better?" he asked.

"Yes. I think it was all the turns."

"I'll go slower when we leave. Come here, check this out."

They walked over to a lookout point with a broken guardrail. The closer she got, the louder the buzz became. She studied it for a moment.

"Looks like someone missed this turn. This road must be dangerous at night," she said, blocking out the noise.

"It is," he said. "Especially if you've been drinking."

The buzzing sound roared back.

Get out of here, Mr. O. Leave me alone. You usually don't bother me when I'm with someone else. Why now?

Damon leaned over and grabbed on to the rail. "This is what I wanted to show you, but we can leave. You don't look so hot."

"No, I'm fine. Just keep talking." She stepped back from the rail, the buzz sound losing power.

"You know the person who missed this turn."

"Really, who?" she asked.

He stood upright. "Piper," he said, using air quotes. "It's weird, though, I never heard a crash." He tapped the rail.

"What, Piper?"

"Allegedly. I don't buy it for a second."

"Her DUI?"

"Yep."

"Wait, I thought this was going to be about your dad? Where's the segue?"

He held up his finger. "You do pay attention. Nice. He got her DUI tossed out. You think having your stuff posted all over teenage sites was bad? Her arrest was blasted all over the news. 'Rock Star's Daughter Busted' was the headline on most of the tabloids. But now it's not on her record."

"Lucky for her," she said. "I'm also curious why you're so convinced Piper wasn't driving?"

"Brains, too," he said. "You know, Sophomore, keep this up, and I might be impressed. First of all, the Judge's good friends with Peyton's dad, so I think he's the one who called in the favor."

"I'm so lost," she said. "Why would Peyton's dad care about Piper?"

"Let me start from the beginning. Last August, everyone was at Peyton and Cory's birthday party at the yacht club—"

"They have the same birthday?"

"Yes, but that's not the point."

"Sorry, I was just wondering when."

"I don't know, mid-August. Why, so you can buy your boyfriend a gift?" He shook his head. "This part isn't about him."

"I know, but my mom's birthday was August eighteenth. I guess I was curious. Never mind, go on."

"Now, you have to understand it's not unusual for Piper to be loaded on something, so for her to be sober at her friends' birthday party was pretty bizarre. I remembered asking her why. She told me her dad was flying in early in the morning and she didn't want to be hungover. She seemed pretty excited."

"So, what happened?" Her patience was slipping.

"By the end of the night, she *was* wasted, and I figured she gave in to temptation and the festivities got the best of her. But I got to thinking and found it weird she couldn't form a sentence. Kind of like the way you acted the other night. Piper can usually maintain. So, I knew something wasn't right. I tried to keep an eye on her, but I lost track of her."

"So maybe she got behind the wheel and drove up here," she said. "Thank God for this guardrail."

He shook his head. "At the end of the night, everyone left at the same time. I followed Peyton's car, figuring she could lead me to Piper. I wasn't sure who was driving, because Peyton was drinking as well. It was a foggy night. I had low visibility, and I had to be careful not to be spotted. When I hit this road, I turned off my light, and about halfway up I parked and walked the rest of the way, knowing it's a dead-end and I'd eventually find her. I hid behind a tree when another car drove past me. I'm pretty sure I wasn't seen. When I reached the top, I couldn't see much except for two people moving a body from the back seat to the driver's side, then getting into the other car."

"What? Are you sure?" she asked.

"Yes. And later it was confirmed it was Piper in the driver's seat. See, I know she was framed."

With wide eyes, Aries said, "Who? Who would do that to Piper?"

He glanced up the road before turning back to her. "Peyton and Cory."

19

*A*ries stood away from the guardrail, keeping the buzzing sound at bay.

"I don't believe it. Peyton, *maybe*. But Cory, no way." She shook her head. "It doesn't make any sense. Piper's their friend."

"Friend? Ha, they don't know the meaning. Check this out." His phone beeped. "Hold on." He turned away, glanced up the hill for a moment, then put his phone back in his pocket.

"What's wrong? Was that the Judge?"

"No. Nothing. Why?"

"You're acting different, and you look kind of pissed off."

"Not at all." He brushed his hand through his hair. "Now where was I?"

"Piper." She pointed at the guardrail.

"Right. I'm sure they didn't intend on getting her arrested—"

"I'm pretty sure you weren't going to say that before your text message." She narrowed her eyes. "What's at the top of the hill?"

"Nothing." He waved his hand, dismissing her question. "Anyway, when the accident happened, Peyton most likely panicked and figured nobody would be fazed by Piper drinking and driving. But little Miss Golden Child? Now, that would shock the entire city. Especially with her dad running for Congress."

"Then why would her dad take the risk of having Piper's DUI thrown out?" she asked. "And why would your dad go through with it?"

"Supposedly, it was all done legally," he said. "The police never gave her a breathalyzer test."

"I find that hard to believe, especially if she was as out of it as you say."

He sighed. "I was being sarcastic. Of course that's not the truth, but that's how my dad got her charges dismissed. I'm sure her blood alcohol level report somehow magically disappeared. That's what happens when you're Camden Price and own half of Southern California."

Aries took a moment to absorb his story.

"Come here." He motioned for her to come closer.

"No, I'm good right here."

"I want to show you something else."

She took a couple steps toward the rail and stopped, testing whether she'd be allowed to approach it this time without the noise shooting through her head.

"I don't bite," he said.

She walked up to him, happy to be free from the chaos.

"Look down over the rail," he said.

She froze. "I'm afraid of heights."

"You're not going to fall." He placed her in front of him, wrapping his arms around her waist. "I got you."

Trusting him, she peered down.

"What do you see?" he asked.

"A long way down."

"Nothing else?" He moved her to the side, looking over the rail. "That's weird."

"What?"

"Every other time I've come up here, there are flowers right below this broken part," he said. "See how that rock juts out? Usually, the flowers are thrown on it."

As she scanned the bare rock, the buzzing sound blasted through her head. She covered her ears, knelt down, and moaned.

"Are you sure you're okay?" he asked.

She ran into the street. *What do you want? Why can't you leave me alone?*

"Find out who's leaving the flowers," Mr. Overzealous said.

Okay. Just go away.

Damon rushed up to her. "What's the matter?"

"Nothing," she said.

"Does this have to do with your fear of heights?"

She nodded. "Do you mind if we go now?"

"No, let's get out of here."

Damon drove slowly on the ride back, checking up on Aries at each stoplight. He pulled into a gas station around the corner from her apartment and parked.

"In case your dad's home, I thought I'd walk you the rest of the way."

"It's not just the motorcycle," she said. "The fact that you're a boy would cause him to freak out."

"I want to make sure you get home safe."

"I can take it from here."

He grabbed her bag, wrapping his arm around her. "C'mon."

Since her dad wouldn't be home yet, she agreed. As they walked, she said, "Thanks for telling me about Piper."

"You needed to know. Now will you please stay away from Douglas?"

"I don't think you'd lie to me, but I'm not sure if you witnessed the truth. Like you said, it was dark and foggy that night."

"Maybe you don't want to believe your Prince Charming would do such a thing," he said.

She stopped. "Are you one hundred percent sure it was them?"

Keeping her gaze, he said, "Ninety-nine percent."

The look in his eyes caused her skin to tingle. She blushed. "Well, that's not one hundred."

"Very good, Sophomore. You might get into college now."

She elbowed him. "Shut up. But you're saying there's a doubt?"

"Let's say it was definitely Peyton's car and an SUV. I can't say for sure, but I'd bet it was your boyfriend's. And it was absolutely a girl and a guy who drove away."

"That doesn't necessarily mean it was Peyton and Cory," she said.

"Maybe not, but ever since that night, Peyton's had this weird hold over Douglas."

They stopped in the alley behind her apartment building. "How do you know?" she asked.

"Because Douglas couldn't stand her. None of us can."

"Really?"

"Yes, really," he said. "Now wipe that grin off your face."

"I'm not—"

He pulled her close to him. "Actually, don't...I kind of like it."

She feared her knees might give out if she looked at him. "I have to ask, did you and Cory used to be friends?"

He stepped back. "Way to ruin the moment, Sophomore."

"We were having one?"

He gave her a sly smile.

"Well, were you friends?" she asked.

"Something like that."

"What happened?"

As Damon opened his mouth, her father's truck appeared in the distance. "You have to get out of here."

He understood, dropping her bag and ducking behind the dumpster.

She tried to act casual as her dad parked and stepped out of the truck, carrying two grocery bags. "What are you doing out here, Kiddo?"

"I needed some fresh air."

"I thought we could order a pizza," he said. "What do you say?"

"Sounds great." She followed him up the steps. Hanging back, she waved to Damon.

Ryan set the bags on the counter. Reaching in, he pulled out a bag of peanut M&Ms. "I got your favorite," he said, tossing the bag to her.

"Thank you." She opened the package, popping two in her mouth.

As Ryan ordered the pizza, she changed into pajama bottoms and a tank top. She tied her hair back and turned on the computer. She'd developed a new addiction to browsing various social media websites. Shaking her head, she frowned at the dancing girl who now had Jamie Adler's face digitally mapped onto her body. Derogatory words were posted about Jamie, and she was shown in obscene positions next to Troy Perry, the senior she'd made out with.

Poor Jamie. There has to be some way to shut down this website.

Starving by the time the pizza arrived, she turned off the computer and hurried to the kitchen. Ryan handed her a soda as he cracked open a beer. They sat on the couch, but Ryan didn't turn on the television like usual.

Instead, he said, "I had no idea things were that bad at school. Why didn't you tell me?"

Reaching for a napkin, Aries said, "I didn't want you to worry."

"That's my job. You don't have to go to school tomorrow. Maybe I can take the day off and we can look for a new school."

"There aren't that many, remember?"

He took a gulp. "I was tired, but that's no excuse. I'm sorry."

"You're forgiven. And it's okay. People are leaving me alone for now."

"How'd they get that picture of you and Mom?" he asked.

"Someone stole my phone."

"What? Why didn't you tell me that either? What if I needed to get ahold of you?"

"I thought you'd be mad," she said. "I know you don't have the money to get me a new one. And I kept hoping it would turn up."

"I'm buying you one tomorrow." He reached for a slice.

She took a bite. Setting her pizza down, she asked, "Dad, were you and Mom happy?"

"Yeah." He shrugged. "I guess. I mean, we were married for thirteen years, so we had some rough patches, but for the most part I'd say we were." He got up and grabbed another beer. "Can I get you anything?"

"No, I'm good." She opened the box, pulling out two more slices. "I know you were young, but would you still have married her if she wasn't pregnant with me?"

"Not at twenty; probably not. But I loved your mother."

"I know. But in hindsight, do you think you would have?"

He took a sip. "I can't really answer that question. But you were the best thing that ever happened to us. That I know for a fact."

They ate for a few minutes. Avoiding eye contact, she asked, "Did you ever use drugs?"

"Is this about your mom?"

"I'm wondering if you guys did them together."

"I wasn't expecting the heavy line of questioning here." He scratched his chin before proceeding. "Okay, I experimented here and there. I was stupid and reckless in my teens. But you're way too smart for that."

"I know. This isn't about me. I have no desire. What about Mom? Do you think it's true?"

"I don't know. I was working a lot, trying to save extra cash to lead the new lifestyle she wanted. I think your mom got bored. She started meeting new people and making new friends, and all of them were well-off. She started hanging out in Laguna Beach about two, three times a week. She said she needed to be familiar with the art galleries if she ever wanted to sell her work there. Your mother always did have champagne taste, and she wanted to associate herself with people who lived that lifestyle. I couldn't give her that, so I think she wanted to give it a try herself."

Aries placed her plate on the coffee table. She had a hard time formulating her next question, but she willed the words to come out. "Do you think she was having an affair?"

Ryan snapped his head in her direction. "What would make you think that?"

"I don't know, her wanting a different life and spending most of her time in Laguna. Maybe there was a man she met there."

"Your mom loved meeting new people, anything social really. She craved attention from men, but one thing I can guarantee is, she was faithful."

"How?"

"Because she wouldn't do that to me - and more importantly, she'd never do that to you."

"Maybe," she said. "But do you ever really know someone? I mean, you still don't know if she OD'd by accident or not."

"When did you get so grown up?" He reached over and rubbed the top of her head.

"You never talk about her. And you moved on so quickly with Kimberly. So maybe you were both seeing other people. I can handle it if you were."

He leaned back and regarded her for a moment. "Kim and I are taking it slow. She started cutting my hair after your mom passed. I spent about a half-hour in her salon every five weeks or so, and we found out we had a lot in common. She's a great listener, she's helped me a lot. But not a day goes by when I don't think about Elizabeth. And it kills me to think what it must be like for you. Sometimes I want to talk about her, but I don't know how to broach the subject with you. I'm still trying to figure this whole single dad thing out. I won the lottery with you, Kiddo, but sometimes I get down, feeling like I'm not doing enough for you."

She shook her head. "You do more than enough."

He didn't look convinced as he went into the kitchen to retrieve another beer. Taking a sip, he looked straight ahead.

"But I'm not sold on how your mother died."

"Me either. I think maybe she was murdered."

"I don't know," he said. "But I'm going to find out."

"How?"

"I don't want you to worry about that. Just focus on being a kid. It goes by too fast, and I don't want you dealing with adult problems."

She smiled. "I'm glad you don't believe it either."

She helped him clean up and said goodnight. Walking down the hall, she stopped halfway.

Turning to face him, she said, "Dad, one more thing."

He stood in the kitchen. "Yes?"

"We didn't move to Newport Beach by coincidence, did we?"

He stared out the window, then back at her. "No."

20

GEMINI RISING

*G*reg ate his lunch alone, sitting on a patch of grass behind the school. He couldn't be around his usual friends, disgusted by all their drama. He punched the ground a couple of times. How'd he let Stacy talk him into posting private information about Aries's mother and humiliating her all over social media? Having failed at keeping Stacy in check, he switched his priorities to protecting Aries. She'd never forgive him if she found out the truth, and he wouldn't blame her.

How much longer could he stand being blackmailed? All the secrets and lies he'd been harboring were taking a toll on him. Secrets regarding Jake, Piper, and half of Newport High were becoming too much for him to handle. He wanted to get as far away from the high school as possible. As far away from *her* as possible. Maybe he should come clean about everything while he still had the chance.

He ran his hand through his hair, recalling the night he had sex with Stacy. He never knew such pleasure. The way her silky smooth skin felt against his, the intoxicating smell of her natural pheromones, and the sweet taste of her mouth. But now he never knew such pain. He regretted ever meeting her. The way she manipulated him was inhumane.

He wiped a bead of sweat off his forehead. Closing his eyes, he grimaced as he relived the night Jake Coleman took his last breath, which happened to be the same night he had sex with Stacy. She'd left without so much as a goodbye. Jake jumped on his motorcycle and took off before anyone could stop him. To this day, no one except Stacy could figure out why he'd left the party.

Greg couldn't keep up the façade much longer before cracking.

His phone vibrated in his pocket, causing him to jump, bringing him back to reality.

He pulled it out. "Hey."

"So I'm reduced to 'hey?' You'd treat a bum on the street with more respect," Stacy said. "Where are you? I've been looking everywhere for you."

"Maybe that's a clue."

"Ha. You can't avoid me forever," she said. "Too much is at stake. *Remember,* Greg?"

"What do you want?" he asked.

"I'm bored."

He almost chucked his phone across the street. "Take up a new hobby. Look, I don't know what to tell you. You have plenty of friends. Bug one of them."

"But you're so much more fun. My place after school," she said. "We can strategize our next move. And if you do a good job, you might get lucky."

"You'll croak?"

"Ooh, I like the hard-to-get attitude," she said. "You're turning me on. See you after school."

"I'm busy," he said. "Haven't you tortured the poor girl enough?"

"Who, Legs?" She sighed. "I'm beginning to think you really

like this girl. But Mr. Good Boy all of a sudden, maybe I have something else in mind."

"Good," he said.

"Or maybe not."

"You're ridiculous."

"Like you're not," she said. "Fine, we can talk about this tomorrow."

He hung up on her, shaking his head. He had to make things right again.

21

Through her peripheral vision, Aries caught Cory staring at her. It bordered on creepy.

Unable to concentrate on the nutrition facts label worksheet, she asked, "What?"

"Nothing," he said. "You seem different."

"How?"

"In a good way. You look really pretty."

"How'd I look before?"

"I mean, you always look good," he said. "Never mind, I'll shut up now."

She laughed. "Thank you."

"For shutting up?"

"No, for the compliment." After talking with her father the night before, Aries finally blocked out the other side and caught up on some much needed sleep.

"You have a game tonight?" she asked.

Cory tugged on his jersey. "What gave it away?"

"I don't know," she said. "Maybe you were just trying to show off. 'Look at me, everyone, I'm a stud football player.'"

He smiled. "We have a game. You going?"

"No."

"Just like that? No?"

She shrugged.

"Well, at least let me borrow a pencil for good luck."

She studied him for a moment before reaching into her bag. "You really are superstitious."

"Yes." He took the pencil, holding on to her hand. "I want you to go."

A light cast around Cory as she blocked Gladys from communicating. Her new strategy for distracting the deceased souls involved staying in a real conversation with the living.

"I don't have anyone to go with. It's not fun sitting by myself."

Shut up, Gladys. Aries cut her off before Gladys could say she'd go to the game with her.

"You can go with Piper," he said. "I'm giving her and Michael a ride."

"Which includes Peyton and Paige, correct?"

"Yeah, so?"

Rather than explaining the dynamics of girl relationships, she said, "I don't think my dad will let me. I didn't leave him with too much confidence after last weekend."

"That's right. Is there a chance he'll let you go paddle-boarding tomorrow?"

Ryan worked on Saturdays, so she said, "Yes."

"Is there somewhere you'd like to meet?"

To avoid him finding out she lived in a tiny apartment, she suggested the most well-known place within walking distance, the Newport Beach pier. They agreed to meet there at noon.

Miss Townsend's substitute teacher kept yelling at the class to be quiet, but nobody paid attention to him. Aries finished the assignment right before the class ended.

Putting away her binder, she said, "Good luck tonight."

He held up her pencil. "Already got it."

Peyton waited for Cory. She smiled at Aries, but all Aries could see was Peyton's expression from the reflection off the glass house.

Trying to get the evil image of Peyton out of her head, she nearly bumped into Jamie. Since they had something in common after both being victims of social media, Aries said, "Sorry about the videos."

Jamie didn't look at her. "Don't be," she said and walked off.

Aries shook her head, shocked by Jamie's attitude.

Her day picked up after history class, when Paige walked over to say hello.

"Hi, Aries. Are you going to the game tonight?" Her ponytail bobbled as she spoke.

"No."

"Why not? Everybody goes to the games."

"I'm starting to get that."

"We're going to a new restaurant after," she said. "It's pretty awesome."

"I'm sure it is, but I don't have a ride."

"You can go with us."

Aries appreciated her effort and wanted to be friends with Paige, but she still didn't trust her, so she said, "I have to spend time with my dad tonight. Next time?"

"Okay, I'll let you off the hook this time. But you need to hang with us and redeem yourself. Plus, Cory will be there." She looked Aries up and down. "And I bet Damon, too. You'll have your pick."

Aries rolled her eyes. "I'm not like that. I don't even know them."

Paige laughed. "Sure. I bet you know why Damon's not here today."

"He's not? How do you know?"

"I pass by him every day after second period, and his motorcycle isn't where he usually parks."

Aries shrugged. "Okay, well, I've got to go. Have a nice weekend." *Who does Paige think she is to inquire about the boys? She needs to mind her own business.*

Paige gave her a funny look and sang the words, "Have fun with Cory tomorrow."

"How'd you know?"

"Peyton," she said and bounced off.

Aries couldn't concentrate in her next class. Did Cory tell Peyton about their plans? Did she overhear their conversation? The image of Peyton's evil reflection continued to flash through her mind, causing her anxiety. She had to get out of there.

"*Relax,*" the boy said. "*Who cares what people think? Life's too short. And I can testify to that.*"

Who are you? Can you help me? You're the only spirit I've ever contacted that's around my age. She scribbled on the desk, trying to keep her vibration high. *You know who Peyton is. I can sense it.* She erased the marks on the desk. *Or maybe you don't. I don't know how to trust my intuition sometimes.*

After class, she made her way to her tree, enjoying the fresh air. She couldn't wait to eat.

Sitting down, she leaned her head against the trunk and indulged in a turkey and cheese sandwich. After she had her fill, she pulled out her notebook and sketched a sailboat. She added some waves until an intense pain jolted through her left side. The pain went away as fast as it came on. A spirit tried to communicate, but she couldn't understand. She flipped the page in her notebook and scribbled in circles for a while.

Still unable to make out the words, she said, "Slow down. I don't understand."

The soul projected a peaceful aura, which she appreciated, but the words sounded foreign. She recognized the aura.

You're back, she said to the boy.

Aries slowed down her scribbling and looked down at what she'd drawn. A hardhat and hammer.

"My dad!" she screamed.

Springing up, she darted through the front entrance of the school. Running across the street, ignoring the red light, she was out of breath by the time she reached the bus stop. The schedule showed the next bus arriving in five minutes.

Fifteen minutes later, Aries arrived near her dad's construction site. She'd only been there once before, but it didn't matter because the boy from the other side was guiding her. Crossing the street, she ran down the sidewalk until she found an opening to the fenced off area. Jackhammers and drills echoed throughout the site as she walked across loose boards and gravel, heading toward the middle of the infrastructure. Glancing up, she shielded her eyes from the sun.

"Dad. Dad, are you up there?"

A couple of men stopped working and looked down. Ryan stepped off the scaffolding onto the building.

"Aries?"

Part of the top level of the scaffolding collapsed, and a moment later a box of heavy tools crashed onto the lower level where her dad had been standing a moment before.

All work stopped, and a man yelled out. "Everyone okay?"

"Nobody's hurt," another man yelled back. The noise resumed.

Aries closed her eyes and whispered to the boy, "Thank you."

A moment later, Ryan climbed down and ran over to her. "Are you okay?"

"Yes, I'm fine. Are you?"

"I am now. Did you see that? If you hadn't called my name, I'd most likely be heading to the hospital." He shook his head. "What are you doing here? Did school let out early?"

"I-I was having a hard time today," she said.

He hugged her. "Let me try and see if I can leave."

"No, it's fine. I just wanted to see you and ask if it would be okay if I went home."

He checked her over. "Sure."

"Thanks, Dad."

"Oh yeah, come with me."

He escorted her over to his truck, reached into the cab, and handed her a bag. Her face lit up when she pulled out a cell phone.

"It's the latest version and has everything you wanted," he said.

"I can see that. Thank you, thank you." She jumped over and hugged him goodbye.

Aries strolled down the street, distracted by all the new gadgets on her phone. As she rounded the corner, oblivious to traffic, a motorcycle roared up and stopped in front of her.

"You better watch where you're going, Sophomore."

"LeMoore? What are you doing here? Stalk much?"

"I should ask you the same thing. Shouldn't you be in school? How'd you find me?"

Confused, she said, "What are you talking about?"

"Seriously," he said. "What are you doing here?"

"Um, it's none of your business, but my dad's building the new hotel over there." She pointed behind her.

He shook his head and laughed.

"What's so funny?"

"You know who he's working for right?"

"R&B Construction."

"Not what I meant."

She sighed. "Well, what do you mean?"

"The guy who owns the land. Who he's building the hotel for?"

She put her hand on her hip. "Of course I don't know that. How would I? Enlighten me, Mr. All-knowing."

"Ha, if only. A complete jackass, that's who."

"The Judge?"
"Not bad. Good guess, but no."
She crossed her arms. "Then who?"
"Camden Price."

*a*ries and Damon remained by the side of the street in a standoff.

"Just hop on," he said.

"No. This isn't some type of coincidence, running into you. You had to be following me."

"Get off your high horse there, Sophomore. Trust me, I have better things to do than follow you around all day."

"Why weren't you at school?" she asked.

"How do you know I wasn't? Stalk much?" he said, attempting to imitate her voice. "You don't think it was weird for me to see you on the street just now? I had to do a double take, and I almost ate it. Why aren't *you* in school? Admit it, you came looking for me."

"No. I went to see my dad, remember?" She held up her phone. "He just gave this to me. And how on Earth would I know to look for you here?"

"Okay, so I guess we can establish that this *is* a strange coincidence. Can you get on already?"

Chuck broke through. *"Go with him."*

Really? I don't feel right about this.

"*Go.*"

Damon sighed. "I don't have all day. You in or out?"

"Where are you going?"

He thought for a moment. "Somewhere I think would interest you."

She put her hand on her hip, scrutinizing him. *Is this what you're talking about, Chuck?*

"*Yes.*"

"Always a mystery, LeMoore," she said and swung her leg over the seat, situating herself.

Damon sped off, winding down Pacific Coast Highway.

While at a stoplight, he glanced back. "You look miserable."

She wiped her eyes. "I'm not. I'm enjoying the ride."

"You need sunglasses."

The light changed, and he peeled away. He turned off the highway into a parking garage in Laguna Beach. She stood, adjusting her shorts and fixing her hair.

"C'mon."

Damon grabbed her hand, directing her into a chic boutique. He found a sales associate and asked her to show him some women's sunglasses. The associate guided them to a counter.

"Damon, no, I'm fine," she said. "You don't have to buy me anything."

He pulled out a credit card and flicked it against his hand. "The Judge is good for at least one thing."

The saleswoman pulled out a couple of designer sunglasses.

"I can't," she said.

"Here, try these on." He put a pair on her. "Those are hot."

She looked in the mirror, admiring them.

"We'll take 'em," he told the lady.

A display rack of glasses fell over, causing the saleswoman to jump. After regaining her composure, the woman fixed the display. Damon stood, perplexed.

Aries asked, *Mr. Overzealous, was that you?* A moment later she said, *Chuck, are you here? Gladys?* Maybe Gladys didn't appreciate her getting close to Damon because she wanted her to be with Cory.

With no response from the other side, she said, "Damon, I think that's a sign. I can't let you buy these for me."

"No worries," he said. "Remember, technically, I'm not."

Aries gasped when the lady rang up the total. "These are way too expensive."

"Well, enjoy them."

She wore the sunglasses out of the store, and Damon stepped back and admired her for a moment, nodding in satisfaction. He wrapped his arm around her and guided her into an art gallery.

She pushed her sunglasses up on top of her head and scanned the room. Amazed by some of the pieces hanging on the wall, she said, "You're not going to buy me a painting next, are you?"

"Ha, you're funny, Sophomore. Check out some of the prices."

She took a closer look at some of the price cards. "Whoa."

"The Judge won't miss a few hundred dollars," he said. "But thousands…then we might have some problems."

She walked around in awe as inspiration swept over her. One painting in particular caught her eye. For some reason, it made her face light up. It had a simple depiction of dolphins, but the colors and detail were brilliant, making the piece unique.

Damon observed her. "You look happy."

She smiled. "I am. Thank you for bringing me here. I have a feeling my mom came to this place and would've loved this." She touched the painting.

"It's not hers?" Damon asked.

"No."

You were inspired by this, huh Mom? Aries drew a breath, smelling a tobacco pipe. *Grandpa?* He didn't respond, but he was there. *Did my mom know the artist?* The tobacco smell grew stronger. Aries touched the painting one last time.

Damon found an employee, a good looking man, wearing an expensive Italian suit. "How may I assist you?" he said in a British accent.

"I'm wondering if you have anything by Elizabeth Dade?" he asked.

The man faked a laugh. "No, never heard of her."

An elderly couple walked in, and the man directed his attention over to them. Damon followed him. "One more question. Is Mrs. Price in today?"

"No, she's usually here on Tuesdays and Wednesdays."

"Thank you."

Damon held the door for Aries.

"Mrs. Price?" she questioned as they walked out.

"Yeah. Camden bought this gallery for her. The woman's insane."

"Sounds like the whole family is."

"No. I mean literally. She was hospitalized last year," he said. "Either depression or bipolar. Can't remember."

"With all the money that family has, what on Earth could she be depressed about?"

"Trust me, money's not everything."

"I guess you're right," she said. "I'd give all the money in the world to have my mom back."

Damon rubbed her arm, his eyes trying to meet hers. "I know."

Unable to look at him, she feared she might start to cry.

He stopped and glanced around. "You hungry?"

"You even have to ask?"

"I forgot who I was dealing with."

They walked across the street to a restaurant with a rooftop patio and incredible ocean view. After they placed their order she said, "Yesterday, you were going to tell me about you and Cory. You guys used to be friends, so what happened?"

"Seriously? You're not going to let it go, are you?"

"Of course not."

The server dropped off their burgers and fries. Damon dumped ketchup onto his plate, then hers. "Yes, we were friends. We've played baseball together since, I don't know, I was in second and he was in first grade. DB, Paige's brother, and I were the oldest. Cory and Brandon always wanted to tag along with us. But during Cory's freshman year, he started dating a girl my age. She liked him, but she was never his girlfriend. He was more into her, if you know what I mean."

Aries bit into her hamburger. Wiping her mouth with a napkin, she said, "Let me guess, you moved in on her?"

"No, ma'am. I honor the Guy's Code. She came on to me. Numerous times. But one night at DB's house, she caught me at a vulnerable moment, and that's when Douglas walked in."

"He *saw* you guys?"

Damon put down his soda. "Yes."

"Oh." She sunk into the seat. "Well, then you're the jerk. Cory has every right to be upset with you."

"You're right. But I apologized God knows how many times. Thought we were cool, but then last year I'd been seeing a girl for a couple months. I liked her a lot—"

"And Cory got together with her."

"He fu—"

"Got it," Aries said.

"I don't think you do. He did it to even the score."

"How could he do that?" She couldn't imagine.

"He's a complete douche."

"Okay, well now it sounds like you guys are even. Can you go back to being friends?"

"It's not just the chick. He got me kicked off the baseball team. And the list goes on."

"How?"

"Long story. But he's got Coach Anderson so far up his you-know-what, he gets whatever he wants."

Cory wouldn't behave in that way…would he?

But she really didn't know Cory that well. She finished her meal as Damon continued to eat. She didn't really know him either.

She excused herself to use the restroom. On her way back, she recognized a familiar woman sitting at a table by herself. She double-checked to make sure it was really her.

Hurrying back to Damon, she said, "Look who's here," pointing to the woman with her back to them.

He peered over. "Who is she?"

"Miss Townsend."

"The hot health teacher?"

"Yes. Did you have her for health?"

"No. She started a couple years ago. Unfortunately, I got stuck with Anderson."

"She was out today," Aries said. "We had a sub."

"Teachers have lives, too, you know."

"I know."

As the server cleared their plates, an attractive man walked up to Miss Townsend. He kissed her on the cheek and sat across from her. He appeared to be about 15 to 20 years older than Miss Townsend.

"Good for her," Aries said. "Her boyfriend's handsome."

Damon turned to look, letting out a quick laugh. "Miss Townsend's a dirty little—"

"Shut up."

He shook his head. "I can't believe it."

"Believe what?" she asked.

"I take that back; I can believe it."

"You're so frustrating sometimes," she said.

He paid the bill. "It's one of the many things you love about me, Sophomore."

"No, really it's not." She leaned forward. "I take it you know her boyfriend."

"Yes. Yes, I do. If that's her boyfriend, which, let's give her the benefit of the doubt, he might not be. But if it is, then your teacher over there is having an affair with a married man."

"Out with it, LeMoore. Who is he?"

"The one and only Mr. Price."

23

*A*ries sat underneath the Newport Beach pier, waiting for Cory. With the temperature in the 80s, the beach was packed for a mid-September afternoon. Umbrellas covered the sand as far as she could see. Drawing an infinity sign in the sand, she tried to connect with Gladys.

Are you here, Gladys? She tried to concentrate. *Gladys, I need to talk to you. I believed you when you told me Cory's a good person, but now I'm having a hard time. What he did to Damon doesn't sound good at all.*

She made a connection, but not with Gladys. *"You need to follow your instincts."*

She sighed. *Hi, Chuck. I wish I knew what they were right now.*

"Keep listening to your intuition, pay attention to the questions, and follow through on finding the answers."

So much easier said than done.

"Life isn't easy, Aries."

You don't have to tell me that. She kept making the infinity sign deeper until she hit wet sand. *Why was my teacher having dinner with Camden Price?*

"There you go. Your intuition is telling you to find out."

"Really?" she questioned.

Aries jumped when Cory dropped the boards on the sand. "I know, sorry I'm late. I couldn't find a parking spot," he said. "Thanks for waiting."

She stood. "Did you win your game last night?"

"How do you not know? What, did your phone die?" He pointed both hands at his chest. "But of course."

She smiled.

He gazed over at the surf. "You okay to start here? Looks a little rough, but once we make it past the waves, should be pretty easy."

She nodded and followed his lead, lying on the board and ducking under the waves. Once they passed the breakers, they both stood up.

"That felt good," Cory said, brushing the hair out of his face. "You okay?"

"Yes," she said, even though the cold water made her skin prickle.

Looming in the distance, the Wedge taunted her, bringing back memories of Paige's party. They were heading in that direction, with the Wedge growing larger by the second. As they got closer, she locked her eyes on the rocks, and her foot slipped, causing her to fall on her knees. Over the noise of the water and her paddling, the soft sound of her mother's voice teased her. But the sound came from her memory, not the other side. She kept her gaze glued on the rocks.

I really did hear you that night, Mom.

"Are you okay?" Cory caught up to her. "Man, you were paddling like a maniac. I could barely keep up. I thought we were out to chill? I didn't know you wanted to race."

She stayed on her knees and caught her breath. "Sorry. I had a flashback of the party." She glared at the Bradleys' house.

"Maybe Paige is home. Do you want to see if she has the footage from that night?"

Her eyes lit up. "Yes."

They paddled to the shore a short distance from the Wedge, battling through the surf onto the beach. Cory carried the boards up to the house, setting them on the patio. He did a special knock on the door.

A girl looking almost identical to Paige answered the door. She had the same sun-damaged hair, overly tanned skin, and frail frame. Aries and Cory were giants next to her.

Cory said, "Kaylie, this is—"

"I know who she is. Hi, Aries."

"Hi."

Kaylie hugged Cory. "Come in." She stood at the bottom of the stairs and shouted, "Paige, your friends are here."

Paige walked down the stairs, wearing pajamas. She tied her hair back when she reached the bottom. "Hey, guys. This is a surprise."

"Aries wanted to check out the video, is that cool?" Cory asked. "And can we borrow a couple towels?"

"Sure. Kay, go grab some towels." Paige glanced back into another room. "My mom's home."

"We'll be quick," he said. "We can turn the sound off."

"Okay." After Kaylie handed them each a towel, Paige directed them upstairs to her bedroom.

Paige picked up some clothes off the floor, throwing them into a walk-in-closet. "Sorry it's such a mess." She opened a chest, pulled out a box of video storage cards in plastic protectors, and rummaged through them.

Aries read some of the titles; most of them were labeled "Dance Competition."

Paige searched through a couple drawers, then her closet. "It's not here." She checked under her bed, with no luck. "Hold on." She opened the door and shouted, "Kay Kay, come here."

A moment later, Kaylie entered the room. "What's up?"

"Where's the disc from the party?"

She shrugged. "I only watched it with you guys."

"It's not here," Paige said.

"Well, I don't have it," Kaylie snapped back before leaving the room.

Paige held up her hand. "Sorry, I don't know what happened to it."

Aries slouched. "It's okay, thanks for looking."

"It's weird," Paige said. "I have no clue where it could be."

"Do you think Peyton took it?" Aries asked.

Paige stared at Cory.

"So that's a yes?" Aries asked.

"The video is in the house," a spirit said.

"No," Cory said. "I doubt it."

Who are you? What should I say? She waited a moment, sensing the spirit, but he wouldn't respond.

"Is there anywhere else the video could be?" Aries asked.

Paige shrugged.

"Look in her parents' bedroom," the spirit said.

Really? "Do you think your parents found it?"

"Ha. I'd be grounded for life if they did," Paige said. "That's a definite no."

Did I misunderstand you?

"No, it could possibly be used for insurance. Ask about what they saw on the video," The spirit said, before breaking the connection.

"What made you guys think I was drugged?"

"Sweetie, you were definitely drugged. You can see your entire demeanor change," Paige said. "But we were trying to figure out who did it."

"Who?" Aries said, shifting her eyes back and forth from Paige to Cory.

Paige glanced at Cory. "Damon," she said.

Aries shook her head. "You guys are wrong. There's no way."

"Sorry, sweetie." Paige gave her a sympathetic look.

"I don't believe it." Aries faced Cory. "You're awfully quiet. What do you think?"

He shrugged. "Looks that way."

"Okay," Aries said. "Explain to me why you guys are so convinced?"

"You're not the first girl he's liked that's been drugged. He seems to be forming a pattern," Paige said. "But in the video, you're standing next to Michelle and about to reach for a cup when someone wearing a leather jacket switches the drinks."

Aries shook her head. "He didn't switch anything. He wouldn't have had to; he's the one who brought me my drink."

"I think he was making sure you got the right cup, and not Michelle?" Paige said.

"A lot of people wear leather jackets. You didn't see the person's face, right?" Aries asked.

"No, but…" Paige crossed her arms.

"And could you tell if the hands were male or female?" It had to be Peyton and they were covering for her.

"What is she, CSI Newport Beach?" Paige asked. "We didn't pause it and inspect the hands."

"Then how can you be so sure it's Damon?"

"You don't know him," Paige said. "We grew up with him. He's one of my brother's best friends."

"Would your brother be friends with someone who drugged girls?"

"No, but he's oblivious," Paige said. "He doesn't know."

Aries kept her gaze on Cory. "What do you think?"

"Does it matter? You're just going to defend him." He stared out the window.

"Oh." She didn't mean to upset Cory. "Well, I guess I'm having a hard time believing he'd drug me, that's all." Something buzzed next to Aries's ear. She stepped back, swatting at the air.

"What are you doing?" Paige furrowed her brow. "What's that noise?" she asked, glancing at the window.

"You hear it, too?" Aries asked.

A few bees swooped down from the ceiling toward them. Paige screamed, running down the stairs.

Cory jumped off the bed, grabbing Aries as he headed for the hallway. He slammed the door behind them. Once at the bottom of the stairs, he scrutinized her.

"What is up with you and bees?"

"I don't know." Aries took a defensive stance.

He shook his head. "Crazy. Does this sort of thing happen to you a lot?"

All the time, so get used to it. With a puzzled expression, she said, "No."

Cory went back upstairs to investigate as the girls waited in the family room.

Aries fixated on her mother's painting. "Paige, where did you guys get this painting?" She pointed at it.

"I don't know."

"How long have you had it?" Aries asked.

"A couple years, maybe. Why?"

"It's really cool. I like it," Aries said.

Cory returned. "I opened the screen, and the bees left, thank goodness."

Mrs. Bradley entered the room, and Paige made the introductions. "Mom, where did you get that painting?"

Mrs. Bradley crossed her arms, with her face expressionless, frozen from too much Botox. Her perfect platinum blonde bob didn't have a hair out of place. She wore an expensive outfit and had manicured nails with a huge diamond on her finger.

"Your father got it. Some auction at work. I really don't understand it."

No, of course you wouldn't. The Bradleys didn't deserve her mother's painting. It belonged with her.

"Do you know when he got it?" Paige asked.

"I'd say a little over a year ago." She pressed her lips together. "A year-and-a-half."

Around the time of her mother's death.

"Thank you, Mrs. Bradley," Cory said. "We should get going."

Paige whispered something to Cory as he guided Aries to the door. Cory and Aries said goodbye, grabbed their boards, and headed down the sand back toward the water.

"What did Paige tell you?" she asked.

"She felt bad that she didn't have the video."

Sure she did.

They paddled against the wind, taking double the amount of time to get back. But they had a clear view of Catalina Island, and not a cloud in the sky. As she struggled with the paddle, she envisioned her mother's painting hanging in her apartment.

They reached the pier, and she had fun riding the waves back into shore, like a surfer.

Cory motioned for her to sit next to him on the sand.

She sat, admiring a couple sailboats out in the distance before asking, "What does Mr. Bradley do?"

"I'm not sure exactly, but he works with Peyton's dad. That's why Paige is friends with Peyton, I assume."

"He seems to be popping up a lot lately."

"Who?" he asked.

"Peyton's dad," she said. "I saw him yesterday."

"Where?"

She told Cory the details, including Miss Townsend.

"What? No way," he said. "How'd you know it was him?"

"Damon." She pressed her lips together, regretting saying his name.

Cory fell silent, facing the water. His brows furrowed, and his smile faded.

"Say something."

A moment later, he said, "What are you doing here with me? Damon busy?"

"What? No."

"Look, I think I made it pretty obvious that I like you." He stood, shaking the sand off his boardshorts. "Never mind, let's go."

She got up and faced him. "It's not like that. I just moved here. It's not like I have any friends."

He shook his head. "He's obviously playing some sick game with me, and I hate to see you get caught in the middle. The guy's a lunatic."

"He told me about your girlfriend and that he was sorry, but then you got him back, and you got him kicked off the baseball team."

"Ha. He got himself kicked off when he attacked me in the locker room. And yeah, he nailed..." Cory ran his fingers through his hair. "My girl, but what the hell is he talking about? I never did anything with his chicks."

She glanced at the sand, then back at him. "Well, he said you did."

He appeared to be deep in thought. "I know who he's talking about, but you want to know the difference between me and him? I didn't sleep with her."

"Sorry," she said. "But he's convinced you did."

"I'm not like that. I'd never do that to her." He stared into Aries's eyes.

"To her? Don't you mean him? You guys were friends."

"No, I mean her. We *were* friends." He exhaled slowly. "Sorry, I get worked up when it comes to LeMoore." He rubbed her back. "I guess I need to know where your head is. That's the important question."

The way he tilted his head and smiled at her made it seem as though she didn't have control of her legs. They could give out at any moment.

Caught up in his gaze, she said, "I like you." She giggled. "Did that sound lame?"

"No, it sounded pretty awesome." He pulled her in, moved some stray hairs out of her face, and leaned down to meet her lips.

She moved her head over his shoulder and hugged him. He held her tight for a moment. Letting go, he regarded her with a strange expression.

"I'm going to sound stupid," she said, "but I've never kissed a boy before." Embarrassed, she had no clue what to do, but maybe he could teach her.

"Not stupid at all. I kind of like it."

She smiled. "I should probably get going."

"Can I give you a ride home?"

"That's okay." She couldn't run the risk of having her dad home. "I don't live far."

"Okay." He hugged her again. "Bye."

She hesitated. "Cory, I need to know who the girl Damon said you slept with is."

He glanced in the opposite direction before saying, "It's not important."

She bit her bottom lip, sick to her stomach. "I know her, huh?"

He nodded. "Yes."

---

*a*ries walked along the shore, heading back home. She couldn't get rid of the knot in her stomach. Some girl had been with both Damon and Cory. Not like either of them belonged to her, but she still hated the fact.

Oh Mom, how do I control my heart? You would know exactly what to do.

She took a seat by the water's edge, entranced by the endless motion of the waves and sandpipers one step ahead of them. Closing her eyes, she tried to contact the spirit from Paige's house. After a few minutes, she gave up and began to meditate.

Damon couldn't have drugged me.

"Good, go with that," Chuck said.

She smiled. *I was hoping I'd get to speak to you. Are they blaming Damon because they don't like him, or do they really have proof?*

"*What do you think?*"

She turned her head right, then left, relieved no one was near her. As a wave rushed up the sand, she said, "I think I could use your help. You know who drugged me. Just tell me. Why do I have to play these mind games with the spiritual world?"

"I am helping you, Aries. It doesn't work that way. I'm not playing games. The physical world, your world, is different. Your guides come from a loving energy, a positive light, and so do you. I don't want to see you draw from negativity. It won't turn out well."

She sighed. "Okay, if we're all peace, love, and harmony, then shouldn't I know who's trying to harm me?"

"You're in charge of your destiny, always remember that."

She sat up straight. "Wait, so is my mom not from a loving energy?" Her pulse started racing as her skin tingled. "I can't contact her…is that why?"

"Settle down. No, it doesn't mean her energy is evil. It could be that you're not letting her light shine."

"My grandpa said it was me, too. But why? I'd do anything to speak to my mom. Anything."

"Maybe your desperation isn't coming from a good place," he said. *"Are there some negative feelings you're harboring?"*

She picked up a handful of sand, squeezed it, then let it fall through her fingers. "No."

"Then relax, and when the time is right, I'm sure your mother will shine through."

"I can't relax. I want to speak to her more than anything in the world."

"What's the first thing you'd say to her?"

"I don't know." She patted the sand for a moment. "I guess I'd be so excited to connect, I'd thank her."

"Then what?"

"I'd tell her how much I love her and how I miss her so much, sometimes I'm in physical pain."

A pelican soared right over her, dropping even lower toward the top of a wave, waiting to pounce on an unsuspecting fish.

"She already knows that," he said. *"She's watching over you."*

"Right now?"

"Always. Now, what else would you tell her?"

She waited for a family to walk past her before saying, "I'd ask her about her death and then advice on what I should do about Damon and Cory."

"Let's start with her death," he said. *"Do you want to know the truth?"*

"Without a doubt."

"Do you think she'd want you to know?"

"I don't see why not," she said. "I think she was murdered and she'd want me to find justice for her."

"That could be dangerous. I sense you feel that way, too."

"It'd be so much easier if you were a therapist, because then I could deny it, but there's no use lying to a spirit."

"No," he said. *"Go with your feelings. What exactly are you afraid of?"*

"My safety, my dad's, too. I guess the truth. It might be more than I can handle. Pretty much all of it. Knowing and proving who killed her. My biggest fear, though, is never finding out what really happened."

"If that's your biggest fear," he said, *"then lead with it. Use the fear to guide you to the truth."*

"There are so many things that don't make sense," she said. "I feel like every day there's a new mystery to solve. And I don't know who I can trust."

"Yourself. All the answers lie within you."

She wrapped her arms around her knees. "Whatever that means." The whitewash inched closer, almost reaching her toes. "And what about Cory and Damon?" she asked.

"The best advice I can give you is to follow your heart. I used to tell my daughter that."

"But what if my heart likes them both?"

"I'm afraid that won't work. Make it your decision, not theirs. I suggest the sooner, the better."

"I guess you're right," she said. "It's so hard because they each have a different story about each other. And I don't know them well enough to detect which one is telling the truth."

"Perception, my girl. Haven't you heard the expression 'There're three sides to every story?'"

"Yes," she said as a woman jogged by with a black Labrador. The dog tried to run toward Aries as the woman tugged on the leash, continuing her stride. *Black leather.* "Ohmigod," Aries said.

"What is it?" he asked.

"I was wearing Damon's jacket. He put it on me before we went to the party. I knew it was someone else. Thank you, Chuck."

"Don't thank me. I told you the answers are within you."

She wanted to scream. "Do you have any idea how frustrating that is?"

"Unfortunately, yes."

"I feel better, though," she said. "Well, at least about the jacket. I'm still upset about the mystery girl. I really hope it's not Peyton. I don't think I could be with either of them if it's her." She smirked. "Or anyone I know. I can't picture them with another girl."

"Not really my area here," he said.

She laughed. "Sorry. I want to help you now. Tell me who Sarah is. Can't you guide me to her? I could give her a message for you."

"You know her."

"You said that, but I'm telling you, I don't know a Sarah… wait, does she go by a middle name?"

A huge wave crashed, causing a thundering echo. Aries jumped back, and Chuck was gone.

Taking several steps away from the water, she sat down again and lay back, stretching her arms above her head. How could she bring positive energy into her soul to connect with her mother? What the heck could Chuck be talking about?

For several minutes, nothing came to her. Then it hit her. She sprang up and ran across the sand, headed for home. She checked the alley to make sure her dad wasn't there. No truck. Sprinting up the stairs, she couldn't get the key in the door fast enough.

Out of breath, she slammed the front door, checking all the rooms to ensure she was alone. Reaching into the refrigerator, she pulled out her father's six-pack of beer.

25

*a*ries pulled the tab back on a can of beer.

She said, "This is for you, Mom."

She gulped it down until the taste registered. Leaning over the sink, she spit as much out as possible, then ran the faucet, letting the water saturate her tongue.

How can anyone drink this stuff?

She had no idea what urine tasted like, but she imagined it would be close to beer. Putting back the remaining cans, she called Piper.

Relieved when she answered, Aries said, "Hi. Do you have any plans for tonight? I need your help with something."

"Sorry, I do. My dad surprised me, and he's staying the night. He has a gig in L.A. tomorrow," she said, the excitement in her voice escalating. "Hey, you want to go to it?"

More than anything. Aries tried to keep her cool. "Oh, yeah. Well, I'll have to check with my dad first, and I highly doubt he'll let me go on a Sunday night."

"I hope you can. The more, the merrier," Piper said. "If you're looking for something to do tonight, a bunch of people are going to the Balboa Fun Zone. I'm sure you could get a ride with Cory."

"Maybe. Thanks, Piper."

Aries put down the phone and turned on the computer. She searched *the* website and saw a picture of Jamie. The caption read, "What goes around, comes around…karma, slut." Next to her picture was one of Troy kissing a beautiful blonde with long curls and porcelain skin.

The front door opened as she turned off the computer. "Hey, Dad!" she shouted. Turning the corner, her smile faded as she saw Kimberly.

"Hi," Kimberly said. "Your dad and I were thinking of seeing a movie tonight. Would you like to go?"

"No, that's okay."

"C'mon, Kiddo," Ryan said. "It'll be fun."

"Maybe next time."

Ryan threw his keys on the counter and kissed Kimberly. "Make yourself comfortable, babe. I'll be quick."

When he went to take a shower, Aries hurried into her bedroom. She had no intention of having a fake conversation with Kimberly.

She debated on whether or not to call Damon. He could help with her plan of getting drunk and contacting her mom, but he most likely wouldn't go for it. The original plan called for Piper to be just as drunk as her - or better yet, on drugs - so she wouldn't notice Aries having her own private conversation. Damon would probably worry about her, and she wouldn't get the connection time she needed.

She lay on her bed, thinking of alternatives, when her phone rang. Sitting up, she said, "Hi, Piper."

"You still looking for something to do tonight?" She sounded pissed. "Or need help with whatever?"

"Yes," Aries said, hesitant from the tone of Piper's voice.

"Good. I don't feel like being around my usual crew. Can you come over?"

"I'll call you right back."

When her father returned from getting ready, she asked, "Dad, can I spend the night at Piper's?"

"Sure, I don't see why not."

"Will you drop me off before you and Kimberly go out?"

"Why don't you see if she'd like to go see a movie with us? I'd like to meet her."

Aries would rather die before asking Piper to do that. "Her dad's home, and she wants me to meet him. So maybe next time."

"Nice. Get his autograph for me."

She curled her lip. "No, that would be so embarrassing."

When Ryan and Kimberly were ready to leave, she called Piper back.

TWENTY MINUTES LATER, they pulled up to the circular driveway.

"This is incredible. You'll have to get me a tour sometime," Ryan said.

"Me, too," Kimberly said. "I wish we weren't in such a hurry."

Aries rolled her eyes. "Okay, see you tomorrow."

"Be careful," Kimberly said.

Aries didn't acknowledge her. *Shut up.*

Ryan honked the horn, waved, and drove away. *Can he be any more embarrassing?*

Piper opened the door before Aries reached the front step. Pulling Aries inside, she said, "Good, you're here. So, my dad said he'd like to spend time with me, right?" She dragged Aries through the house so fast, Aries barely noticed Marisol waving to her from the kitchen.

Through the glass windows, Aries took in a huge crowd, figuring at least fifty people were in the back yard.

Piper flung open the screen door. "This is his idea of being with me. Are you f'ing kidding me?" she said, raising her voice.

The music blared, so most likely no one heard Piper.

Robby Zacora staggered over to them and put his arm around Piper. "Excellent, you invited a friend." He threw his hand in the air. "Invite them all," he slurred. Stumbling back, he caught his balance. "What's your name, beautiful?" He kissed the top of Aries's hand.

"She's fifteen, Dad," Piper said through clenched teeth.

He laughed. "That's an unusual name."

"That's her age," she said. "Her name is Aries."

"Still unusual," Robby said. "Brilliant. I should've named you Aquarius."

"Go back to spending time with me...oh, I mean your party," Piper said.

"Is this a party? Well, then let's..." He blurted out a string of obscenities. "Party." Robby turned and dove into the pool, with his drink still in his hand.

The singer and drummer from IDK and a famous model with a group of women who also looked like models hung out on the opposite side of the pool. Some women weren't wearing bikini tops, and from the skimpy material covering their bottoms, they might as well not be wearing those either.

Marisol walked out, carrying a pitcher of margaritas in each hand. She set them on a table next to Piper and Aries. "Senoritas?"

"Por favor," Piper said. "You're a lifesaver, Marisol."

Marisol poured two glasses, handing one to each of them, then walked over to a group of people sitting at the bar.

"You don't have to drink that," Piper said.

"No, I want to. This is what I needed your help with."

Piper raised a brow. "Seriously?"

"Yes."

"Well, then you came to the right place. Just don't expect me to hold your hair. I don't do puke."

"I don't plan on throwing up," Aries said.

"Nobody does. C'mon." Piper led her to a secluded couch by the firepit, off to the side of the pool. Piper glared at her dad. She raised her glass. "Here's to family time." She drank almost half the glass.

"I'm sorry," Aries said. "I noticed your dad has the same 'Z' tattoo as you."

She rolled her eyes. "Yeah, for my thirteenth birthday he took me to get it. I thought we were finally bonding, but he was just drunk and forgot to get me a present." She rubbed the tattoo. "I can't stand it. So, what's going on with you and Cory?"

"Nothing." Aries took a sip, enjoying the cocktail. *So much better than beer.*

"That's too bad," Piper said. "You guys would make a cute couple. Your babies would be ginormous."

"How about you?" Aries asked.

"Cory's really not my type," she said.

"Who's your type?"

"I'm kidding," she said. "I don't have one."

"Michael?"

She shrugged. "He's fun, but no."

"Have you ever thought about being serious with someone?"

Piper glanced over at the crowd surrounding her father. Everyone appeared to be having a good time. "Sure, I've thought about it." She looked up. "Once."

"With Michael?"

Piper shook her head. "No. Tell me, what are you escaping from?"

"Reality," Aries said. *So I can talk to my mom.*

"Right on." She raised her glass. "Salud."

Piper made her way through the crowd over to the bar area and brought back a full pitcher. Refilling their glasses, she said, "Please don't tell anyone about this. Everybody thinks I'm finally getting to spend time with my dad." She nodded toward the pool. "And this is so typical of him."

"I won't say a word."

The famous model screamed when Robby picked her up and pretended to throw her into the pool. When she screamed again, he set her down and started making out with her.

Piper picked up the pitcher. "Let's get out of here."

Aries followed her upstairs toward her bedroom. Piper shut the door and rummaged through a drawer.

Holding up a baggie, she said, "You ever 'shroom before?"

Aries had read about the hallucinogenic drug, mushrooms, but she'd never seen them before. "No."

"You want to see the most amazing colors of your life?"

"Well, yeah," Aries said. "But I'm not going to do drugs, if that's what you mean."

"Right, I'm so stupid. Your mom. Sorry. But you can't OD on these. It's just mushrooms."

"How do you know? It's poison, right?"

She shrugged. "You're the one who wanted to escape reality. Can't think of a better way."

Aries held up her glass. "I'll take it one sip at a time."

"Suit yourself." Piper reached into the bag, putting a handful in her mouth. "Oh God, they taste like crap."

Aries laughed at the faces she made.

Piper poured the rest of the pitcher into her glass. "C'mon, we're going to the park. I need to be outside when this hits."

Following Piper wasn't a good idea, but the effects from the margarita made Aries happy, and she didn't care about anything in that moment, so she trailed behind her.

They walked for a few minutes, passing a tennis court,

public pool, and some soccer fields. As they walked up a steep hill, Piper said, "Look at the moon. It's amazing."

Aries glanced at the full moon.

"Those flowers are so pink. Oh my God, have you ever seen a flower so pink?"

Yes. What the hell is she seeing?

"And the orange ones." She laughed. "They're *so* orange." She veered over and snagged a couple of flowers.

They reached the top of the hill and walked into a miniature park. A boy and girl were kissing on top of a slide.

Piper ran toward the swing set and sat on a swing. She kicked her feet in the air and leaned back, pumping her legs as high as she could. "This is awesome."

Aries sat on a swing, but she stayed still. The motion might make her dizzy.

The girl climbed down the slide and approached them. "Piper?"

Piper dragged out the word, "Yes." She laughed.

The beautiful girl standing in front of her looked familiar.

"Poppy." Piper jumped up and hugged her. "It's been forev."

"I can see you're up to your usual antics. Molly, weed, 'shrooms, or all of the above?"

Piper hung on to Poppy. "Look at the moon."

"Yes, I see it. Troy, let's go. Trouble seems to follow Piper, here."

Aries stood with her mouth open when Troy Perry came down. *The boy Jamie cheated on Brandon with.*

"Hey, Piper," he said.

"It's been real," Poppy said. "We're going to take off. Be careful." She hugged Piper goodbye.

They walked away. "Who's that girl?" Aries asked.

"Poppy Davenport," Piper said. "She got kicked out of Newport, goes to a private school now, and she blames me. Peyton couldn't be happier, though. Thanks me all the time, but

I didn't do a damn thing. Now Peyton thinks she's *The Queen.*" Piper laughed and lay flat on the sand. She flapped her arms and legs. "Sand angels. Come make 'em with me."

Aries sat down.

"No, make angels."

"No, thanks, I'm good right here."

Piper sat up. "That was exhausting."

"You all hung out together?" Aries asked.

"Who? Oh, yep, the four of us," Piper said. "And then there were three. Dunt dunt dunt."

"You guys really are the P-pack," Aries said. "So it's true, to be popular, you have to have blonde hair and your name has to start with a P. I feel like I'm in some parallel universe. P names are ubiquitous."

Piper started laughing so hard, she began to cry. In-between breaths, she tried to say, 'P-pack.' She tried a dozen times, then rolled over until her laugh turned into a coughing fit.

"It's not *that* funny," Aries said.

Piper kept coughing.

"Are you okay?" Aries patted her back and brushed some sand off her.

She stopped. "P-pack. You're classic, Aries." She stood, swinging her hands in the air, repeating Aries's name, then sang it as loud as she could.

Aries lost the effects of the alcohol, realizing where the expression "buzzkill" came from. "You're right, this is exhausting," she said to an oblivious Piper.

A buzzing noise started in her right ear, then switched to her left. The noise echoed so loud, she grabbed her head.

Piper stared at her. "What was that?"

"You heard it?"

"Heard it, heard it, heard it," Piper said.

Aries feared her head could split in half. "Leave me alone, Mr. Overzealous!" she screamed.

The noise grew louder.

"What the hell?" Piper said, swatting at the air.

"You can hear the buzzing sound?"

Piper kept swatting, but nothing was around her.

How can she hear you? she asked Mr. Overzealous.

The noise stopped, but Piper made the same arm motions.

"Can you hear a buzzing sound?" Aries asked.

"Nope. But I can feel the buzz." Piper laughed again.

"Then what are you doing?"

"Having fun. What are *you* doing?"

Trying to figure out what Mr. Overzealous wants. The buzz exploded, then stopped.

Tell me what you want.

Only one word emerged from the ringing in her ears that replaced the grating buzz sound.

"Guardrail."

oppy and Troy faded in the distance as a boy on a skateboard with a hoodie covering his head approached the pair. While Piper worked her way up the slide, Aries kept an eye on the skateboarder. After he exchanged words with Troy and Poppy, he started in their direction.

When the boy got closer, she could make out his face. "Piper, come here," she said.

Piper put her hands in the air as she slid down. "Yeah?"

"Michael's here," Aries said.

Piper jumped up and ran toward him.

Aries sat on the bottom of the slide, relieved to have a break from babysitting. *Who are you, Mr. Overzealous?* Precisely one month after her mother's death, he began haunting her with loud buzzing noises and periodic gifts of bees, moths, and flies.

What is this truth you're talking about, and why do you care? What's in it for you? And how are you related to me? She fired away with questions, even though she would get no answers. She had no contact with Mr. Overzealous. He was a rebel, showing up only on his own terms.

She peered over by the bushes where Piper made hacking

noises. Michael rubbed Piper's back, while she hunched over a bush.

"I thought you didn't do puke?" she mimicked to herself.

Walking over toward Piper, Aries asked, "Are you okay?"

"She's fine," Michael said. "I can take it from here."

Aries scrutinized him. "What are you even doing here?"

He looked her up and down.

She gave him a dirty look. "You just happen to be in Piper's neighborhood?"

"None of your business." He turned back to Piper. "What do you want to do, go home?"

Aries directed her attention to the street as a pair of headlights approached. Someone in an SUV parked, and four kids spilled out.

"Great," Michael said.

Paige made it over to them first. "You guys having a party and didn't invite us?"

"What are you doing here?" Michael asked. "How'd you find us?"

"More like what's *she* doing here?" Peyton pointed at Aries.

Aries rolled her eyes, causing Peyton to drape herself around Cory.

"You and Pipes are on Newport Dish," Cory said. "Someone posted it about fifteen minutes ago."

Michael smirked. "Of course. Hey Jamie, you missed Troy. He's with Poppy."

Peyton curled her lip. "Gross."

Jamie crossed her arms. "What makes you think I care?"

Dressed in all black, Jamie looked tough. Pretty in a natural, tomboy way, she had blonde hair, with dark roots pulled back in a ponytail. Aries liked the silver ring Jamie wore on her thumb but didn't comment. She didn't particularly care for her.

Sirens echoed in the distance. "Let's get out of here," Michael said. "I got Piper. Meet back at her place."

"C'mon." Cory grabbed Aries's hand.

The sirens intensified as the five of them jumped into Cory's car. He left his lights off and worked his way toward Piper's house, cutting the engine right before a squad car drove down the main street.

Peyton laughed as she got out. "You guys are so paranoid. Like the cops are really after us."

Cory locked the car. "Somebody could've called them on us. You can't even cough after ten o'clock in that park."

"Whatever," Peyton said. "Is the music coming from Piper's?"

"Sounds like it," Paige said.

"Oh yeah, her dad's home." Peyton laughed. "Mystery solved. Now we know why she went to the park. He's never going to change, and she falls for it every time. So lame."

The crowd in the back yard had thinned out, and Robby and the famous model had disappeared. Aries followed everyone over to the firepit. The only place left to sit was next to Jamie.

"Hi."

Jamie rolled her eyes.

Note to self, do not speak to Jamie Adler.

Cory and Peyton interacted, Peyton trying her best to stake her claim over him. Aries tapped her foot, anxious to go home. Paige walked over, handing everyone a bottle of beer. When Paige reached her, Aries held up her hand.

"No, thank you."

"Figures," Peyton said.

Paige didn't move. "C'mon, we're going to have a group toast."

"I don't really care for the taste."

"Well, what would Her Highness like to drink, then?" Paige asked.

"My head hurts," Aries said. "I'll just have water."

Peyton laughed.

Cory headed over to the bar as Jamie twisted off the cap and chugged her beer.

Paige chuckled. "Whoa, hold up."

Jamie raised a brow. "There's plenty more."

Cory came back, handing a bottle of water to Aries.

"Thank you," she mouthed.

When Piper and Michael arrived, Piper didn't seem as sloppy. She must have puked up the effects of the mushrooms.

"Whoo, let's get this party started!" she said.

"Couldn't have said it better myself." Paige put her arm around Piper. "Let's drink to that. Cheers."

Piper raised her beer. "Salud." They all clanked bottles.

Back to being an outcast, as if Aries were watching them on TV and not an actual participant.

Two adults standing near the bar glanced back at the commotion, flashing brief looks of disapproval. They didn't say anything, though. Wouldn't most adults try to stop teens from drinking?

"Let's go swimming," Michael said. "Who's with me?"

"I am." Paige hopped up.

Everyone migrated toward the pool, while Aries stayed put.

Mom, if you can hear me give me a sign.

She sighed at the silence. She'd give anything to go home and have her mother and father waiting for her on the couch. She missed the days of watching movies and eating popcorn with them. She shifted her eyes from the flames dancing in the firepit to everyone having fun in the pool. She didn't belong there.

She continued her one-sided conversation with her mother.

Dad and I haven't watched a movie since you passed. She shrugged. *I guess it's not the same. I don't think anything ever will be.*

Sensing Gladys's presence, she embraced defeat.

Hi, Gladys.

"*Go have some fun. Join the group.*"

I don't feel welcome.

"Nonsense. Cory would be thrilled."

I think you're the one who would be thrilled. He seems pretty entertained.

The P-pack had stripped down to their underwear.

Looking back at her, Cory smiled. She managed a quick smile back.

"Do you need a bigger sign than that?"

I'm not in the mood. She pulled out her phone, contemplating whether or not to have her dad pick her up.

Cory snuck up from behind, sitting next to her. "Hey, we're not fun enough for you?"

"No, it's not that. I'm just really tired, and I have an annoying headache."

"Let me see if I can help." He rubbed her temples for a moment.

"Thanks, but I think I need to lie down," she said as more students from Newport High entered the back yard.

"Word travels fast around here," Cory said.

"Apparently."

He put his hand on her knee. "C'mon. I know what you need."

Peyton's stare pierced through Aries as Cory led her to the bungalow. Peeking inside, he said, "The coast is clear." He held out his hand.

Grasping his hand, she took in the contents of the room. A king-sized canopy bed and fake candles lit around a fireplace intimidated her with their romantic ambience.

Unable to stop him, he led her inside and squeezed her hand before shutting the door.

27

SCORPIO MOON

*S*tacy logged on to Newport Dish and uploaded several photos of Aries. She finished typing captions for the pictures and hit the post button. She took pleasure in tormenting Aries, making her life miserable. But lately, for some reason, Aries seemed to be coming out on top, which infuriated Stacy.

The competition to see who could get the new girl had become a tradition at Newport Beach High School. Watching Cory and Damon battle for Aries was hysterical at first, but now she worried they may have real feelings for her. Shaking her head, she reassured herself. *No, impossible. She's a total freak.* She laughed out loud at the thought. *Sorry, Legs, but you don't have what it takes.* How someone like Aries could possibly think Cory - or even Damon, for that matter - would be interested in her seemed more ridiculous by the second. *Please.*

She couldn't be one hundred percent sure it was only a game for Cory and Damon, but they were always in some type of contest. Besides, they'd made bets to see who could get with a girl first when they were friends. So why would they stop now that they were enemies? Stacy had used her tactics to control the status of a girl's reputation many times in the past, and they'd always worked without a hitch. What made this time different? *So damn frustrating.* But she couldn't lose control. She needed to step up her game.

She stared at the pictures of Aries on her computer screen. "You're not one of Newport Beach's elite," she whispered. "Not if I have anything to do with it." She crossed her arms and smiled. "And I have everything to do with it."

The general population of Newport High disgusted her. They were all complete morons, so easy to control. Almost too easy.

Except for Jake.

Jake was the only person who'd discovered the truth about her.

About to destroy her reputation forever, Stacy had spent weeks trying to find dirt on Jake, But he was too damn clean. So, doing what she did best, she lied. The lie she'd made up about him would've been a work of art, but she never got the chance to tell it. Jake being gone didn't stop her from feeling gypped of the opportunity.

Jake's death did make her sad. She never meant for anyone to get hurt physically, or even worse, as it turned out to be. But also, it made her secrets a lot easier to hide with him out of the picture.

She pushed away the thought and focused on Greg. Poor Greg. She pitied him, yet at the same time she yearned for him to want her.

He thinks I'm manipulating him because of the night Jake died. If only he knew the half of it.

She called Greg. Like usual, he let the phone ring for a while. She rolled her eyes.

He's going to pick up. He always does.

"Hello—" He started to use her real name.

"It's Stacy, remember?"

He sighed. "What do you want now?"

"What are you doing?" she asked.

"I'm busy," he said. "Why aren't you?"

"Because I want to see you," she said in the voice he couldn't resist.

"I don't know."

She smiled. *He falls for it every time.* "Please," she said in her most seductive tone.

"What did you have in mind?"

"I don't know," she said. "Maybe a movie."

"Um."

"Where it's nice and dark, and who knows?" She pressed her lips together, waiting for his response.

"You haven't done anything stupid to Aries lately, have you?"

Her good mood vanished. Controlling her anger and assuming her most innocent tone, she said, "No. Of course not." She paced, collecting herself. "C'mon, Greg, she's so last week. And this using secret identities thing turns me on."

He took a moment before saying, "Good. Then yeah, I'll be over in a few."

"Can't wait."

After saying goodbye, she threw her phone on her bed.

God, you really are predictable and pathetic. You haven't seen stupid yet.

28

*A*ries awoke to the sunlight barging its way through the shutters. She stretched out her legs, refreshed. She could get used to sleeping in such a comfortable bed. Still fully clothed, she ran her fingers through her hair, then got up to make the bed.

She exited the bungalow and tiptoed around empty beer bottles, not wanting to wake Cory and Piper, who were passed out on lounge chairs. Making her way into the house, she found her overnight bag in the front room and snuck out the door.

Walking toward the front gate, she called her dad. She smiled when he arrived Kimberly-free.

As soon as she jumped in, he asked, "Want to grab breakfast?"

"You read my mind."

He pulled into a local diner. After ordering, he asked, "So how was it? I guess I can't compete with a rock star."

She put a napkin in her lap. "It was okay. Robby should stick to guitar, and not fatherhood. Trust me, I'm lucky to have you."

He smiled. "Thanks, Kiddo, but I'm the lucky one."

The server set down their plates, and Aries dumped half a bottle of syrup over her pancakes.

Ryan finished a sausage link before asking, "Have you heard of a girl at your school named Peyton Price?"

Putting her fork down, she said, "Yes. Why?"

"Just curious. How well do you know her?"

With a furrowed brow, she said, "She's in a couple of my classes. How do you know of her?"

"Her father's a bigwig around here. Are you two friends?"

Aries let out a laugh. "Hardly."

They ate in silence for a while until she received a message from a spirit.

"Mom knew him," she blurted out.

Ryan choked on his coffee. "What? Who?"

"Peyton's dad, Camden."

"What makes you think that? And how do you know his name?"

"I found his business card in one of Mom's boxes. Is he the reason we moved to Newport?"

He shook his head. "Well, sort of. But I think his card belonged to me, not your mother. The resort I'm working on belongs to him. It was a job I couldn't refuse."

She held his gaze for a moment before he broke off and went back to shoveling potatoes into his mouth. Either he was covering for Elizabeth, or he didn't know she had Camden's business card.

The buzzing sound from Mr. Overzealous tried to break through. She kept talking to her dad so he'd go away.

"Where's Kimberly?"

"She's at work."

"On a Sunday?"

"She mentioned something about doing hair for a bridal party. I don't know. Speaking of work, I need to check on the site today for a few hours. Then do you have some time for your old man?"

She smiled. "Of course. Maybe we can finally see a movie."

He stood, threw down some money on the table, and put his wallet in his back pocket. "You got it, Kiddo."

After Aries hopped out of the truck, she headed straight for her computer. She clicked on the latest information posted on Newport Dish. The flashing caption read, "Look at Newport Beach High's Latest Couple." Several pictures followed: Cory leading Aries inside the bungalow, a picture of the canopy bed through the window, and finally a picture of Aries and Cory sitting on the edge of the bed.

Every few seconds, a student from the high school would chime in with rude remarks about her. The latest read, "Looks like Cory's really slumming it these days. I guess quarterbacks aren't what they used to be."

Another student responded, "Yeah, surfers are the new QB. Sorry CD but looks like Troy Perry's taking over your status with the ladies."

Had Cory been with Jamie? A lump formed in her throat. Or maybe they were talking about Poppy Davenport, which made more sense.

Poppy's probably the girl Damon and Cory fought over.

A buzzing noise echoed through the room. She looked toward the window as several flies tried to shove their way through the screen.

Covering her ears, she said, "I get it, Mr. Overzealous, and I'm trying to figure out the truth. But can we please come to an agreement on how you contact me?"

"You need to hurry."

The buzzing sound remained the same. "I'll do anything if you just lower your frequency."

Sitting on her bed, she closed her eyes, trying to relax. Maybe then Mr. Overzealous would calm down as well.

"What is it you want from me?" she whispered.

The buzzing stopped. "Hello? Mr. Overzealous? Please come back." Something in her closet rattled.

Opening the door, she found her mother's box turned upside down. As she flipped it upright, Camden Price's business card fell to the floor.

Holding up the card, she asked, "Does the truth have to do with this?"

She couldn't hear Mr. Overzealous, but she could sense his presence. A moment later, he said, *"Yes."*

She paced across the room, with her heart pounding in her chest. "How?"

With no response, she rubbed her hands together, attempting to remain calm.

The buzzing sound started up again, barely audible this time. She said, "Thank you for not hurting my ears. Again, how?"

She hated how the other side communicated. Losing control, she yelled, "I'm sick of all these games."

"You're welcome."

"For what?" Her frustration reached a record high.

"I won't make loud noises now that I have your attention."

"You always had it!" she screamed.

"Ouch. Now you're hurting my ears."

"Was that supposed to be a joke?" Her body tingled from the energy surrounding Mr. O. She focused for a moment. "You had a dry sense of humor when you were alive, witty yet charming. You were well-liked and had a lot of charisma. I'm receiving images of you being a real ladies' man, a player if you don't mind my saying."

"I knew you were a smart girl."

Letting out a sigh, she asked, "Did you know my mom?"

The window rattled as a gush of wind whirled through the room. She tried to connect the dots. "Somehow my mom, you, and Mr. Price are all connected. How'd you know Mr. Price?"

"I worked for him."

A chill ran down her spine. She closed her eyes, tempted to push her luck with one more question. "Did you know my mom?"

"Yes."

29

*a*ries tossed and turned all night, thinking about Mr. Overzealous.

Talk to me. I need to learn more about you, so I can find out the truth for you.

If Peyton weren't so horrible to her, she could ask her about her father's business.

"She doesn't pay attention to his job," a spirit said. *"She only cares about herself."*

Obviously. Who are you?

"Peyton's grandmother's cousin, Iris."

My throat hurts. Did you die from some type of cancer in that area? Or did you have a lot of sore throats when you were alive?

"Laryngeal cancer is what caused me to pass over."

Sorry. Well, thank you for contacting me. Can you tell me why Peyton hates me so much?

"I didn't contact you,"

Aries glanced up. *Why else would I be communicating with you?*

"It's all you."

Okay, sure. Well, can you tell me about Camden? Waiting a moment, she whispered, "Iris, are you here?"

A moment later, Aries sat up.

Damon.

He might be able to help her. The clock read 5:55 a.m. He'd most likely be sleeping.

She hopped out of bed and made breakfast, scarfing down two bowls of cereal and a banana.

After showering and picking out an outfit, she called Damon. He didn't pick up, so she left a message.

"Hey, it's Sophomore." She rolled her eyes, embarrassed to be using his nickname for her. "Can you give me a ride today? I'll be at the bus stop by seven-fifteen." She hung up, hoping he'd get her message in time.

She tapped on her dad's door and whispered, "I'm taking the bus today."

Ryan mumbled something, and that was good enough for her.

She arrived at the bus stop a little after seven. Since a couple occupied the bench, Aries stood next to the sign.

At 7:30, the bus arrived, but Damon hadn't. She hesitated before stepping on with the other passengers, disappointed he didn't show up. She wanted to ditch school and follow Mr. Price around all day. The image of a cliff flashed in her head as she tapped her nails against the window. Maybe Damon could take her to the guardrail after school.

"That's a start," Mr. Overzealous said.

Aries could feel him smile. *Right back at you, Mr. O. I appreciate a smile much more than your annoying buzzing sound.*

"Good. And it's Mr. C."

What's your name?

The bus came to an abrupt stop, flinging Aries into the seat in front of her. *Great, not only does my shoulder hurt now, I lost Mr. O. - I mean C.*

She had to find Damon. It wouldn't be hard to convince him to ditch school, and she wanted to get started on her new strategy right away. Perhaps Damon could help her find information about a deceased male who worked for Camden Price. Shouldn't be too hard now, since his last name started with the letter C.

Aries surveyed the parking lot for his motorcycle. With no luck, she headed to class. She sat down at an empty table. Cory would either show up late or not at all. How did he feel about all the Internet rumors? She drew shapes in her notebook, trying to purge her mind of all the horrible things that were said about her.

Miss Townsend lectured for fifteen minutes, while Aries tried to contact Mr. O. After giving instructions, Miss Townsend distributed an assignment. When she reached Aries, she said, "Sorry, since Cory is absent today, you'll have to work on this alone. It's due at the end of the period."

"That's okay."

Miss Townsend gave her a sympathetic look. "You're always welcome to come in at lunch if you don't finish."

"I'll finish. But thank you."

Miss Townsend had seen the website. *Why is she so nosy?* Aries's initial love for health class began to dissipate.

Halfway through the assignment, she stared at the empty seat. *Cory's not only popular, he's handsome, athletic, and kind.* He'd been so nice to her. Why? She tapped her foot. It didn't make sense.

"Relax, dear."

I wish I could, Gladys.

"The reason Cory's not in school has nothing to do with you. In fact, he contemplated going just to be with you. Something about a misunderstanding with you two."

I hope you're right. But I'm not too impressed with your track record, so I still have my doubts.

"I'm sorry you feel that way. I only have your best interest at heart."

Then can you at least tell me where Cory is today?

"He's at his Grandpa Joe's gravesite. Today was his birthday. Would've been seventy-two."

She grinned, delighted to get a straight answer from Gladys. *Oh, that's sweet. Happy birthday, Joe.*

She finished her assignment right as the bell rang.

On her way to history class, she ran into Jamie. She seemed different, almost happy, her usual sarcastic expression replaced with a smile. It made her seem human.

"Hi, Aries," she said.

"Hi." Aries took a step back, shocked.

"Today is going to be interesting."

What's this about? "I'll take your word for it," Aries said, still unsure of Jamie's purpose for acknowledging her.

Jamie squinted her eyes, staring at her for a moment too long.

"Well, I need to get to class," she said, waiting for Jamie to move. When she didn't, Aries put down her head, gripped her backpack strap, and walked around her.

What is it with the people at this school?

After a couple hours of being in a somber mood, Aries made her way to her tree. For some reason, the tree cheered her up. She ate lunch and finished her math homework. After she put away her book, she spotted Damon. Running over to him, she tapped his shoulder.

"Hey, stranger. You get my message this morning?"

"Uh, yeah."

She pushed his arm. "What's up with you?"

"Nothing," he said as he turned and headed toward the building.

"Okay," she said.

She followed him into the classroom and took a seat.

"How was your weekend?" she asked.

Damon spoke without looking at her. "Just dandy."

"Alright, LeMoore, what's going on?"

He flashed a sarcastic smile. "Not a damn thing, but apparently a lot happened for you over the weekend."

Her stomach dropped. *Not him, too.* "Oh, the Internet. I was trying to forget about it. Well, obviously, it's not what you think."

He smirked. "Whatever. Nice try, Sophomore."

She looked him in the eye. "Damon, please tell me you don't believe the rumors?"

He didn't answer.

She crossed her arms. "You of all people should know it's a bunch of crap."

She flung open her Spanish book. She hated that damn website, and at that moment she also hated Damon for believing it.

Minutes felt like hours as the tension built. After class, she chased Damon into the parking lot.

"Can we please talk about this? Go for a ride at least. Please?"

He looked her up and down. "Desperation isn't a good look for you." He turned without giving her a chance to respond. She leaned against the wall as he walked away.

She hadn't felt that desolate and alone since her mother passed. With all her emotions colliding into one disastrous storm, she stood frozen, staring down at the sidewalk.

Hearing Damon's motorcycle in the distance snapped her back to reality. Maybe he'd come to his senses. She had a glimpse of hope.

The glimpse shattered when Damon wasn't alone.

What the hell is he trying to prove?

She stood wide-mouthed as he rode away with Jamie Adler sitting in her spot.

30

*S*tanding with her feet cemented to the ground, Aries remained a statue with her mouth open as Damon and Jamie faded into a speck in the distance. A speck she wanted to stomp on.

"Unbelievable," she said, shaking her head. *Fine. He wants to play games, whatever.* She didn't need his help.

A Mercedes pulled up to the curb, Peyton's face appearing as the window went down. "Aw, don't look too disappointed. What would Cory think?" She laughed, put the window up, and sped off.

"Jerk." Aries forced herself to walk toward the bus stop. *Forget about Peyton. She's jealous, and spiteful. And a complete bitch.*

The image of Damon and Jamie had been imprinted on her mind. *What's he doing? And Jamie? How could she be so blind?*

"Don't blame her. It's not her fault," Aries whispered. "It's Damon's."

Aries stomach and heart ached at the same time. Did her reaction mean she was in love with Damon? She shook her head. *No, he's all wrong.* She remembered the first time she rode on his bike, the way he felt when she wrapped her arms around him. She could smell his musk scent cologne.

"Ahhh!" she screamed. *He's so infuriating.*

"Hey Aries, are you okay?" Michelle stood up from the bench.

"Hi, yes, I'm fine. I haven't seen you in a while. How are you?"

Michelle gave her a strange look. "I saw you at Piper's. So, you and Cory, huh? Pretty awesome."

She couldn't remember Michelle being at the back yard party, but a lot of people had showed up late.

"Are you waiting for the bus?" she asked.

"No." Michelle waved her hand at a truck rolling to a stop across the street. "My ride's here. I hooked up with Brandon at the party." She smiled. "Maybe we can double date."

"Your parents let you date?"

"I don't know," Michelle said. "I never asked." The truck made a U-turn and pulled up. "He's here, see you later."

"Wait. Didn't he used to date Jamie?"

She shrugged. "Please, not from you, too. Okay, bye."

Aries waved. "Bye."

Why did she care about Damon and Jamie? If she were to write down every quality she wanted in a boy, it would be Cory. So how come she couldn't stop picturing Damon's green eyes and sexy smile?

Damn him.

Mr. Overzealous interrupted her. *"I hate to burst your bubble, but what makes you so special that two handsome boys – who according to you could basically have any girl at your school – are fighting for you?"*

So now you're not going to annoy me with buzzing sounds? You're going to insult me? Thanks, Mr. O.

"*C.*"

She rolled her eyes. *O to me. You don't think I have enough problems? Now I have to question their motives, too? Why wouldn't they want someone like me? Oh, let's see. Maybe because I'm too tall, my ears are too big, chest too flat, I'm a big dork, I don't have blonde hair, and my name doesn't start with the letter P. Or I know, is it because I talk to dead people?*

"*Well, they don't know about the dead people, so I'd go with the first scenario.*"

Her face turned red and eyes swelled as she fought back her rising anger.

"*Sorry, don't get upset. Bad joke. Look at you, you're stunning. Trust me, when you're older, there's going to be a heck of a lot more than two men fighting for your attention.*"

She sighed. *Sure. But you're right about questioning their motives. They hate each other, and yet they're both trying to be with me. You know there's more to this story, don't you?*

"*You're getting off track.*"

Of course, you're not going to tell me. I know, I'm in charge of my own destiny. Blah, blah, blah. And I know either one could have any girl they wanted, okay?

"*Are we still stuck on that? Girls, women, you're all the same.*"

Really, how?

"*You're all crazy.*"

Whatever. And now Damon's with Jamie, but he doesn't even like her. He told me she's too easy, and also bitchy. I hope she talks his ear off, teaches him a lesson.

"*Well, there are ways to keep her from talking.*"

Thanks a lot.

"*I'm just saying.*"

And then there's Cory and Peyton. I mean, she's beautiful; she's got a body to die for. Oops, sorry, not literally.

"*You're funny, Aries. No, you're right, if I were a teenage boy, I'd die for her body, figuratively speaking.*"

Exactly. And she throws herself at him. He's the quarterback with a reputation to uphold. Aren't boys supposed to brag about how many girls they have sex with?

"Yes."

So what's Cory's deal?

"Well, as a guy, I'd say he's probably already been with her. And as a guy on the other side, I can definitely say he's already been with her."

I feel nauseated. Really?

"You already had a gut feeling."

Still, having it confirmed doesn't make it any easier. She cringed when she asked, *Damon and Peyton?*

"You really want to know?"

No. The bus approached in the distance. *Yes. Wait, no.*

"I think I'm dizzy. Do you girls take lessons at a young age on how to confuse the hell out of a man, or is it innate, a gift given at birth?"

Ha, ha. So Damon and Cory are in some competition to see who can sleep with me first?

"Your words, not mine."

See who gets to the virgin first?

"Settle down."

You're the one who put this in my head.

"I said to question their motives. I would warn any young girl when it comes to teenage boys."

Well, at least I haven't even kissed either one.

"Au contraire."

She narrowed her eyes. *What?*

"Think, it'll come to you."

She pressed her lips together. *Cory. He did lean in and kiss me when we were sitting on the bed. But he respected me when I told him my head hurt. And it wasn't open mouth, so it doesn't count. Right?*

"Sure."

She checked out the bus route and nodded at the last stop.

"I like the way you think," he said.

I hate that you know what I'm thinking.

"Go on, say it."

She smiled. *You're growing on me, Mr. O, and I'm going to check something out for you.* His smile washed through her.

When the bus came to its final destination before turning around, she exited and walked a quarter-mile to the correct street. She avoided the scenery of the ocean in an attempt to forget about Damon.

He's an idiot.

When she reached the bottom of the street, she had another quarter-mile hike up the winding road. She'd never been one for exercise, so she distracted herself by using the alphabet to come up with words to describe Damon. Annoying, bad boy, condescending, difficult, edgy, foolish.

At the letter "I" when she reached her destination, she stood back, not quite ready to approach and look over the guardrail.

Irritating. She bit her lip, blushing. *Incredible.*

Standing in the middle of the road, she faced the direction of the ocean, trying to envision the night Peyton's car broke the guardrail.

Who could have been driving? She faced back toward the rail, staring at the wide open crack.

Mr. O, are you here? I really need to ask you a question. She had no contact with him. *Were you always this rebellious when you were in the physical world?* She never took her eyes off the rail. *I know you want me to find out the truth, but for some reason I always thought you meant my mother's death. But did you mean the truth about what happened to Piper? This confusion is making my head hurt.*

Mustering her courage, she walked over to the guardrail and willed herself to peek over. The more she leaned, the more her heart raced. She took a good look and jumped back.

Damon was right. A bouquet of flowers covered the rock

jutting out. She peeked over the rail again. *A bouquet of orange poppies.*

Something forced her to look up the steep street, almost as though someone had physically moved her head. She froze as a figure in the road stared down at her.

31

The figure at the top of the hill darted out of sight. Aries envisioned herself running up the road and confronting the person, but in reality, she'd never make it in time. The person would be long gone. Frustrated, she checked her watch. Speaking of time, she needed to hurry back to catch the next bus.

Who could the mystery person be? Maybe Poppy Davenport? She could've been the one who drove into the guardrail and framed Piper. Could leaving poppies be some sort of clue? Aries shook her head. Too obvious. Maybe Peyton was trying to pin it on Poppy.

What am I missing?

She gave up on trying to come up with an answer and made her way back down the hill.

Up ahead, the bus pulled over to the curb. She ran toward it as a couple passengers got off. Taking a seat, she leaned back and closed her eyes. It would be so much easier if Damon would help her.

If someone got off at the bus stop by his house, she'd take it as a sign for her to talk to him in person. If not, she'd try to make up with him at school.

When the bus stopped near Damon's house and two people exited, she straightened her posture and stepped off. She rounded the corner, losing courage when she saw a man waxing an expensive looking antique car in the driveway. Taking a step forward, her gut warned her to turn around and go home.

An older version of Damon, the man polishing his car had a full head of salt-and-pepper hair. He was around the same height as Damon, with a well-kept body, and gave off a strange aura.

As she took another step, her throat constricted, and the hair on her arms stood up. Her physical symptoms weren't related to seeing Damon, but from his father. She'd never met the Judge before, yet she despised him. The feeling didn't come from Damon's opinion of the man either.

This man is evil.

She commanded her legs to move, but she couldn't get any closer. Spinning in the opposite direction, she took off toward the beach, finding her way to the Wedge. Walking along the top of the rock formation, she sat down when she reached the end. Putting her shirt over her knees to block the biting onshore wind, she tried to stay warm.

"Your instincts are right about James LeMoore." Chuck's voice cut through the blustery air and pounding waves.

Hi, Chuck. She smiled. He reminded her of a grandfather figure, or a wise uncle. *Yeah, I received the message loud and clear from the feeling he gave me. I know he had Piper's charges dismissed, but I'm sure there's more to the story.*

"There always is."

She held her hair to the side to keep it from blowing in her face. *I need a break. I wish I could solve everything and move on. I know I'm missing something big, and most likely obvious, but I can't figure it out. I can't figure anything out.* She sighed in frustration.

"It's more complicated than you think, but you can work it out. Give it time."

A powerful set of waves crashed against the rocks, peppering her with whitewash.

"What's troubling you now?" he asked.

Shaking her head, she mumbled, "There's no privacy with the other side."

"No. And of course I know what you're thinking, just thought you might want to talk about it."

I do. With my mom. Besides, you told me it's not really your area.

"No, it's not. I guess I'm making up for missed opportunities with my daughter."

Sarah?

"Yes."

I wish I knew who she was. I could help you both.

"I'm here to help you," he said as more whitewash splashed over the rocks.

She scooted back. *I don't know, Chuck. I really like Cory. But I still can't figure out why he'd be interested in me. The popular boys usually don't even look at me, let alone talk to me. It feels good to be accepted for once, but I can't stop questioning his sincerity. I know I'm being insecure. And then there's...*she sighed. *Never mind.*

"Go on. It's important to let it all out."

Damon. Just saying his name right now makes my body ache with jealousy. I can't believe he'd take Jamie out. I don't understand. Is he giving me a taste of my own medicine? If so, he's only going to hurt her. He's so immature.

"I tried to warn you before. You need to make a choice and stick to it. Looks like Damon's making the choice for you."

You're saying it really is over for me and him?

"I'm not saying anything except for you to focus on what it is you want. Would it be so bad if you end up with Cory? Isn't that what

you wanted all along? With Damon out of the picture, you can now give Cory an honest chance."

But I'm not sure Cory really wants me. Maybe he just wants to beat Damon, and when I do pick him, he'll laugh and leave me.

"That's love, my friend. It's always a gamble, but you need to give it a shot. Listen to your heart."

She smirked. *Thanks, Chuck.* The breeze picked up as the last few moments of the sunset slipped away. She let out a quick shiver, and Chuck faded away.

The sun dipped below the horizon, casting bright colors of burnt orange and gold through the atmosphere.

I hope you're up there admiring this amazing sunset, Mom. She smiled. *Maybe someday I'll be able to watch one with you again.*

She jumped off the rocks onto the wet sand, heading back home. As Paige's house came into view, the door opened, and two figures emerged.

Dashing to the lifeguard station, she climbed the steps and shielded herself from being seen. She peeked around the corner as Paige and a boy walked out onto the patio. The boy had his back to Aries, making it difficult for her to identify him. The pair talked for a while.

Aries shook out her hands, anxious to get home, but she couldn't risk being seen. She tapped her foot, getting more antsy by the second. The sky had turned gray, and she didn't want to walk home in the dark.

Paige started to make out with the boy. Catching a glance of his profile, Aries recognized him. She leaned back against the tower, covering her mouth.

Every day reveals a new secret.

32

*A*ries waited on the lifeguard station for a few minutes after Paige went back inside the house. She climbed down, still in shock from having discovered the new couple.

Paige and Michael? But doesn't he have a thing for Piper? How were they able to keep their relationship a secret?

"Because nobody cares," a spirit said. *"Everyone's too self-absorbed."*

I've noticed. But thanks for the reminder.

Dreading walking alone in the dark, she whispered, "Do you mind staying with me?" The wind picked up, along with her pace. She broke out into a sprint for a few minutes, easing into a jog. "Are you here?" she asked, out of breath. She continued to jog, and several minutes later she reached her apartment.

Thanks for nothing, she said to the random spirit.

On her own for dinner since her dad had another late night of work, she made a salad, sprawled her homework across the kitchen table, and began working out trigonometry problems. Thirty minutes later, she finished the assignment and took a break.

"I could sure use your help, Mom." She sighed. "I know it's

trivial, liking two boys who couldn't be more different, but it still hurts the same. You probably think I'm stupid. You never had a problem knowing what or who you wanted. I wish you were here to help me. Or at least help me from the afterworld. Even some guy named Chuck found me, but you can't." She shook her head. "Don't you care about me?" She blinked back the pain and grabbed her guitar. Strumming the strings relaxed her, and she came up with some lyrics for a new song.

She wrote down a line.

Gone but not in my heart.

Inspiration kicked in, and she couldn't scribble fast enough.

Gone but not in memory. Never ever really gone.

She crossed it out, shaking her head.

That sucks.

She picked up her guitar and continued to play.

Smelling tobacco, she heard her grandfather's voice. *"I think you're on to something. You have so much talent. Just like your mother. And I don't even think she could help you with your predicament between the two boys. Matters of the heart are never easy."*

"I miss her." Aries set the guitar on the ground. "And I'm frustrated. She always gave the best advice."

"Time. You always know in time."

She turned the page in her notebook. "I'm hearing that a lot lately."

"Have you ever thought maybe you don't want either boy? There could be a reason why you're stalling."

"No, but I guess it's something to think about. Thanks, Grandpa."

The smell of tobacco vanished.

She made a list of everything she couldn't figure out.

Mother's Death

1. Camden Price
2. Mr. O

3. Art Gallery

4. Laguna Beach

Putting down the pen, she took a break for a moment. She shook her head.

No, I doubt that has any correlation.

The windows rattled, startling her. She picked up the pen, skipping a couple of lines and continuing to write.

Guardrail

1. Cory

2. Peyton

3. Piper

4. Poppy

5. Damon???

The phone rang, causing her to jump.

"Hello?"

"Hi Aries, it's Cory."

"Hey," she said, sounding surprised. She mouthed the letters, "OMG" as she sat on the couch.

"How are you?"

"I'm doing well," she said. "You?"

"Good. Hey listen, the reason I'm calling is, I wanted to make sure the rumors weren't getting to you, and I hope nobody bothered you at school today."

"No, not really. But some people think it's true."

"People suck."

She laughed.

"I'm sorry I couldn't be there today." He went into detail about his day at the cemetery.

Cutting him off, she said, "I know."

"How do you know?"

She bit her bottom lip. She couldn't tell him the truth. *Oh, because your deceased grandmother already filled me in.*

"I meant, I know you were probably doing something

important. I'm glad you're not sick." She put her hand on her forehead. *Stop talking, stupid.*

"Yeah, okay."

She needed to recover quickly. "Trust me, I know birthdays aren't easy. I went through my mother's last month."

"You're the only one who understands. I almost cried like a baby."

"Tough guy like you? Not very quarterback-esque."

"Hey. I thought I could tell you anything?"

"You can. And I'm glad you called."

"Me, too. This is the best I've felt all day. I want to see you."

She smiled. Her dad wouldn't be home for at least another hour, but she felt awkward inviting him over. "You'll see me tomorrow."

"Maybe I don't want to wait that long."

Her stomach dropped. He had a way of boosting her confidence in the same way her mother used to do. "I don't know what to tell you."

"Generally, the polite thing to do would be to invite me over."

The kitchen lights flickered. She didn't know if it was a sign or not.

"You know I'm big on etiquette, so—"

"Hang on a sec," Cory said. Muffled voices filled the background. "Sorry, Abby here wants to talk to you."

Aries furrowed her brow. "Okay."

"Hi," Abby said, letting out a giggle.

"Hi."

"Aries," Abby said in a serious tone, sending a chill up Aries's spine.

"Yes?"

"Get out of the house."

---

33

*A*ries dropped the phone and sprinted out the door, down the steps into the empty street. Her entire body prickled from fear. She rounded the alleyway when a pair of hands grabbed her from behind, diverting her direction and pulling her backwards. She screamed.

"Hey, relax, it's me," Cory said.

She shook, trying to catch her breath, staring at him in disbelief.

Abby caught up to them. "Hi, Aries." She laughed. "We got you."

Aries gave her a dirty look. "What?"

Cory put his arm around her. "We were in the neighborhood and—"

Aries threw his arm off. "This is a trick? Some sort of sick game?"

"No, not at all," he said. "See, Abs, I told you we should've knocked."

"We didn't mean to scare you," Abby said. "We thought you'd open the door and look around and then see your present."

"My present?" she asked, confused. "And how did you know where I live?"

"I have my ways," he said. "We set it on the doormat. But I think you trampled it."

Moving past them without saying anything, she walked back to the apartment. Picking up a bouquet of yellow roses with a card inside, she smiled at Cory.

"Sorry, we didn't mean to scare you, I promise. My intentions are good."

She glanced down at Abby, her anxiety fading, lost in the innocence of the child's eyes looking up at her.

"Open the card," Abby said.

Keeping her eyes on Cory, she opened the envelope.

He smiled. "Go on, read it."

She held his gaze for a moment longer. He looked nervous.

She opened the card.

A,

Will you go to the homecoming dance with me?

C

"Really?" She covered her mouth. It was as though she'd won a contest she didn't enter.

He nodded.

She blocked Gladys from coming through, while Cory looked at her, waiting for his answer. Headlights illuminated the alleyway.

"Well?" Abby said.

"Oh, no," she whispered. "My dad's home."

Luckily, the three of them were outside the apartment. Looking confident, Cory stood straight with his chest back as Ryan got out of the truck. He chucked the roses off the balcony when Ryan wasn't looking. Ryan walked up the steps with a frown.

"Hello, sir, Cory Douglas." Standing eye-to-eye, the two engaged in a firm handshake.

"Mr. Dade," Ryan said.

Aries flinched. *He's so embarrassing.*

Cory nodded, keeping his stare. "Mr. Dade, I was absent from school today, and your daughter was nice enough to give me the homework."

Neither one so much as blinked. Aries couldn't tell which one would win the staredown.

"Mmmhmm," Ryan uttered.

"This is my little sister, Abby."

"Hi," Abby said. "Do you have a dog?"

Ryan shifted his eyes down at Abby. Aries named Cory the victor of the staring match.

"No, we don't," he replied.

"You should get one. Aries was so good with Nana."

"What?" Ryan said in a firm voice.

Cory pulled Abby close to him. "I showed her a picture of a dog your daughter drew in class. Abby named the dog Nana. She means Aries is a great artist. Well, we should get going. Nice to meet you, Mr. Dade."

Ryan wasn't buying it, his eyes shooting daggers through Cory's skull.

"Bye, guys." Aries opened the door, with her dad practically on her heels.

He threw his keys on the counter. "This is what I get to come home to?" He walked straight to the refrigerator, cracking open a beer. "You don't think my day is hard enough? Now I have to worry about you and some boy? I thought I could trust you?"

"You can. I didn't let him inside. And he had his little sister with him. They were here all of about ten minutes."

He combed his hand through his hair. "How many times have you been to his house?"

"What?"

His face turned red. "You heard me."

"Once. During the day. We went paddleboarding, and we took Abby with us. He's just a friend."

"You think I wasn't a teenage boy once? There's only one thing on his mind, and I guarantee it's not paddleboarding. I don't want you seeing him outside of school."

"He's my friend who happens to be a boy. I don't have a lot of friends around here, you know."

"He's not your friend. He's succeeding in making you think he is, but trust me, I know boys. I need to be able to work twelve-hour days without worrying about you sneaking off with this boy who's trying to get his way with you. Promise me you won't see him."

She couldn't make any promises, and she hated her dad at the moment for putting her in such a messed-up situation.

"If you really trusted me, you'd allow me to be friends with whoever I wanted."

"I don't trust him."

"But you trust me?"

He chugged the rest of his beer, crushing the can and tossing it in the garbage. "You're all I've got, Kiddo. I can't handle this. Not now."

She couldn't look him in the eyes. "Then I won't see him."

"Thank you."

She walked to her bedroom, closing the door. Peeling back the sheets, she threw herself on the bed. Holding her face in her hands, she held her breath. Her body shook as she tried not to make a sound. She had no control over her emotions, feeling as though they'd been tossed into a meat grinder and squashed into pure frustration. She felt embarrassed by the way her dad acted toward Cory, guilty about hating him, and annoyed at having to make a promise she wouldn't be able to keep.

"No use trying to control your emotions, dear," Gladys said. *"Don't worry, you'll think of a compromise. You must know how*

much your father loves you. He'll do anything to protect his little girl. He's an admirable man."

I know, but if he really trusted me, then it wouldn't be an issue.

She laughed. *"He's going to act that way no matter how much he trusts you, and no matter how old you are. Even if you were twenty-one, he'd have the same reaction. It's true about what he said; it's the boy he doesn't trust."*

Great.

"Cory understands. Every boy knows it's not easy meeting the girl's father."

Her emotions were somewhat solid again. Thank you, Gladys.

She settled into her pillow, looked up at the ceiling, and whispered, "Mom, if you can hear me, please talk some sense into Dad. You know I'm trustworthy, and I wouldn't do anything to compromise my values." She exhaled, releasing tension in her body. "I love you." She reached up to turn off the lamp when something caught her eye.

The bouquet of roses lay dispersed across her dresser.

*a*ries awoke to the sound of a fly buzzing, emanating from around the flowers on her dresser.

Good morning, Mr. O.

He didn't respond, but she could sense his presence.

How do you expect me to get dressed when I know you're in the room?

The spirits were always with her, but it would be awkward changing in front of a man who once worked for Camden Price.

"*It's not the same as the physical world,*" he finally replied. "*All I see is your energy. But if it makes you feel better, I won't look.*" He chuckled.

Actually, it does make me feel better. She smiled. *What is it you want from me now?* She opened her closet, pulling out shorts and a halter top.

"*It's the other way around. Your energy brought me here.*"

She pulled her hair back into a ponytail. *Really? Well, can you tell me what energy I need to use to reach my mom?*

"*Afraid I can't help you there.*"

Well then, I guess there's a malfunction in my energy. So, you can go back to buzzing someone else.

"No, you need reassurance. And you're on the right track."

Okay. By the way, how'd you get the flowers onto my dresser?

"The secrets of the afterworld. But it wasn't me."

She put her hand on her chest. *My mother?*

Ryan knocked. "You up, Kiddo?"

She opened the door. "Yes."

"I made your favorite."

She inhaled the aroma of blueberry waffles. "You're the best." She rushed into the kitchen and dug in.

Halfway through breakfast, she asked, "What made you do all this?" pointing at her plate.

"I couldn't sleep. After tossing and turning all night, I realized how hard things must be on you. And I know you're alone a lot. I guess what I'm trying to say is, I do trust you. It's hard because you're my everything, and I want to protect you, but I also want you to be able to make your own decisions. You're going to be an adult in a few years. I think you're old enough to choose the right friends. So, if you want to see that boy, you can."

Her mouth hung open. Regaining her composure, she said, "Really?"

"With a few boundaries."

She smiled. "I figured."

"He can't come over when I'm not here, and I don't want you at his house without an adult there, too. But if you want to go paddleboarding or work on homework, that's fine. But I want you to tell me first. Deal?"

"Deal."

As he went to the stove to refill his plate, she mouthed, "Thank you, Mom."

Thirty minutes later, she arrived at school, ready to ace Miss Townsend's test. She had the first half of the exam finished when Cory snuck into class late.

"Hey, do you have a pencil I can borrow?"

She reached back for her bag and pulled one out. He grabbed her hand, lingering for a moment.

"Thanks."

Miss Townsend shushed Cory as she handed him the test. Rolling her eyes, she turned and walked back to her desk.

Aries finished early and took out a book. She didn't read a word; she just stared at the pages, lost in a daydream about going to the dance with Cory. But as he worked on the test, she worried about Damon. What would his reaction be when he found out about her being Cory's date at homecoming? Would he care? She pondered her dilemma until Cory handed in his test.

After he returned to his seat, Miss Townsend stood and made an announcement. "Today after school, we're having our first recycling event, and I was just informed by Mr. Haggerty that he'd like two volunteers from this class to attend. I know it's late notice, but it's always nice to support a good cause, not to mention impress the principal. The recycling club is down in enrollment this year, with just a few added freshmen, so I'd love to have a sophomore and junior representative." She glanced over at Cory and Aries. "Any volunteers?"

Paige spoke up right away. "I'd love to, Miss Townsend, but I have dance after school."

"I understand," Miss Townsend scanned the room.

Aries did want to get into a top university, and since she didn't play sports or do any other extracurricular activities, the recycling event might be a good place to start for her college resume. She raised her hand.

"I'd like to help."

Miss Townsend smiled. "Thank you, Aries. How about you, Mr. Douglas?"

"I have football practice." He smiled at Aries. "I can help after."

"The event won't take that long, but thank you."

Peyton raised her hand, never taking her eyes off Aries. "I'll help," she said.

"Great, I have my two," Miss Townsend said as the bell rang.

Before Aries could stand, Cory grabbed her arm. "Hey, I never got my answer."

Peyton loomed over them. "What was the question?" She waited for Cory, with her hand on her hip.

None of your freaking business.

Aries stood, wrapping her backpack around her shoulders.

"I'll talk to you later." She flashed Cory a smile that disappeared as soon as she turned toward Peyton.

"See you after school," Peyton said in an overly friendly voice.

Aries didn't acknowledge her. Heading for the door, she overheard Peyton say, "What's her problem?"

Aries grabbed her trigonometry book out of her locker, slamming the door.

Why does Peyton always butt in at the worst time? She's so damn annoying.

Turning the corner, her anger intensified as Damon kept his eyes locked on her, despite Jamie draping herself all over him. Aries walked in slow motion, holding his stare until she entered the math building.

She fumed in math class with her book open, oblivious as to whether it was on the correct page or not. She didn't know or care. She kept picturing Damon leaning against the wall in his sexy pair of jeans and white T-shirt snug around his chest and arms. His jet-black hair, with just the right amount of gel, and the curvature of his mouth when he looked at her drove her crazy. But then what about Cory? She loved the fact that he was one of the only boys she had to look up at due to his height. She could actually wear heels to the dance.

Thirty minutes later, she walked to her next class with the

scene of Damon and Jamie replaying over and over in her mind. She snapped back to reality when Piper bumped her.

"Hey," she sang the word. "Rumor has it you're going to homecoming with Cory."

"And who started this rumor?"

"Who cares? Way to go." She headed toward her desk.

Aries turned to take her seat and knocked into Paige. "Sorry."

"Yeah, you are," Paige snarled. She whipped her head around and walked toward the front of the room.

Her mouth dropped. What did she do to her this time?

Michael nudged her. "Sit down already."

"Um, yeah."

He gave her a strange look. "Looks like you're going to the dance with us. Word of advice, handle your liquor this time."

"'Us?'"

"We always go as a group. Me, Piper, Cory, and his chick. I guess this year, you're the chick."

She hung her head.

"Don't look so bummed," Piper said. "I'm glad Cory chose you."

"Who are his other options?"

Michael rolled his eyes. "Oh, please. Poppy, P—"

Piper hit him. "Shut up." She turned to Aries. "You were his only choice."

Aries had a lump of jealousy lodged in her throat, thinking about all the girls Cory had most likely dated. She resented him for being his flavor of the month.

After class, Piper waited for her by her locker. "Are you okay?" she asked.

"Yes, why?" She attached the lock.

"You don't look so hot."

"I'm fine."

Piper regarded her for a moment. "Look, I hope it's not about Cory. He really likes you."

"No, not at all. I'm good."

"Good. Eat lunch with us today. I can't believe you haven't yet. Where do you go?"

"Today I have to go to the library. Major English assignment."

Piper curled her lip. "That sucks. Tomorrow, then?"

"Okay."

They said goodbye and walked in opposite directions.

During Spanish class, nerves took over Aries as she bounced her feet up and down. Without looking at her, Damon put his hand on her knee to get her to stop. He continued to work on the assignment. There had to be something she could say to him to ease the tension. Drawing a blank, she finished the classwork.

When the period ended, she blurted out, "How are you?"

He stood and stared at her for a moment, then walked out of the room.

She followed him. "So that's how it's going to be?"

"How'd you like it to be, Sophomore?" he said over his shoulder.

She grabbed his arm and stopped him. "Normal. I want my friend back."

"Looks like you already have one."

"What do you mean?" she asked, confused.

He sighed. "Give me your phone."

"Why?"

"I'll show you."

She handed her phone to him.

He took a moment to download an app. Handing the phone

back, he said, "There, now you'll get an alert every time something pops up on Newport Dish."

She clicked on the alert and stared at a picture of Cory and Abby at her apartment. The caption said, "QB slums again. Douglas decides on Aries as his homecoming date."

"Damon, I can ex…"

She glanced up. He was gone.

35

*A*ries found Miss Townsend near the cafeteria, surrounded by recycling bins. Miss Townsend said, "Hi, Aries. We're trying to get organized here. You can sign in by the benches." She went back to directing a few boys who were separating the bins into different categories.

Aries signed in and went over to where several girls had gathered. A few of them had made fun of her after Paige's party.

A girl wearing a NBHS Recycling Club T-shirt turned around and said, "Is it true? You and Cor—"

Peyton walked up, interrupting. "Miss Townsend told me to come get everyone. She's ready to start."

The girls all said hello to Peyton in unison, as if she were some A-list celebrity. Aries rolled her eyes as she walked over to Miss Townsend.

"The recycling club will sort empty milk cartons, cans, bottles, and paper, placing the items into the correct bins," Miss Townsend said. "Peyton, Special Education is joining us today, and Mrs. Clarkson specifically asked for your help."

Peyton nodded.

"Aries, would you make posters for the different bins?"

"Sure."

"Great. I want our school to win the green ribbon this year. So, we need to clearly advertise to the students how important it is to recycle."

Aries painted a poster for the empty milk cartons, drawing various pictures of milk. Taking a break for a moment, she couldn't believe her eyes as Peyton interacted with the Special Education students. Peyton did a couple of dance poses and sang a popular song, causing the students to laugh and clap. She then knelt next to a boy in a wheelchair and gave him a high-five.

He said, "Go, go."

Peyton said, "Hold on tight."

Pushing his wheelchair, she zigzagged in between the bins. He acted like he was on a roller coaster, having the time of his life.

Wow, Peyton actually has it in her to be silly and fun. It was nice to see a different side of her, but something inside Aries didn't trust it.

Peyton wheeled the boy over toward her. "Look at the pretty pictures," she said to the boy, triggering a smile out of him.

"I like it," he said.

"I know, me, too," Peyton said. "Isn't she talented?"

He attempted to nod.

"Christopher, this is Aries."

Aries waved. "Hi."

He blushed.

"He's shy," Peyton said.

"He's not with you," Aries said. "You're so good with him."

"He's used to me. I help Mrs. Clarkson sometimes. She knows I volunteer at the children's hospital every summer."

"Wow, that's so nice. I didn't know that about you."

"There's a lot you don't know."

"I'm sure. It's really impressive, though."

She smiled. "So is your poster."

"Thank you." Aries couldn't hide her shocked expression.

"Over there." Christopher pointed.

"Of course, Your Majesty." Peyton joked with Christopher. She bowed, then pushed him toward the other students from his class.

Aries shook her head, admiring Peyton for the first time. Several yards beyond Peyton, a couple of boys were picking up trash. She'd recognize that stance anywhere.

Putting down the paint brush, she walked toward the boys. "Hey."

Damon nodded.

"You don't strike me as the type to volunteer to pick up trash," she said.

"Is that supposed to be a joke?"

"No. It's supposed to be an educated observation."

"I got detention, Einstein."

"Oh. See, I knew you wouldn't have volunteered."

"Whatever. I should get back to it." He turned.

"Damon, wait."

He flipped his head around. "What?" Dropping the trash bag, he put up his hands. "What do you want from me, Sophomore?"

"I want my friend back. I want you to talk to me. And I want…well, more like I *need* your help with something."

He shrugged. "It's not all about what you want."

"You just asked me what I wanted."

"Why do you want to be my friend so bad, Sophomore? You're a good girl. You shouldn't be hanging around someone like me."

"And why is that? What's so bad about Damon LeMoore?"

He picked up a piece of trash. "Your Prince Charming has never had to do this. Go be with him and stop wasting my time."

"What else do you have to do? How am I wasting your time?"

"You know what I mean." He took a step back.

"What are you doing after detention?"

"Rearranging my sock drawer."

She narrowed her eyes. "You're so annoying."

They stared at each other for a moment. Their gaze intensified before he made the first move, slightly bumping into her.

"Grabbing a bite to eat with you." He smiled. "Better answer?"

"Much."

"Hey, LeMoore," Mr. Haggerty shouted. "Social hour's over, get back to work."

"I'll find you," he said. He picked up his bag and headed back toward the principal.

She walked back to finish the posters. Peyton's smile practically covered her entire face. "So, what was that all about?"

"What?" Aries didn't have time for her.

"You and Damon looked awfully close over there. Like a couple."

"We're just friends."

Peyton pressed her lips together. "Ummhmm. Anyway, Mrs. Clarkson took her class over to the bus, and Miss T said we could leave."

"I didn't finish the posters," she said.

"Miss T said you didn't have to. And I'm giving some girls a ride home. I can take you home, too, if you want."

Damon was still picking up trash. "Thank you, but I'll feel better if I finish the poster."

Peyton glanced over at Damon. "Okay, I understand." She gathered her purse, pulling out her keys.

She couldn't figure out Peyton's angle, but it would be a relief not to be her enemy anymore. "It was really nice of you to offer me a ride. And I'm glad I got to see you interact with Christopher."

Peyton smiled. "Yeah, I guess. You really have a gift, you know. I wish I could draw."

"Thanks." She picked up her brush.

Peyton took a couple steps. Turning back, she said, "This doesn't mean we're friends."

"Of course not." Aries kept painting as Peyton walked away.

She finished her posters and helped Miss Townsend clean up. After they pushed some bins inside the cafeteria, Miss Townsend asked, "How's everything going with you?"

She nodded. "I can't complain."

"You seem happier. You got the highest score on the test today. Congratulations."

Aries smiled. "Thanks."

They walked outside to gather the rest of the supplies. "H-how's your dad doing?" Miss Townsend asked.

She hesitated. "He's fine. Why?"

Miss Townsend shook her head. "No reason; just thought I'd check in with you."

Aries managed to smile. They stood in an awkward silence for a moment until Miss Townsend cleared her throat.

"If you ever want to talk, I hope you know I'm here for you."

"Okay."

"I've had my fair share with death recently, too."

Maybe Miss Townsend was the one who needed to talk to someone. "I'm sorry. Did your mom pass, too?"

"No, my fian—"

Damon startled her from behind. "Ready?"

"Go on. I can get the rest," Miss Townsend said.

Aries said goodbye and followed Damon toward the parking lot.

As they walked up to his motorcycle, she asked, "What made you change your mind and want to hang out with me again?"

"I couldn't stand the pathetic puppy dog look in your eyes anymore."

"Shut up."

Damon grabbed her by the waist and pulled her against him, whispering in her ear, "Did you just tell me to shut up?"

She melted in his gaze. The way he looked at her, the magic of his touch, and the intoxicating aroma of his cologne had her hypnotized, under his spell.

"Yes," she managed to whisper back. "What are you going to do about it?"

With his eyes locked on her, he leaned in, inches from her lips when a car honking broke the silence. Damon stepped back.

Aries caught her breath as Peyton and Jamie drove away.

---

36

*A*ries enjoyed the cruise down Pacific Coast Highway before Damon pulled into the parking lot of a diner. After being seated and ordering, she let the tension build as neither one said a word.

After popping a couple of fries in his mouth, Damon caved. "So, what do you need my help with?"

Aries set down her veggie burger. "I know you said your dad had Piper's case thrown out, but do you think he kept any records? And do you think maybe he has information on Camden Price? I can't understand why Camden would want to protect Piper."

He shrugged. "I don't think it's Piper he's protecting. Besides, Camden and the Judge go way back. They always have some type of shady business going on, but he's too smart to keep any records lying around."

Aries took a couple bites of her burger. There had to be something lucrative and tangible between the two men.

"If your dad covers up legal matters for Camden, wouldn't he want to have substantial evidence over him? What if Camden turned on him?"

"Why would he?" Damon furrowed his brow. "That would be crazy. I'm sure they have the gentlemen's contract."

"What's that?"

"Handshake. I don't know, basically your standard 'You Screw with Me, and I'll Have You Whacked' agreement."

"Really?"

"I'm kidding."

She sighed. "You're probably not too far off. Maybe your dad would never keep any records in his office, but what about at home?"

Damon set down his drink. "You're not going to let up, are you?"

She dipped a French fry into ketchup. "Nope."

"I don't know what you're looking for, but I can help you find it Saturday night." He tilted his head to the side, with a confident grin.

It took her a few seconds to figure out why he chose Saturday night. "The night of the homecoming dance. You're funny."

"I'm serious. You don't want to go to some stupid high school dance."

"How do you know?"

"Because you wouldn't be chasing me down, desperate to be friends."

"I'm not desperate."

"Fine, persistent."

"I don't know what I want," Aries said. "I haven't even told Cory yes or no, and it's all over social media that we're going."

"Welcome to Newport High." He leaned back, tossing his napkin on his plate. "Wait, you didn't give him an answer yet?" He let out a laugh.

"So."

"It's *so* obvious."

"What is?"

"You'd rather go out with me."

She shook her head. "You're so damn cocky."

"I like to call it confident, but either way, you love it. Let me take you out Saturday night."

"I-I can't."

"You mean you don't want to. You'd rather go to the dance with Douglas."

"I didn't say—"

"It's okay, you didn't have to." He stood and paid the bill. "Let's go."

"Wait." She rushed to catch up with him. "I don't even know if my dad will let me go to the dance, but I can guarantee he won't let me go on a date with a senior." Walking into the parking lot, toward his bike, she pointed at it and said, "Especially one who rides a motorcycle."

Damon ran his hand through her hair, placing some loose strands behind her ear. "Don't worry, Sophomore. I'm confident you'll figure it out."

She leaned into him, feeling safe. She didn't want the moment to end. "I don't know if I'll ever figure anything out."

He held out his arms. "It doesn't take a rocket scientist. C'mon, now."

She smiled. "You're right. How could I ever be so foolish? Please show me the error of my ways."

He wrapped her in his arms. "Gladly."

She pushed him back. "I was kidding."

He rolled his eyes. "Nah, you don't say."

"Well, I never know with you."

He glanced at his watch, then straddled his Harley, strapping on his helmet. "Hurry, hop on."

"Why are you in such a rush to get me home?"

"I'm taking you somewhere, but we're running out of time."

She obliged. When they were stopped at a light, she asked, "How'd I get so lucky to have you help me all of a sudden?"

"I like you, Sophomore."

The light turned green. He revved the engine and sped off, weaving in and out of traffic.

Several miles down the street, he pulled into his garage, cutting the engine. "My mom is home, but she'll most likely be knocked out on some anti-depressants and wine." He checked his watch. "We have a good half-hour before the Judge should be home."

The inside of Damon's house was like nothing she'd ever seen before. It could pass for a museum somewhere in Europe. A gorgeous crystal chandelier hung delicately from the vaulted ceiling. Antique furniture, classic art statues, and rare paintings were the impressive attraction, until she glanced down at the ivory tile framed in gold.

"Is that real gold?" She didn't dare touch anything, afraid she might break something. The elegance couldn't take away her discomfort.

"Unfortunately, yes, twenty-four carat."

"OMG," she mouthed as she gazed out the floor-to-ceiling glass windows at the epic oceanfront view.

He grabbed her hand, leading her toward the back of the house. They passed a woman wearing a long silk robe, sleeping on the couch in front of the television, which she'd left on.

"I told you she'd be out," Damon said.

They reached the end of the hallway to a closed door. He turned the knob.

"I had a feeling it would be locked. Hold on."

Nerves took over as Aries waited for him to return. She should have him take her home, yet at the same time her curiosity had gotten the best of her. The Judge had some of the answers she was searching for, if not all of them.

Damon came back with several tools, and within less than a minute he had the door open.

"I don't even want to know how you were able to open the lock so fast."

"Child's play," he said. "Okay, I don't know what you're looking for, but whatever it is, your best shot is in this room."

As soon as Aries entered the room, she inhaled a strong aroma of masculine cologne. "Damon, I think someone was in here recently. Did your dad go to work today?"

He shrugged. "It doesn't look as tidy as I remember," he said, directing his attention over at a desk with papers strewn across it.

She walked over to the computer and clicked the mouse. A daily planner popped up. "It says Coastal Lounge, five-thirty. What time is it?"

"Quarter after."

"Do you know what this means?"

"It's a restaurant in Laguna Beach. He probably ran in the house to grab something before heading there. He'd never leave his desk like this."

She rifled through some papers, mostly bills, until a bank statement caught her eye. She gasped when she saw the numbers 855,043,721.

"Whoa, get a hold of your dad's savings account. Looks like you have a nice inheritance waiting."

She handed the paper to Damon. He studied it for a moment.

"In the Cayman Islands. How convenient."

"I take it you didn't know about this."

"I just live here."

She sat down, checking the recent history on the computer. "He was looking up the account on the computer."

"Does it match?"

"I'd need his password."

She stood, scanning the room. Passing a bookshelf packed

with legal volumes, she walked over to a file cabinet. When she went to open it, a shock ran through her body, jolting her back.

She shook her hand. "Ouch."

He grabbed her hand. "You okay?"

"Yes," she said as a chill swept over her. The information she came for had to be in the file cabinet.

He reached for the drawer. "Of course it's locked."

"Shouldn't be a problem for super agent Damon LeMoore over there."

He cracked his knuckles. "You're in good hands."

He bent a paperclip into a straight line, inserting it in the lock. He then grabbed one of the small tools he'd used on the door lock and went to work. It took a lot longer than when he manipulated the door.

"So, you're not invincible." She smiled.

Wiggling his fingers in the air like a magician, he said, "Never doubt my powers."

He messed around with the lock for a few more minutes. "Wha-la," he said, pulling open the drawer. "You are in the presence of greatness."

"Ha, highly unlikely." She walked over, flipping through the files. They were listed by name and a court number. "These aren't alphabetical or even numerical. How does your dad know where to find anything?"

He reached around her to take a look. "It's filed by date. See, the first folder is listed September twenty-first."

"Yesterday," she said. "When did Piper get a DUI?"

"Second weekend of August. Not sure of the exact date."

She flipped through the files until she reached a manila folder labeled "Piper Zacora." She froze.

Damon sat on the desk, analyzing her. "I take it you found what you're looking for."

She pulled out the folder, sensing something bad was about

to happen. Did she really want to find out what secrets lie within the folder?

"Go on, open it."

"I don't know if I can."

"What?" Damon questioned. "I didn't say anything."

The voice didn't come from Damon, but a spirit. She assumed it was Mr. O because he kept harping on her to find out the truth.

"This is what you came for. Open it."

Detecting a different inflection, she asked, "Chuck?"

"Huh?" Damon said. "You feeling alright?"

She shook her head. "Nothing. Sorry."

"Everything okay in that pretty little head of yours?" He leaned back. "Well, talk to me."

She held up the folder. "It's labeled 'Piper Zacora.'"

"You're kidding."

He hopped off the desk, snatched it out of her hand, and opened it. He scanned the contents for a couple seconds before stopping and narrowing his eyes on something. His face flushed, and he snapped the folder shut.

"Let's get out of here."

"Get the folder from him," Chuck said. *"You need to know what's in there. My daughter—"* His voice cut off, replaced with static.

Chuck? Chuck, are you there? The connection was gone. She blinked, focusing back on the task at hand.

Reaching for Damon, she said, "Let me see."

He pulled away from her. "I don't think it's a good idea."

"Damon, let me see it."

"No. Let's go."

They squared off, staring at each other as if they were in an old Western film and if either one of them so much as flinched, they'd draw their guns.

"I'm not leaving until you show me what's inside the folder."

She stood with her arms crossed. If she could kill him with her stare, he'd have been dead.

"You're not seeing this file," he said. "We're leaving now. Whether I have to carry you out or not is up to you."

She closed her eyes, clenched her fists, and let out a scream.

"Shut up!" he yelled. "What the hell are you doing?"

Something broke inside the closet. When he turned to look, she grabbed the folder.

"No!" he said, knocking it out of her hands.

Pictures scattered across the floor. She scooped them up, her gaze captured by one in particular.

All the blood drained from her face, and the room began to spin. Damon said something, but she couldn't hear him. His face went out of focus, looking fuzzy before she fell backwards.

37

GEMINI RISING

Greg sat near the shore, staring at the breakers. Tapping his fingers on the sand, he shuddered as he recalled memories of Jake and the night that would change their lives forever. He couldn't reconcile how one night could be both the best and worst time of his life. Filled with complete bliss from the pleasure Stacy brought him, everything went to hell after that. Dammit Jake, he should've known better than to drink and ride.

Greg fought to hold on to his sanity as images of Stacy naked were quickly replaced by Jake's body splattered on the rocks.

It's my fault Jake's dead.

If the police discovered he'd brought the supply of pills to the party, he'd be the one ultimately responsible for Jake's death. Everyone wanted to partake in the festivities. Why would he deny somebody a good time? He punched the sand.

If only he could take it all back, have a mulligan of that night, like in golf. He'd endured so many "if only" moments of late. The regret ate away at him, consuming him from the inside out. Not one day had gone by since the accident where he didn't relive Jake's death. The haunting torture of knowing what he and his friends had done, topped with the unbearable code of silence, had to be worse than serving jail time.

A flash of Jake's motorcycle crashing into a guardrail invaded his mind. He squeezed his eyes shut as he saw Jake flying over the ledge, plummeting to his death.

Greg hadn't supplied a drug to anyone since that night. He knew exactly where Jake died, even though Stacy swore he was hallucinating whenever he brought up the subject. Jake had caused the break in the guardrail. But who'd helped Stacy move his bike and body to a different location? Every time Greg tried to get a straight answer out of Stacy, she'd blame it on the drugs, convincing him he didn't know what he was talking about. But she couldn't fool him. He just needed proof.

He enjoyed playing the part of Stacy's clueless friend, letting her think she called the shots and she had control over him. He needed to wait her out, convince her he was pathetic and in love with her, then he'd make his move. Once he found out who'd helped her, he'd be in control. It was his only way out of the nightmare she'd created for him.

When his phone vibrated, Stacy's picture popped up on the screen. Rolling his eyes, he said, "What do you want?"

"A simple 'hello' would be nice."

"Nothing with you is simple," he said. "Let's cut to the chase. Tell me what you want."

"Well, isn't that a good thing? Simple is boring," she said. "Anyway, I don't want anything. I just wanted to say hi. You've seemed preoccupied these days, so I wanted to catch up with you."

He loved when she used her soft, sensual voice. It was her form of manipulation, but he didn't care. It did things to his body.

"What are you doing later on?"

"Nothing," she said.

"You know it's sexy as hell when you talk like that."

"I know."

He had to control himself. "I'll be over later."

"Great. Can't wait."

He sat on the beach for a few more minutes. Maybe she did have control over him. No guy could resist her body.

Who cares? She can have it.

Bits and pieces of the party flashed through Greg's mind, despite his efforts to stay in the present. He shook Jake's hand when he arrived at the party that night. They had a brief conversation. Greg never realized those would be the last words he'd ever say to Jake Coleman.

38

*A*ries blinked a few times, gaining consciousness as a woman said, "Damon, are you in there?"

How long had she been lying on the floor? She gasped the second she remembered the reason she fell.

Damon pressed his finger against his lips, signaling for Aries to be quiet.

The woman knocked on the door, turning the knob. Aries froze. The door knob shook once more.

When her footsteps faded, Aries got up and whispered, "What do we do?"

He held out his hand. "We wait."

She scanned the room. The file cabinet was shut, the folder nowhere in sight. Damon did a sweep of the room, ensuring it looked the exact same way the Judge had left it.

She hyperventilated. *What the hell are those pictures doing in Piper's file?*

"Stay here," he whispered as he left the room.

With her entire body shaking, she couldn't stay put. She had to get out of there so she could unleash her wrath on the Judge.

Tiptoeing down the hallway, she stopped when Damon attended to his mother. He placed a blanket over her and turned off the television. She looked to be asleep, but he rubbed her shoulder, whispering something in her ear. He then caught Aries's eye, motioning for her to go back. She shook her head, mouthing the word, "No".

He slowly got up and walked over to her. "Okay, she's asleep. Let's get out of here." He locked the Judge's room and escorted her to the garage.

When they were out of the house, she said, "What is going on, Damon? How is this possible?" She paced around his bike.

"C'mon, let's go for a walk."

They headed down a landscaped trail to a beach area in front of the house. Walking across the sand, she studied a party barge navigating its way back to the channel from the open sea. The people on the boat had no idea how lucky they were. To be able to dance, drink, and not have a care in the world. What did that feel like? She shook her head.

"I'm freaking out here," she said. "I'm going to lose it. Seriously lose it."

He pulled her close to him, embracing her in a tight grip. "It's going to be okay. We'll figure this out, I promise." He rubbed her back. "Do you know who the man in the picture is?"

She trembled as she tried to say, "No."

"It's okay. I'm here for you. Please don't be scared."

She stepped back and tried to catch her breath. "Wait, how'd you know…" She pointed to herself. Unable to speak, she shook out her hands.

"I read the names on the back."

When she collected herself, she said, "What was the man's name?"

"Anthony Capozzi."

Feeling like she'd been sucker punched in the gut, she fell to her knees. Pounding her hand against the sand, she screamed, "Why? You had an affair with my mom, you scumbag! Why are you torturing me?" She gulped for air, trying to catch her breath. "I hate you!"

Damon walked over, helping her to her feet. "You've heard of him?"

"Yes," she mumbled. "Sort of." She shouted, "I hope you're in hell, Mr. O!"

"Look, I'm no brain surgeon, but shouldn't Capozzi be 'Mr. C?'"

"Shut up."

"Whoa, Sophomore, I'm trying to lighten things up here."

She glared at him.

"Okay. You want me to take you home?"

"No, I want you to take me to the Coastal Lounge."

"Hell, no."

"Why not? I need your dad to explain to me—"

"Exactly. You are not getting anywhere near the Judge. You have no idea what he's capable of. Those pictures were probably taken by a private detective. I bet someone's being blackmailed. But how this relates to Piper is beyond me."

"It probably has to do with Camden. Anthony Capozzi worked for him."

"Okay, there's your answer. Let's find this Capozzi guy and ask him about your mother."

She couldn't respond. Her mother looked beautiful in the pictures, but Aries's heart shattered into a million pieces when she opened Piper's folder and saw her mother's face next to Mr. O's; most likely the last picture ever taken of her.

"How the hell does he know Piper?" Damon asked.

"He doesn't."

"How do you know?"

"I just do. You're right, Piper wasn't driving. Do you

remember seeing anyone else? This has Peyton written all over it."

"I already told you," he said, looking away.

"You're sure you only saw a boy and a girl?"

"Yes."

"Look at me. How?"

"Hey, I'm not on trial here. I'm trying to help you."

She scrutinized him, unable to read his expression. Did he know more than he was letting on?

"How about you save the badgering for Capozzi?" he said.

She rolled her eyes. "I can't."

"Is he dangerous? Is there something you know about this guy you're not telling me?"

"Yes." She glanced at the ocean.

"Well, what?"

"He's dead."

"Of course. This just keeps getting better. We need to back off. I don't know what I'd do if anything happened to you."

Sitting down, she wrote names in the sand.

"What are you doing?" he asked, reading each name out loud. "Mom, Camden, Judge, Mr. O, Chuck, Piper, Peyton."

She drew a circle around the names. "Wondering how they're all related."

He shrugged. "Is Chuck your dad?"

She shook her head. "Don't ask."

"I won't. But I do want to know why you think your mom and Capozzi were having an affair."

"Because he had his arm around her. And in the other picture, he was looking over his shoulder, like he didn't want to be seen with her. Scumbag was probably married, too."

"Doesn't necessarily scream 'affair.' They could've been working together."

"She was a stay-at-home mom."

"Who wanted to be an artist. And she obviously frequented

Laguna art galleries. She could've been in the wrong place at the wrong time. Maybe this guy was trying to help her. Could be the reason he ended up dead, too."

Damon could be right, but so could she. Pressing her lips together, Aries focused on a couple of pelicans, feeling her mother's love pick up the pieces of her heart.

No, my mother wasn't the type to have an affair.

Damon finally broke the silence. "What are you thinking?"

"What you said. I guess you could be right." Maybe Mr. O *was* trying to help. She wrote the words "Neptune's Window" in the sand.

"Your mother's painting?" he asked.

She nodded. "What am I oblivious to? I'm missing something."

"Maybe not," he said. "Maybe you're the window, not Neptune, and you're seeing more than you should."

"Maybe." She wrote Mr. Bradley's name in the sand.

"Why'd you write his name?"

She shrugged. "Because he has the painting."

He nodded. "Okay, yeah. Makes sense."

The wind picked up, numbing her face. Shivering, she grabbed her knees.

"You're freezing," he said. "I don't want to, but I really should take you home. You going to be okay?"

"I don't know."

"Don't worry, I'm here for you." He helped her up. "We need to be careful."

She erased the names in the sand with her foot. She should be careful of everyone, including him. But something in his eyes dared her to trust him.

"What?" she said.

"I don't know. I don't want to leave you. I wish I could give you the answers."

"I know."

He glanced up, rubbing his hand through his hair. He opened his mouth, about to say something, then hesitated.

She narrowed her eyes. "What is it?"

"Nothing. Let's go."

"You were going to tell me something."

He shook his head. "Like I said, I don't want to take you home. But I should."

He's not telling me something. Calling on a spirit to help me out here.

Damon wrapped his arm around her as they walked back to his house. She didn't want to leave him either. He held out a leather jacket and helped her into it.

Rubbing her arms, he said, "This is the warmest jacket I own. It's going to be a cold ride." He handed her gloves as well.

On the ride back, she didn't mind the frigid air as she reviewed the recent revelations. Closer to discovering the truth about her mother's death, she couldn't grasp what Piper's cover-up had to do with it all, but at least she was headed in the right direction.

They arrived at her apartment. Damon parked behind the dumpster in the alley, just in case her dad came home. She hopped off, handing him his jacket and gloves.

"Thanks for helping me today."

He stood, reaching for her hand. "Like I said, we'll get to the bottom of all this."

She nodded, avoiding eye contact.

He squeezed her hand. "Hey, Sophomore."

She gazed into his eyes. He pulled her close to him and gave her a quick kiss on the lips. She backed away from the bike, her face crimson.

He smiled. "You've got your friend back." He fired up the engine and sped off before she could respond.

She stood in a daze for a moment, with her hand touching

her lips. Shaking her head, she walked up the steps. Before opening the door, she smiled.

Grabbing a snack, she headed to her room and turned on the computer. Newport Dish popped up with a picture of Aries and Damon, looking like they were about to kiss. The caption read, "Uh oh Douglas, looks like your homecoming date has other plans." She closed the site.

You're so immature, Peyton. This has to be from her.

The picture was taken at the exact same location where she'd honked at them.

Aries had more important things on her mind as she searched the web for anything on Anthony Capozzi. When she found what she was looking for, she clicked the mouse, pulling up various articles. He'd been employed by Camden for five years. She read for a few more minutes until she came across his cause of death.

Suicide. No way.

The window rattled.

Am I on to something here, Mr. O?

The phone rang. Shutting down her computer, she grabbed her cell phone. Plopping on her bed, she said, "Hi, Cory."

"Hey. This a good time?"

"Yes. You're not outside, are you?"

He laughed. "No. I learned my lesson last time."

"Good."

"I was hoping to catch you after practice, but you were gone."

"Oh, yeah." She rolled her eyes. "Um, I can explain."

"What?"

"Are you calling about Newport Dish?"

"No. I don't look at that stuff. Especially when I have a big game. And this one is big. Lots of college scouts will be there."

She sighed in relief. "What do you mean?"

"This could make or break where I go to college."

"Where do you want to go?"

"USC. My grandpa went there, unfortunately my dad, too, but whatever. Plus, I want to stay local for Abby."

She smiled. "That's sweet."

"She needs a good male influence in her life."

"So why are *you* staying?" she asked.

"Hey."

"I'm kidding. Makes me jealous I don't have a big brother."

"You have your dad, though."

"True."

"So, about the dance," he said. "Is it okay if I pick you up Saturday night? We'll meet everyone at Piper's."

After their discussion earlier, her dad might be willing to let her go. But then she pictured Damon.

"Aries? Um, okay, I guess you really never gave me a clear answer. I'm so stupid. You do want to go to the dance, don't you?"

The tone of his voice made her picture him as a little boy fishing with his grandpa. She blurted out, "Of course. Yes."

"You had me worried there."

"I'm sorry. I was thinking about my dad and you picking me up."

"Oh, yeah. We can meet at Piper's if that's easier. I understand."

"Okay, I'll let you know tomorrow."

"I can't wait to see how beautiful you're going to look."

Her cheeks flushed. She pictured him dressed up. "You, too."

They talked for a few more minutes until her dad came home. After they said goodbye, she walked out to greet him.

She slouched when he wasn't alone. "Oh, hi, Kimberly."

"Hi," she said in a bubbly voice.

"*Not so fast,*" a spirit said. "*You don't have to be disappointed. Find a way to use Kimberly to your advantage.*"

Ha. How?

"I'm confident you'll figure it out," the spirit said before fading away.

She stared at Kimberly for a moment. *Got it. Thank you.*

"Dad, you know Cory, the boy you met the other night?"

"Yes." He took his arm off Kimberly.

"He asked me to the homecoming dance, and I wondered if that would be okay?"

Ryan took off his hat, rubbing his hand through his hair. "I don't want you dating 'til you're sixteen."

"Oh, babe," Kimberly's face lit up. "Going to the homecoming dance as a sophomore is a big deal."

Bingo. Aries laid it on thick at that point. "Yeah, and he's the quarterback."

"Oh, well she has to go now," Kimberly said. "I can do your hair. I can add some highlights to frame your face. This is so exciting."

"I know," Aries said in a fake voice.

"We'll talk about this later," Ryan said.

"You have to say yes," Kimberly said.

"You can go," he said. "But we're going to discuss the details later."

Kimberly clapped as if she was the one going to the dance.

Aries smiled. "Thank you. I'm tired. I'm going to do some homework and then go to bed."

Ryan nodded. "Goodnight, Kiddo."

"Goodnight, Aries," Kimberly said, turning toward Ryan. "Dad of the Year."

Aries rolled her eyes as she walked down the hall. Glancing over her shoulder, her heart ached at how Ryan interacted with Kimberly the way he used to with her mother. She stopped and stood in her doorway, continuing to stare.

Ryan kissed the back of Kimberly's neck as he said, "What can I get you to drink?"

"I had a couple of glasses of merlot earlier, so I'll stick with red."

She felt guilty for eavesdropping, but she couldn't look away.

Ryan massaged Kimberly's shoulders. "That's right, the meeting you set up. Where did you end up having him take you for drinks?"

"Coastal Lounge."

39

*a*ries spent the entire night trying to contact Mr. O. She could barely function when the alarm clock went off, piercing the morning silence with a trendy pop song.

Rubbing her eyes, she said, "Figures you're nowhere to be found when I really need to talk to you."

She made her way to the bathroom, where she brushed her teeth. "What happened to my mom? Were you there the night she died? Did you try to help her?" She had so many questions for him. "Did *they* have you killed, too? I know you didn't commit suicide." She reached for a towel and dried her mouth. "Was it because of my mom?"

The shower door rattled. She jumped back.

You and my mom knew something.

The door shook again.

"Why won't you talk to me if I'm right?" The shower door moved a third time, but not as loud. "You're not Mr. O. *Mom?*"

She stared at the shower for a moment.

"Kiddo, get a move on," Ryan called from outside her bedroom door.

She hurried and changed. Rushing out of her room, she grabbed a granola bar and banana.

Ryan seemed just as tired as they piled into his truck. On the ride to school, he appeared to be deep in thought.

Turning down the radio, she said, "Dad, I need to ask you something."

"Yes, you can go to the dance," he said on autopilot, his mind clearly somewhere else. "I—"

"No. Um, thank you, but it's something else."

"Sorry." He glanced in her direction, appearing to be back from wherever his brain had wandered off to. "What is it?"

"I overheard you and Kimberly talking last night, and I was wondering, is she helping you discover the truth about Mom?"

With a shocked expression, he concentrated on the traffic.

"Is she?"

"What makes you think that?" he asked.

"My friend's dad just happened to be at the same restaurant as her last night. I don't think it's some strange coincidence."

"Right," he said. "Peyton."

"No, a different friend. Wait, Kimberly met Camden?"

"Yes. Why?"

She shook her head. "You shouldn't put her in such a dangerous situation."

"I'm not. She knows what she's doing. Listen, I don't want you worrying about this."

"Too late, I'm already worried. I mean, Kimberly's not my favorite person or anything, but I don't want her to die."

Ryan glanced over at her. "Nothing is going to happen to her. I can guarantee it."

"I don't want anything to happen to you either." Her stomach hurt.

"It won't. I promise." He pulled up to the school. "I love you, Kiddo. But leave this to me, alright?"

Aries waved goodbye, more worried than ever.

She made her way into the building and headed for Miss Townsend's class. As she walked in the room, Cory ran up from behind, tapping her on the shoulder.

"Hey," he said.

"Hi."

Peyton walked over to them. "I guess I'm going with Danny. Plan is to meet at Piper's at seven." She gave Aries a dirty look, without Cory noticing. "Work for you guys?"

Cory squeezed the bill of his cap.

"Sure," Aries said and walked to her seat.

Danny Aguilar interacted with Jamie, laughing and making goofy faces, while Jamie rolled her eyes. Why would Peyton agree to go with him? He wasn't ugly, but he acted too immature for her. He did have kind brown eyes, and he'd probably have a nice smile when he got his braces removed.

She turned to Cory and said, "Danny's one of your best friends, right?"

"Yeah, why?"

"Just wondering why Peyton would go on a date with him."

"It's not a date. It's more of a group thing. And Brandon's taking Paige."

"I thought he was with Michelle?"

"Kind of," he said. "But I guess she can't go."

"How come Paige isn't going with Michael?"

He laughed. "Yeah, right. They annoy the crap out of each other."

Interesting, they both can keep a secret.

"Oh."

After Miss Townsend handed out a study guide to complete, Cory asked, "Do you have a pencil I can borrow?"

She glanced at his desk. "You have one right there."

"I need one from you for good luck, remember? Game night."

She loved the way Cory smiled at her. Fishing a pencil out of the bottom of her bag, she handed it to him. "Good luck."

They worked on the study guide for the remainder of class.

Piper strolled up to her in the hallway. "Hey, I'm glad you're going with us tomorrow. If you want, you can come over early. It would be fun to get ready together."

"Thanks, that would be fun, but my dad's girlfriend wants to help me." She rolled her eyes. "I really appreciate the offer."

"Yeah, of course. I just wanted you to know, it's nice to hang out with someone real."

She smiled. "That means a lot. I feel the same about you."

"Cool. See you later." Piper waved, sauntering off in the opposite direction.

Aries held her head high, with her shoulders back, walking without slouching for the first time in a while. She smiled the entire way to class.

AFTER RECEIVING dirty looks from Peyton and Paige all morning, Aries ate lunch alone. She rested against her favorite tree, eating and enjoying the warmth from the sun.

"Hello, dear."

She smiled. *Hi, Gladys. I haven't heard from you in a while.*

"You've been busy. I'm happy you and CJ are getting along so well. You're keeping him out of trouble."

He doesn't seem like he needs help. He's a good kid, you know.

"Yes, I know," she said. *"Well, he's not in the clear yet."*

Gladys, does this have anything to do with the night Piper got a DUI? Was Cory involved somehow?

"You know how I told you things don't always seem as they appear?"

Yes.

"Good."

She had a blank look on her face. "Well?" she questioned. Waiting in silence for a moment, she said, "Gladys."

Some leaves crunched behind her as Damon said, "Not quite, it's me. Who's Gladys?"

"Um." She waved her hand. "Nobody you know. Back to stalking?"

"I don't think you'd call it stalking when the alleged victim so *desperately* wants to be your friend."

She made a sarcastic face. "Can I help you?"

He sat next to her. "As a matter of fact, yes."

She gestured for him to continue.

"Let's do some *stalking* together," he said.

"What do you have in mind?"

"Tomorrow night, I'll meet you somewhere, a place you'd meet a girl, so your dad won't mind, and we'll grab something to eat. Not a date, just some food to keep our energy up."

She laughed. "Doesn't sound like stalking. Sounds more like a date."

"I haven't gotten there yet. After we have some sustenance in us, we'll follow Camden around."

"How do you know where he'll be?"

"You trust me?" He displayed his most alluring smile.

"Maybe."

"Better answer than I expected. Okay, it's a date. I mean plan."

"I can't."

"C'mon."

"You know I'm going to the dance," she said.

They locked eyes. "What's more important?"

She sighed.

When the bell rang, he helped her up. "I know you, Sophomore. I know what you want."

She glanced past him as Cory and his friends walked toward

the building. How could he know what she wanted when she didn't?

Turning to leave, he said over his shoulder, "Think about it, but not for too long."

~

SATURDAY EVENING HAD ARRIVED. The big night. Aries ate a handful of almonds and an apple to settle her nerves. She'd never been to a school dance before, either on a real date or as part of a big group, especially a group containing the popular kids. How was it possible to be nervous, excited, and unsure all at the same time?

As she slipped into the beautiful black dress Kimberly had helped her pick out, Damon's words, "What's more important?", kept ringing through her head. She adjusted her gold sling-back heels, looking into the mirror. Kimberly had done her makeup and styled her hair half-up, with wisps of dark blonde highlights framing her face. With the lighter shades of hair, a slight resemblance to her mother stared back at her. Her father would be home from work soon, and she couldn't wait to see his reaction.

She'd purposely neglected her phone all day. But with some time to spare, she checked her messages.

"Hey, it's Cory. Call me and let me know if seven still works."

The next message was from Damon. "Offer still stands. Let me know either way."

She sat on the corner of her bed and said, "I need your advice, Mom."

She smelled a slight stench of tobacco and smiled. *Hi, Grandpa.*

"Sounds like you're in some sort of predicament."

Yes.

"*The way I see it is, you made a commitment to one boy, so there's no real problem here. Your word needs to mean something.*"

You're right. I've dreamt of this moment. I mean, Cory's ideal.

"*I take it your heart's somewhere else.*"

"Yes, it's with my mom," she said.

"*You sure that's the only place?*"

She shrugged.

"*Well, you have the final say, but you know what I think the right thing to do is. But remember, love trumps all.*"

Thanks, Grandpa.

The smell of tobacco vanished.

Aries picked up her phone and left a message. "Can you meet me on the beach as soon as possible? I know this is a strange request, but for some reason I'd really like to watch the sunset with you tonight."

She grabbed a towel, locked up, and walked down toward the beach. Taking off her heels at the boardwalk, she walked barefoot down to the shore and waited.

As the sun made its descent, she squinted at the golden beauty, framed with orange and crimson rays, dancing over the ocean. Her mother would've marveled at the sight.

She sat on the towel and embraced the magic of the sunset. Her mother once described the sun as a magician with endless possibilities.

Drawing a heart in the sand she whispered, "I finally understand how the beach made you feel. And wherever I am, I don't want to miss the beauty of a sunset."

She continued tracing the heart, making it deeper. "I understand what you meant when you said it was all a gift. The gift of being alive. It's the little things in life, you used to say." Her stomach dropped with excitement as she reminisced about her mother. She closed her eyes as she stated, "I'm going to appreciate life's simple pleasures." She opened her eyes with the sensation of serenity splashing over her.

After a set of waves crashed, she turned around. It took her a moment before her eyes narrowed in on him standing in the distance by the boardwalk, scanning the beach for her. As he took a couple steps in her direction, she knew she'd made the right decision.

She turned back toward the sunset to admire it alone one last time before he'd have a chance to reach her. Wisps of lavender and pink had now formed around the sparse clouds. It was the spitting image of the sunset her mother had painted.

She smiled and whispered, "I'm finally looking through the window, Mom. This isn't over yet."

ALSO BY L L LEWIN

Read on for a preview of *Deep Stare*
The second book in the Neptune's Window Trilogy

DEEP STARE: CHAPTER 1

SCORPIO MOON AND GEMINI RISING

*S*tacy Martin stashed a few prescription pills in her clutch. *You never know when these might come in handy.* She never intended on using them to drug someone else. Deranged psychopaths did that for unimaginable reasons. Not her. Besides, she didn't share things well, and she sure as hell would never spare one of her feel good, little round bits of magic. But she had. And the power she felt after the first time she witnessed someone losing consciousness sent her on a three-day high. An instant addiction.

She admired the way her homecoming dress hugged her body in all the right places. Clasping a designer gold belt around her waist, she smiled at all the possibilities to wreak havoc on the students of Newport Beach High School. Who should her victim de jour be? Aries Dade topped the list, seeing how she had become a major thorn in Stacy's side. She took pleasure in tormenting Aries. It had become her mode of survival, like breathing or drinking water.

Pulling out a small flask, she took a sip of vodka. Shivering, she put it back in her clutch. She applied lipstick, blotting with pleasure. Any guy would be lucky to be going to the dance with her. Speaking of guys, she called her partner in crime, Greg Reed.

As she waited for him to answer, she chuckled. She liked the name Greg better than his actual name.

"Hello," he said, sounding distracted.

"Hi. What are you doing?"

"The same thing everybody is doing, getting ready for the dance. What do you want?"

"To tell you how good I look."

"I'm sure you do."

"You'll see," she sang the words.

"Is that it?"

"Yes. For now." The doorbell rang. "Bye, Greg, see you soon."

"Stop call—"

She hung up and greeted her date with a smile.

He stood with his mouth agape. "Wow."

It must have been the only word the moron could articulate.

"I'm glad you like." She slowly turned and paused so he could admire her backside. She relaxed her mouth, almost feeling sorry for her prey. She turned to face him with her smile beaming again. "Come in."

AFTER GREG HUNG up with Stacy, he prayed a silent prayer. "Dear God, please don't let anything bad happen to anyone tonight." He wrapped his tie around his neck and began to fold and loop it the way his dad had taught him. He maneuvered into his coat, holding his arms out and admiring the perfect fit. Something about the way it made his chest and shoulders stand out gave him a boost of confidence. Splashing on cologne, he relaxed.

As Greg walked out the front door, the porch light flickered on and off three times. He checked back, confirming he was alone. He could fix the light later. He took a few steps down the path when a muffled song began to play, sending a chill down his spine.

The song played from his cell phone. He pulled it out of his pocket. Somehow the alarm was going off, but Greg hadn't set any alarms, and he would have never set it to play that song. He collected himself, now more pissed than scared. He called *her*.

"What the hell are you doing?" he asked.

Stacy whispered, "What are you talking about?"

"How did you set my alarm? Were you at my house today?"

"Hold on," she whispered again. A moment later she said in her usual tone, "No I wasn't at your house. And why are you raising your voice at me? I haven't done anything." She paused. "*Yet.*"

"Well whatever sick joke you're playing, don't waste it on me. I'm the only one who knows everything about you."

"Again, would you please tell me what you're talking about?" she asked.

"My alarm on my phone just went off, and I didn't set it."

She laughed. "Get a grip. So what, maybe you did and you don't remember. Like a while ago you wanted to remind yourself that tonight's homecoming. It's nothing to freak out over."

He couldn't get rid of the goose bumps on his arms. "It's not just the alarm. The song that played, it's-it's creepy, and I don't think a coincidence." He said the name of the song and tried to remember how to breathe while he waited for her to respond.

A moment later, she said, "Jake Coleman's favorite song."

"Yes," he said. "Do you think somebody knows what really happened to him?"

"No. I think you're being stupid and paranoid."

Shaking his head, he hung up on her.

"She can't get away with this any longer," he said, staring at his phone.

The song played again.

ACKNOWLEDGMENTS

I'm writing this during Mercury retrograde, so please forgive me if I forget anyone. First, I'm so honored to thank my soulmate, Aaron Peters (the only person I could ever allow to see my first drafts). I am forever grateful for his input and understanding, and for his being my biggest fan. And, especially for letting me take him so deep into Neptune's Window that while we sip wine on our patio, he dreams of jamming on guitar with Robby Zacora (while I visualize lounging in Piper's backyard all day). Aaron is claiming the title of the first "Neptunian". Thank you to my sister, Pamela Lewin. As a Leo she will be upset that I didn't mention her first, but she truly inspires me every day. I love and cherish my amazing parents, Pete and Sandy Lewin, for all their love and encouragement, but most of all for who they are. Thank you to my wonderful in-laws, Bruce and Lorraine Peters for their support and editorial skills, and my first freelance editor, Mike Sirota. Without his brutal, wise feedback I would not be the writer I am today (if you think I pick on Aries, you should see him work over a manuscript). I would also like to acknowledge and thank editor Jennifer Silva Redmond, my amazing cover designer, Henry Hyde (his professionalism, creativity, and advice are top notch), and my fantastic web designer and social media expert Kat Morgan. And I must thank Joanna Penn for helping me find Henry and Kat. Thank you as well to medium Bill Philips (my first experience with a medium and their amazing abilities), and my friend, Debra McGrath (also a medium). According to Deb, I had a spirit-guide with me as I worked on the trilogy, writing his story in modern time. So, I literally had a ghost writer. Final thanks for support, love and encouragement to: Tom Fackrell, Morgan Gruter, Jenny Kelly, Andrew Lewin, John Lewin, Karen Patton, Shawn Pierry, and Victoria Varon. And last but definitely not least a huge shoutout to my teen readers, Ava Patton and Sierra Varon, for their honest, humbling opinions, given in ways only teenagers can.

ABOUT THE AUTHOR

A native of Southern California, I was born in Los Angeles County, and grew up in Orange County. I graduated from the University California, Irvine with a degree in psychology and social behavior. After teaching for several years and interacting with our youth almost daily, I was inspired to write a young adult mystery novel, which morphed into a little bit more. Since everything happens in threes for me (my initials, triple Sagittarius, the third born) the novel (of course) turned into a trilogy, and reaffirmed my belief that three's a charm.

I love all things astrological, metaphysical, and spiritual. With my sun, moon, and rising all in the sign of Sagittarius, I'm as Sagittarius as they come, optimistic, freedom-loving, and ever so tactless. However, in my natal chart, the planet Neptune is also in Sagittarius, so I don't even know how Sagittarius I am. Supposedly, I'm easy to spot. I'll be the one with my foot in my mouth.

My three passions in life are writing, traveling, and soccer. You'll either find me writing at the beach, on an island somewhere, or a soccer field. And my three vices are chocolate, pizza, and champagne, and not necessarily in that order.

I reside with my husband and four cats (don't judge, I'm a sucker for stray animals) in Southern California.